His Kate

Bianca,
Happy Reading!
XD
Sue Krawitz

His Kate

SUE KRAWITZ

ARCHWAY
PUBLISHING

Archway Publishing books may be ordered through booksellers or by contacting:

Archway Publishing
1663 Liberty Drive
Bloomington, IN 47403
www.archwaypublishing.com
1 (888) 242-5904

Because of the dynamic nature of the Internet, any web addresses or links contained in this book may have changed since publication and may no longer be valid. The views expressed in this work are solely those of the author and do not necessarily reflect the views of the publisher, and the publisher hereby disclaims any responsibility for them.

Any people depicted in stock imagery provided by Thinkstock are models, and such images are being used for illustrative purposes only. Certain stock imagery © Thinkstock.

ISBN: 978-1-4808-2833-9 (sc)
ISBN: 978-1-4808-2831-5 (hc)
ISBN: 978-1-4808-2832-2 (e)

Library of Congress Control Number: 2016935185

Print information available on the last page.

Archway Publishing rev. date: 03/10/2016

For Dylan and Devon

In Loving Memory of
Betty Gelfand
Barbara Krawitz
Edwin Krawitz, Esq.
Gene Krawitz
Sue Schaeffer

There's this place in me where your
fingerprints still rest, your kisses still linger, and
your whispers softly echo. It's the place where
a part of you will forever be a part of me.

—Gretchen Kemp

ACKNOWLEDGMENTS

I am indebted to Tim Sappenfield at Archway Publishing for believing in me and my story and for helping to make my dream a reality. I am eternally grateful to Adriane Pontecorvo, concierge (a.k.a. my one-woman team) at Archway Publishing, for working so diligently from my first draft to finishing touches and everything in between. She is a true gem! I also thank Joanne S. and Eric Saxon for their dedication to this project.

This book has been a true labor of love. I thank the extended Krawitz and Gelfand families, who have always been there for me. This book would not have come to fruition without the love and support of my forever friend Carla Baudo. Special thanks to my friend extraordinaire, Michelle Blattner, who read the entire manuscript and shared her feedback, insight, and advice. I also thank friends and colleagues who helped me on this life long journey: Ashley Baptiste, Angela Beckey, Gianna Tripodi-Bhise, Scott Christmas, Jennifer Crockett, Cindy Crowninshield, Jay Doyon, Susie Gelfand, Janeen Gilbert, Bev Giordano, Steve and Kathi Griffith, Jennie Levy, Colleen Lynn, Andrea Meitz, Kate Noon, Nancy Rankin, Lisa and John Rau, Ray Sajorda, Bob Schaeffer, Lisa and Jeff Schaeffer, Josh Schier, and Jennifer Snyder.

I am grateful to the following people who helped in my book research by sharing their personal experiences: Erika Johnson, Mary Keller, Tara McFadden, and Rhiannon Serpico. Also, to

Wendy Werris, my very first reader and editor in the early stages of this project; and to Pagan Kennedy, who shared her expertise in the craft of writing.

Many thanks to Liz and Greg Shockley and the entire Sage Catering team - you are the best! Special thanks to my friends in the Moms Club of Norriton, everyone at Cole Manor Elementary School and my friends in the Parent Faculty Club. Also to my West Deptford and Widener friends, colleagues and fellow book readers on social media for your support.

I want to extend my appreciation to some of my favorite authors for keeping me company over the years and, in turn, teaching me the art of writing: Elizabeth Berg, Judy Blume, Richard Paul Evans, Gillian Flynn, Gayle Forman, Emily Giffin, Jane Green, John Green, Kristin Hannah, Beth Kendrick, Christina Baker Kline, Debbie Macomber, James Patterson, Jodi Picoult, Anita Shreve, Nicholas Sparks, Jeannette Walls, and Jennifer Weiner.

Oodles of hugs, kisses, and love to my sons, Dylan and Devon, who have shown me the strength of the parent-child bond. I love seeing the world through your eyes and watching you grow. You are two blessings, and I am honored to be your mom.

Most important, this book would not be possible without both of you. From the bottom of my heart, I give you my deepest love and gratitude.

Introduction

Some people believe in soul mates—that there is one person in the world they are truly meant to be with. Others do not believe that there could possibly be only one person meant for them. Most people agree that being a parent is selfless, and many parents sacrifice their own happiness for their children. Many people choose to speak their minds because they do not want to live lives of regret. Others keep thoughts and feelings to themselves and do not realize they carry regrets in their hearts. There are difficult choices to make in life. Some choices require making sacrifices for the greater good of others. Some decisions require a person to choose between the right thing and the thing he or she truly wants. This is the story of making choices, sacrifice, regret, and true love.

PROLOGUE

The snow began falling two hours ago, slowly at first and then picking up momentum before slowing down again. Tiny flakes swirled down from the sky, coating windswept leaves that were huddled together in the corner next to the gate. The leaves looked more like mulch, a pile of brown and soggy foliage that had lost a battle with the elements during the past month. With an intricate design of fully bloomed roses embedded into the iron, the gate glimmered in black lacquer and looked at least ten feet tall. Despite the remnants of fall leaves, it was obvious landscapers worked here year-round, maintaining the grounds, shrubs, trees, and flowers.

Today was the first snow of the season, and forecasters were already predicting a long winter. The December sky turned from a blissful blue to a large gray mass of billowy clouds. Temperatures dropped, and a light breeze whispered eerily through the trees hibernating in the distance as if ordering birds to fly south. On the other side of the gate, evergreens blanketed in white stood across the highway as still as statues. The highway was a blaze of lights, full of cars with people headed home early from work or to the mall to finish their Christmas shopping. Red brake lights lit up the road like a thousand Rudolph noses, and the pearl headlights of oncoming cars shone like stars in heaven. PennDOT trucks dumping sand and salt crawled by in each direction with orange hazard lights blinking across the snowy mist.

Greg Janera walked slowly, keeping his eyes focused on the ground in front of him. He dusted the snow from the sleeves of his jacket, balancing the plant he carried, and ran his hands through his hair, causing snowflakes to stick to his fingers. Snow fell from his jacket, and the front of his jeans and work boots were coated with the white powdery precipitation. It wasn't the type of snow for making snowballs or snowmen, but rather the soft, peaceful kind. It was just the way she would have liked it. Greg drew a deep, ragged breath and exhaled slowly, remembering that perfect night less than a year ago with snow just like this. As he walked farther, he took shallow, rapid breaths while glancing up at the lampposts. This helped him stay on the right path. He walked for several more minutes until he reached her. Greg stood still, taking in the feeling of her presence, his eyes glazing with moisture. He hunched over and then looked to the sky, somehow managing to whisper a prayer. Greg shook his head, still not wanting to believe this was real. Then his heart felt a surge, and he squatted down so he could be closer to her. Gently wiping away the snow from the granite stone that rose about six inches off the ground, he saw six yellow roses placed neatly on the ground, their petals covered with snowflakes. Blinking back a tear, he slowly traced his right index finger over her name, one letter at a time. It was engraved in the stone and made his finger tingle from the cold. "You will forever be in our hearts" was etched on the opposite side of her photo. He looked away for a moment and realized he was the only one there. It wasn't the best weather for people to visit their loved ones, he thought, but he could no longer wait to do this.

The past month and a half had gone by in a blur, and he still felt his mind was playing tricks on him. He turned back and stared at her picture. She wore a bright smile, her eyes gleaming and full of life. He gazed wistfully. She was so happy that day, so full of hope and love. Even though the photo was tucked away at home, he knew every inch—each curve of her face, every strand of her hair, her two precious dimples, her small silver earrings. He could close his eyes and see her smiling and laughing, carefree and happy. The day the photo was taken had been a good day, but knowing there would never be another overwhelmed him with sadness. His heart felt clamped in his chest, and he tried to stop the tears, but they trickled down his face, catching in the stubble on his cheeks and chin. He wiped his face with the back of his hand and then picked up the small poinsettia plant he'd brought and placed it beside her headstone. It was lined in gold foil and had vibrant red leaves. He remembered that four years ago she had had more than a dozen poinsettias in her home. She told him they brightened up the cold, dark days of winter and helped her get in the Christmas spirit. He hoped this plant could somehow comfort her, make her feel she wasn't alone, make her feel she was still loved.

He stared at the two dates written under her name and shook his head, wanting to believe this wasn't real, that it was all just a bad dream and he would wake up and hear her say, "See, silly, here I am." He turned away and put his hand over his face upon realizing this nightmare was real and nothing could undo what had happened. Twenty-nine years old. She was too young to die. She was too beautiful. She had too much life left to live. It shouldn't have ended like this. He turned back and put his hand on her name and wiped away fresh snowflakes. He stared at her picture again. "I'm sorry. I'm so sorry," he whispered.

Greg reached into his inner jacket pocket and pulled out the envelope. The two pages inside were already worn despite the fact that he'd received them just a week ago. He had already read them dozens of times and couldn't get her words and feelings out of his head. He stared at the envelope, and when he flipped it over, he noticed the tiniest heart in the top right-hand corner. *Right*, he thought sadly. *It had been right.* It just could never be, not the way they both wanted it. Greg clenched the envelope in his hands before placing it back in his pocket. Lost in thought, he sat motionless while a gust of wind swirled snowflakes all around him. Despite the cold, Greg felt sweat bead up on his neck and trickle down his back. It would be pitch dark soon, and as much as he didn't want to leave her, he knew he would have to go home before it got too late.

He wiped away some more fresh snow from her headstone, and just as he was about to tell her everything he should have while she was still alive, he heard footsteps in the distance. Turning, his face fell slightly at the sight of her. She wore a long blue coat, and auburn curls crawled out from under her hat. A matching cream-colored scarf was wrapped loosely around her neck. As she got closer, he noticed tissues bunched up in one hand while the other held a bouquet of flowers. Her face was dotted with tears, and when their eyes met, Greg was once again taken aback by the resemblance. He held his breath, his heart thumping in his chest. His mouth went dry, and his stomach felt woozy. He wondered what she would think of him being there. Would she understand? Could she forgive him? Greg thought about how he could express his sorrow. Would she believe that he held regrets in his heart that he could never undo? Regrets that would stay with him for the rest of his life. He turned back toward the headstone until the sound of her voice pierced the night sky.

"Hi. You must be Greg."

CHAPTER 1

As she flipped through the latest issue of *People*, Heather Damon sipped an iced coffee and then set it beside her on a square glass table. She had stayed in last night and woken up early, the morning sunshine filtering through her bedroom window. A light breeze had swept open her curtains, pulling the scent of her fresh gardenias through her room. She lay in bed under a crisp white sheet and relished this momentary calm feeling. There wasn't a trace of humidity, a rarity for the city of Philadelphia in mid-June. When she got out of bed and saw no new texts or messages on her phone, her first thought was to call him. She had held the phone and stared at his number, her finger hovering over the call button. Heather knew he was having doubts about their relationship and whether they should progress to the next level. Shaking her head and wrinkling her nose, she tried to forget how she'd dragged him to Tiffany's last month to look at jewelry—not just ordinary jewelry, like bracelets and earrings; she actually showed him a ring. And not just *any* ring.

Why in the world did she have the saleswoman take out that breathtaking Tiffany Grace engagement ring? Granted, the princess-cut diamond complemented with brilliant round diamonds was gorgeous. It looked elegant when she tried it on, especially with the perfect pale-pink manicure she had gotten earlier in the day. But could she have been any more obvious? In the back of her mind, she knew it was a stupid idea, but somehow she could not resist putting that ring on her finger. Of course, two other salespeople came over and commented about how beautiful it looked while casually asking about her upcoming nuptials and if she needed assistance creating a wedding registry.

All the while, Greg stood off to the side, hands in his pockets, probably wishing he was anywhere but the jewelry section of Tiffany's. Only after he had gone home did she realize that his quick good-bye kiss on her forehead meant she had scared him. She had already apologized three times, but she knew he would never forget the look on her face while that ring was on her finger. As irrational as it seemed to her, she was the one who suggested they take a break to let things blow over, to give him time and space to think about their relationship. She just never thought it would take this long. She knew they loved each other, but she also was starting to think that wasn't enough. She wished she could crawl inside his mind, even for five minutes, so she could discover his true thoughts and feelings. Would this discovery make her happy? Sad? Something in between?

She looked out over her balcony and took another sip of her drink. Reading an article about a woman who overcame breast cancer, she suddenly felt grateful for her good health. The woman in the article was only five years older than her, but luckily the doctors caught it in time, and her treatment was successful. It was a reminder that life was short and precious. It made her think of him, made her want to reach out and wrap her arms around him. But she quickly dismissed that thought, determined to stop dwelling on the situation.

Instead, she let her mind stir about the day ahead. She looked up to the sky, where clouds formed what looked like a giant teddy bear. She smiled; hoping a child nearby could appreciate it before it drifted away and turned to a meaningless white mass. Heather didn't have set plans for tonight. She wondered which of her friends might be free to go out. She was big on going out on Saturday nights when she didn't have to work. To her, it meant a celebration of the end of the work week. It was also a way to get ready for the new week ahead. She didn't care as much about where she went, just as long as she was out having fun. A few drinks, dancing, and good music never hurt anyone— and after all, she deserved a little fun.

Her job at the hotel was demanding, with long hours. She was responsible for satisfying her clients' every last whim and making each and every event go off without a hitch. She prided herself on working hard and looking her best. "Polished and professional, with a hint of glamour at all times," was her mantra. Heather was known to drop a good chunk of her salary on spa manicures and pedicures, keratin treatments, seaweed wraps, hot-stone massages, and facials. Another good piece of her salary went straight to designer suits and shoes, handbags, accessories, and jewelry, and Heather didn't feel there was anything wrong with that. She worked hard for her money; she refused to feel guilty for reaping the rewards. She did save for the future, of course, but more often than not, her credit cards got a good workout.

Heather turned the pages of her magazine and came to an article about a missing boy who had vanished ten years prior. The boy's photo looked to be his kindergarten picture. He wore a big smile, had tousled brown hair, and was missing his two front teeth. There was a picture of his grief-stricken parents and younger sister that did something to her heart. A pit formed in her stomach, and she clamped her hand over her mouth as she read. She felt an overwhelming compulsion to help find the boy, comfort the mother, or donate money to the reward. *Just do something to make a difference,* she thought. The little boy was only five when he was abducted from a Little League baseball game. The mother stated that she had turned her head for an instant—and then he was gone. Just like that. In one second, her world had turned upside down, and she'd been living a nightmare ever since. The police and detectives combed the area for weeks, took evidence, and interviewed every single person at the baseball game as well as all neighbors, school personnel, family, and friends. There were possible sightings and vehicle descriptions, but not one lead had panned out. It tore her up inside to see such a horrendous thing, and this all took place just thirty miles outside of Philadelphia. Small tears began sliding down her cheeks. She wasn't normally a crier. A few of her friends regularly cried watching Hallmark commercials, and she used to laugh how something so mundane could make someone cry. But now, here she was, tears streaking her face over a little boy she didn't even know. She bookmarked the page so she could contact someone on Monday and do anything she could to help. Closing the magazine, she placed it on the table and wiped away the tears with the back of her hand.

Getting a hold of herself, she closed her eyes and tried to visualize her serene place: where the ocean meets the beach. The picture formed easily in her mind: It is dusk, when the sun is fading into the soft pink, purple, and blue horizon. Small waves are licking the beach, washing away footprints and sand castles. In her mind, this beach is pristine. White sand, delicate seashells, and clear, warm, ocean water were the answer to all that bothered her. Her eyes were closed for ten minutes before she realized this was only making her feel drowsy. She stood up, stretched her arms above her head, and then breathed in deeply, the same way she did during yoga class. Standing in tree pose, her long limbs felt warmed up and relaxed. She stood still for a moment before opening her eyes, asking herself why so many bad things have to happen.

She grabbed her cell from the table to send him a text; she just wanted to feel something familiar and be comforted. Yes, she hated to admit it, but she also needed to find out where they stood. *I deserve that much, right?* She was the other half of this relationship, after all, and she wasn't going down without a fight. She still loved him. She was still in love with him and wanted their relationship to move forward, not end. But once she held the phone, her hand twitched. She quickly put it down, hitting the power switch as she did so. As much as she wanted to talk to him, she remembered her promise to give him space. *Let it be.* After all, it was a Saturday off from work, so she decided it was for the best to try to relax, with or without him. She relished the golden sunlight, determined to have a good weekend despite being on a now three-week break from her boyfriend of three years.

Kate Shuster walked through her neighborhood on the same route she had taken nearly every Saturday over the past year. She rose early, threw on shorts and a T-shirt, pulled her hair back in a ponytail, and left her one-bedroom apartment at Fourth and Pine, making her way toward Rittenhouse Square. The shopkeepers waved to her as she passed all of the businesses that had become familiar fixtures since moving to this neighborhood: the antique store, the neighborhood tailor, the coffee shop. She was glad it was Saturday and the end of such a crazy week at work. Her team had put in sixteen-hour days designing press kits for an upcoming medical education conference in Boston, planning a grand opening for a hip new restaurant called Three B (owned by Bianca, Blaze, and Becca) in the East Village in New York City, as well as coordinating all social media, radio, and television advertising for a new Jeep dealership in West Chester, her hometown. It was a bonus to have late-day meetings with the owners and marketing team and then go visit her mom, Ellen, after work. It wasn't far from

Philly, but a convenient way to tie in work and family, especially since she didn't get there as much as she wanted. She took a sip from her reusable water bottle and adjusted the strap on her small backpack, which only held her house keys, cell phone, five dollars, paperback novel, lip balm, and sunscreen. Kate preferred walking outside on a nice day to working out on the elliptical machine or spinning at the gym. It was much too nice out to be cooped up indoors. She trekked up Walnut Street toward the park, where she loved to sit outside, read, and, as much as she hated to admit, people watch. She would usually spend the better part of the day there, resting on the soft grass and reading, taking in the sunshine and relaxing from her busy work weeks. She preferred to spend this time alone but occasionally met up with her best friend, Jennifer, in the afternoons or evenings. Jennifer was more the type to sleep in on a Saturday, which Kate fully understood considering her twelve-hour shifts at the hospital.

Kate took a short detour through Washington Square and then walked toward all the high-end Walnut Street shops in which she had never even set foot. Her only local haunt was the Barnes & Noble. She was known to spend hours looking at all different types of books, everything from women's fiction, classics, mysteries, drama, and romance to history and biographies. Kate went through about a book per week and frequently asked the employees to give her new recommendations. She also scanned Amazon and the *New York Times'* bestseller lists weekly for new books. She credited her mom for her love of books since Ellen was an avid reader who read to her regularly as a child. Kate could remember frequent trips to the library in search of new books and her mom reading to her at bedtime every single night, no matter how tired she was.

Kate smiled and looked around as she got closer to the park. The sidewalks were busy with people, everyone out running errands, grabbing coffee, or going to work. Music emanated from some of the Walnut Street shops as it was too nice out to keep their front doors closed. Cars drove up Walnut, stereos cranked, some horns beeping, some brakes screeching. Kate loved the sounds of the city but was anxious to reach the park where she knew it would be a little quieter to read and relax. She crossed Seventeenth Street and let her arms swing gently by her side. She was almost there.

Greg Janera was sound asleep this morning even though his black lab was wagging his tail so fast that he almost knocked over two empty glasses and a half-eaten, now stale bag of potato chips on Greg's nightstand. The dog moved his head toward Greg's face, but Greg pulled the covers over his head to avoid the dog's sloppy tongue. At that moment, he wished he had stopped drinking earlier last night. His head was telling him he made a mistake mixing beer and shots, and his stomach was still churning from the hot wings, ribs, and God only knows what else. But it was his friend Chad's twenty-fifth birthday, and since everyone was staying downtown, no one needed a designated driver. It had been a while since he hung out with the guys, and it was cause for celebration: his first friend to hit a quarter century old. He and his other friends would be hitting that mark over the next year. Events like these made him appreciate this time with his friends before everyone grew up, got married, and had families. He knew life would be different then and hoped that these milestones would take their time in reaching them. He rolled over and saw his dog giving him grief. "Okay, Rocky." Greg yawned, sat up, and put his hands on his head to stop the throbbing. He felt in no condition to take Rocky on his regular walk through Rittenhouse Square, so instead he grabbed his leash, threw on basketball shorts over his boxers, and took him out to the tree in front of his apartment, hoping Rocky would be quick so he could go back to bed. He stood outside, trying to shield his eyes from the blazing sun while Rocky sniffed all around the tree. "C'mon buddy," Greg pled to his dog. He gave the leash a small tug, which made Rocky go. Greg rushed back inside and dumped some food in Rocky's bowl before climbing back into bed and pulling the covers once again over his head.

Kate reached Rittenhouse Square and scoped out a spot near a tree where she could sit in the sun but also be close to the shade. She took in the sky overhead: a perfect blue with soft clouds doing nothing to block the sunlight. Kids playing, couples walking hand in hand, friends talking on the benches: everyone enjoying a beautiful Saturday morning. Kate felt at peace. After sitting down and closing her eyes for just a moment, she rolled her shoulders a couple of times to relax, appreciating the calmness. Kate ran her hand through the grass, taking joy in the thick, soft blades that tickled her fingers. Each blade was the perfect shade of green and had a freshly cut, clean, crisp smell. She applied more sunscreen to her arms, legs, and face, and some balm to her lips. She loved the close-knit community in the park. Even though it was in the middle of the city, the park, with its many bright trees, soft grass, and fountain, always felt like a private oasis. It was set far enough away from the Financial District where many people worked, yet close enough for employees to take a quick walk before or after work. It was also a popular spot for her and her coworkers to eat lunch when they had the luxury of leaving the office. She gazed one more time around trees and benches and then took her novel out of her bag and began reading where she left off last night.

About an hour later, Rocky returned to Greg's side and began pawing his arm. Greg rolled over and tried to shoo him away but the dog was relentless. "Okay, Rocky, just one more hour and then I'll take you to the park." The dog heard blah, blah, blah "park," and instinctively jumped on Greg's bed and began licking his face and wagging his tail so fast that the bed shook. Greg covered his head with the sheet for a minute, but Rocky's nonstop licking forced him to get up and take a quick shower. Ten minutes later, Rocky was panting at the foot of Greg's bed while he threw on a T-shirt and shorts, ran a brush through his hair, and grabbed his wallet. The shower cleared his mind and washed the musty bar smell out of his hair. He felt better but still could have used a few more hours of sleep. He walked into the kitchen with Rocky following close behind, grabbed a slice of leftover pizza from the refrigerator, took a couple of bites, and washed it down with a gulp of flat Coke and four Advil. Sometime soon he was going to have to clean out his fridge. Not that there was much in there, but something smelled like it had been in there a little too long. *Old enough,* he thought, as mold suddenly overcame him and he slammed the door shut. Rocky followed his every move, and finally Greg led him to the front door and they stepped out together for their walk.

Heather decided she was in need of retail therapy, so she called her girlfriend Laurie, who shared her similar interest in fashion and pampering. Laurie would keep her occupied. That girl could easily try on fifty outfits in twenty stores and find it necessary to analyze how each one looked before deciding to purchase or return it to the rack. The same with shoes; she would try on everything from stilettos to ballet flats to comfort gel running sneakers, analyzing which shoes would look best with the many outfits in her wardrobe. The two of them decided to hit the shops on Walnut Street and then go for mani-pedis in the afternoon. Laurie complained she needed some new summer clothes, and Heather wanted to pick up a new sundress and a birthday gift for her aunt Clara. She always splurged on Aunt Clara, the woman who single-handedly raised her like her own child. She shuddered to think what would have become of her if it weren't for Aunt Clara. She was pretty much the only family Heather had, and she always felt guilty for not visiting enough. Clara lived two hours away, up in Scranton; and with her busy job, she wasn't able to make it up there more than four or five times a year. But she would go for the weekend in two weeks to celebrate Clara's sixtieth birthday, and she had to find the perfect gift. Aunt Clara had diverse tastes and always liked getting a decor item for her home. Heather also always gave her a restaurant gift certificate since Clara was not one to "waste money," as she put it, when she could just cook at home. Heather took her empty iced coffee cup, went inside, and cleaned up the kitchen a bit, showered, and dressed in a pretty pink-and-green sundress with white wedge sandals. It was getting close to noon, so she checked her cell phone again but saw no messages or texts. Tucking the phone in her purse, she brushed off any thoughts of Greg, reminding herself yet again they were on a break. She took the elevator down to street level and started walking toward the Starbucks where she and Laurie agreed to meet. She wasn't going to let anything spoil her Saturday off.

Kate lounged under a giant tree, immersed in her book. She loved romantic novels and usually lost herself when the characters and situations seemed so real that she forgot she was reading fiction. Despite her own upbringing, she believed in true love: that there was one person out there meant for you, the one person who could finish your sentences and know what you were thinking. The person who kissed just like you, lips and tongues intertwined, *making magic*. The person who you were meant to share your life with. Who you would raise children with, children who were a spitting image of each of you and who held each of your best qualities. The person you would grow old with and take vacations with. You'd wake up in each other's arms each morning and fall asleep to the sound of each other's heartbeats every night. Kate knew someday she would meet her *one* who would come in and sweep her off her feet. She smiled at the thought of finally meeting him … her one. All but one of her previous boyfriends had only lasted a couple of months. They would get to know each other and Kate would realize he wasn't *the one*, for any number of reasons. No chemistry. Not funny. Worked too much. Didn't want children. Wasn't considerate. Didn't take care of himself. No connection. Wasn't ready for a commitment. Was a bad kisser. Her one long-term boyfriend of a year and a half seemed perfect until she found out he was having extracurricular activities with one of her now former friends. It wasn't that she was picky, but she knew what she wanted and was not interested in settling. Why should she have to? She was twenty-five years old, a college graduate, working in a good job. She had the whole world in front of her. When she was a little girl, her mom used to tell her that someday she would fall in love with her own prince and live happily ever after, just like Cinderella, from her favorite childhood book. Her mom was also still a romantic, even though she had her heart broken in the worst possible way.

Greg and Rocky walked block after block toward the park. He stopped at Dunkin' Donuts for a coffee, which he tried not to spill while Rocky's leash pulled right and then left and then right again. Greg tried to keep his dog walking straight, and silently wished he had a fenced backyard on days like today. The dog sniffed each tree and then started running in circles when he spotted another dog, probably female, across the street. Greg held on to his coffee and Rocky's bowl, water bottle, and leash for the next five blocks before finally arriving at Rittenhouse Square. He sat down on the first empty bench with Rocky at his feet, took a gulp of coffee, and wished the caffeine would come charging through his veins as if it were dripping from an IV. Rocky sat patiently, staring at Greg while he took a few more gulps of the warm beverage. Then Rocky stood up, wagging his tail as if to say, "Enough coffee already. C'mon, let's play." Greg took two more gulps and got up. Rocky pulled Greg along, trying to get to the other dogs. He wagged his tail as they walked, marking his territory on nearly every tree. They came up to another open bench, and Greg fell into it with Rocky by his feet. "Good boy," Greg said, and patted him on the head. Greg was feeling a little more awake now that the caffeine was starting to course through his body. He held out a treat in his hand, and the dog devoured it and lay down beside him while Greg poured some water into Rocky's plastic bowl. Greg finished the remainder of his coffee, and when he looked down, the dog's eyes were closed. For a second, Greg was jealous that he could fall asleep so quickly. He shook his head and scanned the park, noticing all of the different people enjoying the day. He glanced over his shoulder and saw a small group of runners heading up Walnut Street, probably back to their University City campus. Everyone around him looked so carefree, just happy to be enjoying a beautiful day at the park. If only life were truly carefree. His thoughts slowly turned to Heather. He pulled out his cell phone, pushed two buttons to bring up his number one entry on speed dial, and stared at her name. He looked at the digits of her phone number and remembered how, when they met, she had written her name and number down on a napkin at the bar before she left with her girlfriends. He had only waited two days to call her, and it was only another three days before their first date. He smiled, remembering how they had to run through the rain, laughing the entire time, as an unexpected storm had moved through. They sat on cushions in a quiet restaurant, enjoying sushi and sake. Now she would probably insist on getting a cab if they had to walk more than one block in the rain. But it wouldn't bother him. He always felt their lifestyles complemented each other, like red and green at Christmas. He looked to the sky and then stared at her name again. A lump caught in his throat and he pressed the call button. The call went straight to voice mail, and he hung up without leaving a message. Maybe that was for the best. They were on a break, which she had wanted. Things had changed, and he wasn't sure what he wanted anymore. He clutched his phone, knowing he loved her, but after three years, something was missing. He no longer felt the urge to be with her twenty-four hours a day. She wasn't the last thought on his mind before falling asleep, and he accepted that his life had slowly stopped revolving around her. He still cared for Heather deeply but in a different way. She was four years older than Greg and expected marriage. He couldn't blame her and had wanted this at one point, but wasn't sold on the idea like he used to be. He knew someday he'd get married and have a family, but he wasn't ready yet. Rubbing his forehead, he put his phone back in his pocket. Just as soon as he sat back to try to relax, a long-haired man playing a guitar walked by and startled Rocky, who then stood up and started barking. He smiled at his dog and patted him on the head, teasing him with the stick he had picked up earlier. "Okay, boy," Greg said. He quickly gathered Rocky's stuff, and they started walking through the park toward the fountain.

Kate was still reading her book under the tree but kept taking short breaks to people-watch. She noticed three little girls with their mom sitting on a blanket as the mom braided one of the girl's hair. She smiled at them, and the two girls sitting on the blanket waved at her. Kate waved back and thought about her own mom. She was a strong woman to work full-time but always put her child first. Every year, her mom made Kate a homemade birthday cake featuring the theme that Kate was into at that moment. She took her out for a special dinner on the last day of school each year. She made holidays special by making crafts for her teachers and neighbors, building a snowman on the first day of snow no matter how little snow had fallen, and making unique treat bags for the neighborhood trick-or-treaters on Halloween. Kate knew she had an amazing mom and hoped to be at least half as good when she had children someday. She glanced in the opposite direction and saw college students reading thick textbooks with yellow highlighters in hand. *They must be taking those condensed summer courses,* she thought. She turned around and noticed an older couple walking side by side, the man's right hand on the small of the woman's back. She then caught a glimpse of a black dog out of the corner of her eye and sat up straight as it was headed her way. But when she saw it was on a leash, she leaned back against the tree. She noticed the dog's owner and gave a shy smile. Greg smiled back, and Kate returned to her book, which she finished almost three hours later.

CHAPTER 2

Greg couldn't remember the last time he'd slept so well. No bad dreams. No Rocky waking him up. But the more he thought about it, first in the shower and then while he ate a bowl of cereal, he couldn't make sense of it. He even asked Rocky what it meant and then laughed out loud, realizing his dog couldn't respond. Over the past couple of weeks, he woke once or twice a night, sometimes from a nightmare, sometimes for no reason at all, but each time probably related to Heather. Once he dreamt that the two of them were vacationing in Key West, taking long walks on the beach and hitting Duval Street nightly. On the third day of their trip, adventure got the best of them and they decided to give snorkeling a try. The pair joined a private charter with twenty people, and after a demonstration and safety lesson, everyone, including the captain, suited up in masks, snorkels, fins, and life vests. Once off the boat, each person glided though the warm, clear water, exploring various sea life. That is, everyone except Greg. He was underwater, completely naked, surrounded by his snorkeling group while they all watched in laughter. Although he was a good swimmer, Greg was in a state of temporary paralysis, making it impossible to reach the surface. He struggled to survive but continued sinking farther and farther down to the bottom of the ocean. Not one person had helped him, including Heather. In a cold sweat and arms flailing, he had woken up at three o'clock in the morning, just before he was about to drown. He wasn't able to go back to sleep that night. Instead, Greg sat up in bed, glassy-eyed, watching his sleeping dog snoring away. By the time he got to the office, he had already had four cups of coffee and had sworn off anything involving being in the water. So for him to have slept so well last night could mean that he was coming to a resolution about his relationship. He wouldn't think about it too hard though; it was, after all, just one good night of sleep.

After he finished breakfast and caught up on a few e-mails and texts, he and Rocky stepped out. With his head held high, he admired the streets and buildings and people he loved so much. Sunlight lit up Philadelphia to a golden hue, and although it was hot, the humidity level was low. He took a gulp from his water bottle, keeping his newspaper tucked under his arm, and made a right from Spruce to Twentieth Street, heading toward Rittenhouse Square. Rocky was panting, and Greg could see fur falling from his body as he shook. The dog was happy, though, wagging his tail and sniffing every tree, telephone pole, and sign in his path. As soon as they reached the park, Greg poured cold water into a plastic bowl, and Rocky slurped it up, licking his chops afterward. The dog then yawned and lay down in the shady grass right at Greg's feet.

Greg looked around and wondered why these people weren't spending the day at a pool or down the shore or even the mountains. He opened *The Philadelphia Inquirer's* sports section and read the highlights from last night's Phillies game. Turning the page, he browsed an article on the Flyers but put the paper down because it was hard to think about ice hockey in the middle of the summer heat.

He folded the paper, noticing a man, balding and portly, sitting on the ground watching him. "Excuse me, but if you're done with that, do you mind?" Greg handed the paper over.

"Sure, no problem." The man thanked him, and Greg nodded in return.

Just then, Rocky perked his head up at the sound of a barking dog and tried to break away from his leash, but Greg had a strong hold of it. "Calm down, buddy," Greg said as Rocky looked at him with sad eyes. He pulled out a treat from his pocket and gave it to Rocky, who munched it up within seconds. Greg wiped his forehead and let his thoughts turn to Heather. It was a week since they'd spoken. She had called him at work, and he was right in the middle of a department meeting so he excused himself, answered the call, and told her he'd have to call her back. He called that night, expecting to finally come to some sort of conclusion on the future of their relationship, but the conversation was filled with lulls. They didn't speak about anything important, instead talking about work and, sadly, the weather. It felt awkward and stilted, and he couldn't wait to hang up. No outcome there.

He'd have to really think about what he wanted. He knew it was time for the critical talk: either take their relationship to the next level or break up. It should be as simple as black and white, but relationships were never like that. Real feelings were involved, and someone was bound to end up hurt. The last thing he wanted to do was hurt her in any way, but they couldn't continue the way they were going. He knew dating her with a commitment behind it wasn't enough for her, especially after that incident at Tiffany's. The look of bliss on her face while she tried on that ring made him feel queasy. She was in her element, chatting with the salespeople, and even though he was trying not to listen, he overheard them talking about place settings and bridal party gifts. He had thought up a quick excuse that he had an early meeting at work, gave her a quick kiss, and high-tailed it out of there. He wasn't ready for marriage and everything that came along with it, not by a long shot.

He tried to push the thought of Heather out of his mind and bent down to pet Rocky, who looked content resting in the shade. Greg shook his head thinking how lucky Rocky was, a life without confusing relationships, work, or bills to pay. "If only everyone had it that easy," Greg said under his breath.

Greg looked across the park by the fountain and the sight of a woman gave him déjà vu. "Didn't I see her here a couple of weeks ago?" She was sitting on a small blue blanket in the shady area under a tree, reading a book. Her auburn curls were tied back in a ponytail, and she wore simple denim shorts and a short-sleeved white shirt. Her feet were bare. He saw a pair of pink flip-flops placed neatly beside her bag. Greg watched her for several minutes as she turned back pages in her book.

Kate was reading a thick paperback novel and trying to keep cool in the shade. The temperature was steadily climbing, and she was thinking about all the people she knew and whether or not they had a pool she might be able to use this afternoon. She silently started rattling off names, and when someone from work came to mind, she perked up and fell right back down when she remembered the person was away in Europe on vacation. Unable to think of anyone else, she took a gulp of water and put down her book. Kate lay down on her stomach and scanned the park, thinking about the things she had done over the last couple of weeks: a trip down the shore with Jen, a few summer concerts in the city, and going out with some coworkers after work. It was shaping up to be a fun and relaxing summer, and work didn't seem like it would be off-the-wall busy again until the fall. Gazing at no one area in particular, she realized the park wasn't as crowded as usual, no doubt because of the heat, but there were still a lot of people walking around or sitting in the shade. No matter what, Kate preferred to be outdoors than cooped up with air conditioning. She picked up her book and stared at the cover. In mid thought, she looked up and noticed that same black dog she'd seen before, panting, with its owner holding the leash and heading straight for her. Kate quickly pushed herself up into a sitting position.

"Hi. I know you. I mean, I've seen you here before." Greg and Rocky stood before her as Rocky sniffed the grass surrounding her blanket.

"Hi. Yes, I have seen you two here before." Kate stood up and petted Rocky on the head.

They stood for several seconds in silence. Greg was taken aback by her porcelain skin and shiny curls. She wore small silver hoop earrings but no necklace or bracelet. However, she did wear a ring. A narrow-banded silver ring with a large blue stone sat on her left index finger. A ray of sun caught the stone, and a small rainbow beamed up and bounced in the sunlight. Greg tried to look at it without being obvious. It was actually the type of stone that sparked his curiosity. He didn't think it was sapphire or blue topaz but rather some kind of unique blue stone he'd never seen before. Maybe it was aquamarine.

Greg laughed nervously and looked down at Rocky. He wiped his palm on the side of his shorts and then looked back up and met Kate's deep brown eyes. "I'm Greg." He held out his hand, and Kate shook it.

"It's nice to meet you, Greg. I'm Kate."

"Kate." Her name danced on his tongue for just a second. "This here is Rocky." Greg gave Rocky a pat on his head.

"Well hello there, Rocky." Kate ran her hand across the dog's smooth black coat. The dog wagged his tail and licked Kate's bare feet as if they were steak bones.

"Rocky, stop! Don't do that!" Greg yanked Rocky's leash back. He tapped Rocky on the butt and turned to Kate. "I'm so sorry ..."

Kate laughed and put her hand up to stop him from apologizing. "It's okay, really." She petted Rocky on the head and bent down to be eye level with the dog. She continued to pet him and then smiled up at Greg. In that instant, Greg knew he was going to like this girl.

Greg held tight to Rocky and wiped his brow. He shuffled his feet and glanced around the park. "So you braved the park today too."

Kate laughed. "The heat doesn't bother me too much if it's not humid."

Greg twisted his neck from side to side and then watched a bird land on the edge of the fountain. Rocky was still sniffing the grass, and Greg leaned over and petted him on the head.

"Reading anything good?"

"Just a love story. It's pretty good, though. Do you like to read?" Kate looked up and noticed his deep blue eyes.

"Yes." Greg smiled and looked away before returning his gaze to Kate. "No. Well only if you count the sports section."

"Sure, that counts."

Kate laughed, and Greg smiled, a chin dimple appearing that took Kate by surprise. Her stomach did a tiny flip, and she quickly looked away, as if he knew.

Kate twisted her ring and adjusted her ponytail. She wasn't sure why Greg came up to her and was trying to interpret his body language of shuffling feet and hands combing through his hair.

"Well, I was just going to get something to drink and ..." Greg looked down at Rocky and then back to meet Kate's eyes. "Would you like to come?"

Kate felt herself blush and looked to her side and saw a group of high school girls walking, talking and laughing. So that's what he wanted. He certainly wasn't shy. He was cute, despite being a little sweaty, wearing oversized basketball shorts, and an old Phillies T-shirt. He had wavy, dark hair, and his kind eyes glittered in the sun ... and let's not forget that chin dimple. Kate's mom always told her she was a good judge of character. Kate believed this too; however, when it came to guys, she was right only half of the time. But with that dog, there was no way he was dangerous. In fact, she felt safe and secure standing there with him. Kate smiled and met his eyes. "Sure."

After Kate gathered up her bag and blanket, Greg and Kate with Rocky in tow walked through the park to a little outdoor café on Walnut Street. They took a table under a wide canary yellow umbrella, and Rocky lay down underneath in the shade. Greg poured cold water in Rocky's bowl, and after a healthy drink, the dog lay down to rest.

Greg and Kate each ordered an iced tea from a waitress with jet black hair, half a dozen ear and nose piercings, and thick black eyeliner that almost made her look like a raccoon. As they waited, Kate applied lip balm and Greg checked to make sure Rocky was okay.

"He seems like a great dog."

Greg's face lit up. "Oh, he is. He sure is. I got him when he was six weeks old, and it's really true what they say about a dog being man's best friend."

"How old is he?"

"Six."

"Wow. I thought you were going to say one or two. He seems like a puppy."

"Sometimes he does, and it's great. He loves to run around, chase, and fetch like a little kid, but sometimes he just wants to lie down and sleep like an old man."

Kate grinned. She had never heard anyone talk about their dog like that. "And did you get to name him?"

Greg smiled. He loved telling this story. "It was the only name that really fit. He was my high school graduation present from my parents. They knew I wanted another dog, and one of the teachers at my mom's school had a dog that just had puppies. So I went with her to pick one out, and once I saw him, I knew he was the one." Greg glanced quickly in Rocky's direction. "Actually, if you can believe it, he was the runt of the litter and wasn't doing so well for the first few weeks. He struggled with eating and gaining weight but persevered and never gave up. And I made a promise to him that if he hung in there, I'd always be there for him." Greg shook his head and then smiled. "My first thought was Rocky Balboa. My brothers and I loved watching those old movies when we were kids and he just reminded me of Rocky. Plus I thought it was a cool name for a dog."

Kate smiled. It was a rare occurrence for her to meet a genuinely nice guy. "It just shows how well you take care of him and how much you love him."

"Thanks. He's been with me practically every day since he was born so we're both pretty attached."

"I never had a dog growing up, but someday I'd like to get one. Maybe a Terrier or a Maltese, so she could curl up with me on the couch."

"Small dogs are okay, but I'd feel ... I don't know if this is the right word ...but wimpy."

Kate nodded but thought Greg couldn't be wimpy if he tried. He was a guy's guy. She could already tell he was athletic but not a jock, had a good sense of humor but wasn't the class clown, and was smart but not Ivy League boring. And she could tell right away he wasn't one of those metrosexual guys who got pedicures, wore only designer clothes, or obsessed about his hair looking immaculate at all times. To put it lightly, he was perfect.

The waitress came back and delivered their iced teas just as her cell phone announced a call with loud Goth music emanating from her pocket. Greg added four sugar packets and stirred, and Kate squeezed the fresh slice of lemon into her glass before dropping it in. Greg took a big gulp, and Kate sipped hers through a straw, raising her eyebrows at the tartness and then adding a Splenda packet.

"I'm partial now to black labs after having Rocky. But I had two dogs as a kid: a Siberian husky named Snowball and a Golden Retriever named Bingo. My parents thought it was a good way to teach us responsibility."

"Well it seems like it worked. Rocky is lucky to have you."

"Thanks. But I think I'm the one fortunate to have him." Greg leaned over to peek at Rocky, who was resting at his feet.

Kate suddenly felt a butterfly in her stomach which she tried to quell by sipping some more of her iced tea. "Do you live in town?"

Greg nodded. "Over on Lombard. You?"

"Old City."

"Cool." Greg put one hand around his glass and let the iciness soak into his skin.

"I like it. There's a lot to do, and it's a fun neighborhood."

Greg nodded. "Where did you grow up?"

"West Chester. What about you?"

"The Northeast, not too far from the Franklin Mills Mall."

Kate moved her straw around her glass. Her ring slowly started to change to the color of a pear, and she put her hand down by her side. Greg looked at Rocky, who was standing up and pacing as far as his leash would let him. He wasn't ready to leave, but he knew Rocky would soon start bothering him.

"Do you want to come with us to the dog run? It's over at Twenty-Fifth and Spruce."

Kate shrugged. "Sure."

"Great. Rocky loves it and we can talk some more."

This was unusual, Kate thought. A guy who enjoys talking. In her experience, many guys gave one word answers and didn't ask a lot of questions for fear of getting a lot in return. She smiled to herself, thinking of a guy she met recently at an after-work party who barely gave more than a yes or no response, even to open ended questions. After about fifteen minutes, she had excused herself to make a phone call and "accidentally" lost him in the crowd.

Kate offered money for her drink, but Greg wouldn't accept it. After he paid, they walked toward the dog run, enjoying light conversation along the way. Once they got there, Greg and Kate entered the larger dog section through the double gates. It wasn't as crowded as normal but still a busy Saturday. Owners sat on benches talking about everything from their pets to life in the city. Greg removed Rocky's leash, took a tennis ball from his pocket, and threw it across the green Astroturf. Rocky darted to the other end, grabbed the tennis ball in his mouth, and returned it to Greg. "Hey, boy, there's Cassidy. Why don't you go play?" Like a teenager getting permission, Rocky leapt over to his friend, a Collie, and started to sniff her before the pair tumbled together on the ground.

Kate stood beside Greg, taking it in: the friendly atmosphere of the dog park, the competitive sounds of a basketball game being played just steps away, the happy squeals of children in the playground on the other side of the basketball court. The dog parents in the gate chitchatting with each other about all-natural dog food and BPA-free dog-chew toys. The weather was hot yet comfortable, with a decent breeze, making it seem cooler than it was.

"We can sit over there." Greg motioned toward the wall on the opposite side. "He'll be occupied for a little while."

"How often do you bring him here?"

"About five times a week. It's one of the reasons I moved to my place. I like being close by."

"You are the ultimate dog owner."

They watched Rocky play with Cassidy and two other dogs who Greg knew but had never talked to their owners. The four dogs sniffed each other, tumbled, and chased one another through the park. Kate silently watched them, admiring how well they played with one another and how well maintained the park was.

Greg turned to Kate. "So what do you do for work?"

"I'm in PR at Brice and Bellow Public Relations. Over at Eighteenth and Market."

Greg nodded. "That's only two blocks from my office. I'm in IT at Black Rock Technologies." Greg turned away from Kate briefly to check on Rocky who was still playing with Cassidy. The other two dogs apparently went to play on their own.

"I've only been there about six months but I like it so far. What kind of IT do you do?"

"I'm a software engineer. How did you get into PR?"

"It's a funny story. Getting the job was actually a fluke. Someone I met at a networking event has a sister who works there and gave my resume to HR. Went in for an interview and got the job the next week. It's just ironic that I spent so much time job searching and this just landed in my lap."

"You must have really impressed them."

Kate felt herself blush. "Tell me more about what you do."

"I help design apps. Mostly news-related and educational for students." Greg turned to make sure Rocky was okay. "It pays the bills. I'd eventually like to get into sports or gaming apps or maybe web design."

"I'm sure you do a great job, and I can see you working with sporting apps. I haven't thought about what I'd like to do in the future. Who knows; maybe someday I'll open up my own PR firm."

"There you go. You can be my PR rep when I develop a top-notch sports app that everyone realizes they can't live without."

"There you go, Greg. I would love to be your PR rep."

Greg's dimples appeared as he smiled at Kate and then he looked over at Rocky, who stopped to slurp up water from a large bowl. "I think he needs a hose down. I'll be right back."

Kate nodded and watched Greg lead Rocky to the hoses. She held her hand up to check the color of her ring. It was now a bright shade of pink. She touched the stone and looked to the sky. Turning back to Greg, she saw him turn the nozzle and spray water over Rocky's silky black coat. The dog shook and wagged his tail, and when Greg was done with the hose, he ran his hand down Rocky's back and patted him. He squatted down to speak to the dog, and then Rocky took off back toward the other dogs. Greg rinsed his hands and then rubbed them together. He wiped his hands on his shorts while walking back to Kate.

"Rocky seemed to enjoy that." Kate glanced in Rocky's direction as the dog ran right back to Cassidy.

"He swims down at a creek near my parents. Some dogs don't like to get wet but he loves it."

"I forgot to ask where you went to school."

"Drexel. Did you go in the city too?"

"No, West Chester. It was easier to afford living at home. My mom and I are close so I didn't mind not going away. Did you live on campus?"

Greg nodded. "I had an apartment with a few other guys from school."

Greg and Kate watched Rocky for a few minutes as he played with Cassidy and then a German shepherd and golden retriever. The four dogs ran along the fence, playfully chasing each other. Rocky started panting about five minutes later and ran right back to Greg. He barked twice and then went over to the water bowl and slurped a healthy drink. The weather felt a little cooler, and Greg asked Kate if she'd like to continue walking. Kate agreed, and they walked out of the double gate after Greg put Rocky's leash back on. A breeze rustled the trees as they casually headed back toward Walnut and then kept going toward the Museum of Art. Rocky sniffed the trees as they walked, and Greg and Kate enjoyed light, easy conversation. Kate reached in her backpack and pulled out her lip balm and gently applied it to her lips. Greg snuck a peek from the corner of his eye and smiled as he detected a trace scent of coconut. Once they reached the famous steps of the museum, the temperature felt even a little cooler. They dodged the large crowds of people who seemed to always be at the famous landmark. Then they spoke to each other using only their eyes, smiled wide, and raced each other up the steps.

"I just love the view from up here," Kate said, trying to catch her breath.

Greg scanned the city, straight down Eakins Oval, across the Benjamin Franklin Parkway, and over to City Hall. The sky was clear, and he took in the beauty of the city. Greg's breathing was slowly coming back to normal. Rocky panted and shook fur from his coat.

Kate walked around for a minute to cool off. There were a lot of people walking around, snapping pictures of the city, and enjoying the spectacular view. Kate came up to Rocky and petted his silky coat. "Look, Rocky's footprints. From the movie. This is perfect! Why don't I take your picture with Rocky on top of the Rocky Steps?"

Greg frowned and shrugged. "I don't want to look like a tourist."

"Nah, who cares what people think?"

Greg thought it over. "You're right. C'mon, Rocky." Greg and Rocky stood by the famous footprints while Kate got her phone ready.

"Wait. Squat down so I get the footprints too."

Greg squatted and pulled Rocky closer to him. "Sit, Rocky." Greg patted him on the head.

"Perfect. Okay, Smile." Kate looked at the picture in her phone. "Perfect."

"Let me take one of you now."

Kate shrugged. "Okay, why not?"

Greg took his phone out of his pocket and they swapped places. He snapped her picture. He held back the phone to look at it and smiled. They texted each other their pictures and sat down in the shade to drink some water.

As the crowds increased, they decided to head back to Rittenhouse Square. After going back down the steps and crossing the street, they headed back down the parkway. They made a right turn on Twenty-Second Street, and Greg stopped dead in his tracks at the sight and aroma of a soft pretzel vendor. The warm fresh-baked dough and salt wafted in the air under a red-and-blue-striped umbrella.

Greg's eyes moved from Kate to the vendor and then back to Kate. "Want one?"

"Okay, sure."

Greg asked for two pretzels, paid the vendor, and handed a pretzel wrapped in tissue to Kate.

"Thanks. That is really sweet."

"You're welcome."

Kate looked at her pretzel and then at the pretzel vendor, a guy in his early twenties with light brown hair, cargo shorts, and an Eagles T-shirt. "Could I get some mustard, please?"

Rocky's head jerked toward Kate, and he let out a growl as if someone was trying to break into his house.

"Oh my God! Did he just growl at me?" She could feel the dog's breath on her leg as she stared at Rocky, who was now growling softly.

Greg laughed. "It's just that he hates the word M-U-S-T-A-R-D."

"Why?" The vendor handed Kate two packets of mustard, and she thanked him.

"It's actually a funny story. Last summer, I was eating a soft pretzel with hot, spicy mustard. Rocky kept bothering me for a piece, but I already had it on the whole thing and I knew he wouldn't like it. I told him to lie down, but he wouldn't listen so I broke off a piece and gave it to him." Greg laughed recalling the memory. "He started chewing it and then spit it out. So I said, 'Oh, so you want some mustard?'" Greg spelled the word again. "I gave him another piece, and he did the same thing. So I asked him again if he wanted …" Greg pointed to the mustard packet. "And he growled so loud. And ever since, every time he hears the word"—Greg lowered his voice—"*mustard*, he gets mad. My friends think it's funny."

Kate looked at Rocky and petted him on the head. "Sorry there, Rocky. I won't say it around you again. I promise."

Once they reached Rittenhouse Square, they sat down on Kate's blanket and ate their pretzels, sans mustard. They continued talking for another hour before they each walked home. She didn't expect anything afterward. After all, she'd heard, "I'll call you," or "I'll text you," one too many times before, but she secretly hoped she'd be wrong this time. Greg seemed like a nice, responsible, and caring guy. Plus he was easy on the eyes. Yes, he was very easy on the eyes.

CHAPTER 3

"Okay, so we get there and all my brothers want to do is go swimming."

"Are you serious?" Kate leaned forward on her couch and curled her legs underneath her to get comfortable. A fast-moving thunderstorm had barreled through the city at rush hour, and now the night was cool and crisp. With her windows open, a refreshing breeze flowed through her apartment, and she had to use a lightweight blanket to cover her bare legs. She had a small table lamp turned on, which gave her room a dim glow.

"Yeah." Greg laughed. "And since I was the youngest, I pretty much did whatever they did." Greg shook his head. "My parents were pissed, but luckily for the first couple of days, my dad was too tired to care."

Kate was laughing so hard she could barely speak. "I can't believe you're all just a few miles from Disney World and all your brothers wanted to do was go to the pool!"

"I know. After about three days, my mom had had enough and dragged us to the Magic Kingdom and Epcot anyway, but my brothers, they really just wanted to go swimming."

"What did your dad say?"

"That next year he was going to buy a summer pool membership and save himself the two-day, thousand mile drive.

Each way. I remember he kept harping on the fact that it was two days in the car to essentially go swimming." Greg shook his head, got up, and grabbed another can of Coke out of the fridge.

"What about your mom?"

Greg drank a gulp of soda. "She made us go on all the rides, and even though my brothers didn't want to admit it, we really did have a good time. But she wanted us to be happy, and if that meant we spent our big Orlando vacation at the hotel pool, she decided to let it go. I remember hearing her tell my dad one night, 'Boys will be boys.'"

"That is too much, Greg!" Kate stretched out on her couch and rubbed her stomach to ease the pain from laughing. This was their third phone conversation this week, after two long nights of Facebook messaging, and the more they talked and got to know each other, the more relaxed she felt. It was that easy, comfortable feeling you get when you are friends with someone for years instead of days.

"So every other family vacation we went on, my parents refused to book a hotel with a pool. It was like a dictatorship: they took us to all the attractions, and we had to see all the sights. Looking back, though, I guess they did the right thing. Otherwise all of our vacation memories would have been swimming."

"Where did you go?" Kate took a drink of berry-flavored water and adjusted the blanket over her legs.

"The usual local suspects. Poconos, Jersey shore, Boston, Colonial Williamsburg, Baltimore, DC, New York. After the Florida mess, my dad refused to drive more than five hours each way."

"Well, I bet you guys had fun. And at least you got to swim in the ocean down the shore, right?"

"Yeah. That's the funny thing too. They loved that we wanted to spend most of our time on the beach and in the ocean." Greg paused. "Hey, you know it's probably because they didn't feel like shelling out tons of cash for the rides and games!"

"That's funny, Greg. Your parents sound great."

"They are. Just regular, down-to-earth people. My mom still works at the school, and my dad is an electrician. They did the best they could raising four boys. And they came out of it alive."

Kate laughed. "Now that's an accomplishment in itself!"

"Hey, we weren't all bad! Just four average Philly kids who basically got into everything."

"Somehow I feel you have more stories up your sleeve." Kate raised her eyebrows even though Greg couldn't see her.

"Oh I do. But it's your turn. What was it like growing up?"

Kate sat back on the couch and thought about her mom for a moment. They were a team, two peas in a pod, doing everything together as far back as she could remember.

"Well, I grew up with my mom as an only child, so I don't really have too many good stories to share. So can you tell me another one? I need to vicariously live through a childhood with siblings."

"I'm sure you have good stories, and in time I'll drag them out of you. But, let's see." Greg looked to the ceiling as Rocky lay beside him on the couch. His apartment was a typical bachelor pad: mismatched furniture, large TV, stereo. He didn't put too much effort into keeping it neat and clean, so clothes were haphazardly placed throughout his bedroom, sports equipment strewn about, and Rocky's toys scattered between the living room, kitchen, and bedroom. Every couple of weeks, Greg would "straighten up," which meant picking up stuff off the floor and putting his sports magazines and newspapers in a rack that his mom had bought him when he moved in. His kitchen had the necessary essentials, but he didn't have a dishwasher so he avoided cooking too frequently and would typically eat out or get things that could be heated up. He petted Rocky's coat, and the dog rolled over for a belly rub. Greg smiled and indulged his dog. "Okay, this is a good one."

"Great. Let's hear it."

"So I'm about five or six years old, and my parents go out of town for the weekend for a wedding and leave me and my brothers home with our cousin, Mark."

"Wait, how old was Mark?

"At the time about seventeen."

"And your brothers?"

"John would have been fourteen, Brian twelve, and Dan nine." Greg paused. "So my brothers were on this army kick for at least a year, and they decided to turn the house into a fort. Well, two forts, really … one for each team. And I mean real forts. We turned over all the furniture, couches, chairs, tables, beds, even dressers. We divided into teams. I was with John since I was the youngest, and we literally were at war with each other. I think the only thing we didn't turn over were the refrigerator and stove."

"Oh my God! So what happened?" Kate sat up straighter and adjusted the blanket. She glanced outside at the peaceful night.

"We came up with this game; actually, John came up with it. We had tons of these red-and-blue flags, and we had to put our team's flags on the other team's fort without getting caught. The team with the most flags on the other fort at the end, won."

Kate smiled, envisioning Greg as a little boy playing with his brothers. "What happened when you guys caught each other?"

"The person who got caught would have to take a ten-minute suspension so then it was two on one. Essentially you were getting double-teamed. But I think the best part was that it brought me a lot closer to John. He had these old camouflage clothes that were way too big for me but I wore them anyway so we matched. And we slept in sleeping bags in the fort."

"What did Mark do?"

"Oh, Mark thought it was funny. He was our official referee."

Kate pictured four boys running around the house in chaos. "Did you guys put everything back before your parents got home?"

Greg laughed. "They actually came home right in the middle of our grand finale battle, a few hours earlier than expected."

Kate gasped. "What did they do?"

"My dad laughed because he and his brother did the same thing when they were kids. It was funny because my dad just wanted to know who won. But my mom, that was a different story. She was pretty much horrified."

"So who won?" Kate took a sip of her drink.

"Yours truly and John. You wouldn't expect anything less, would you?"

"No, I wouldn't. But that is too funny, Greg. Sometimes I wish I had brothers or sisters. I don't have any good stories like that."

"It wasn't always fun, you know, growing up in a big family."

"Why?"

"No privacy. I shared a room with Dan and a bathroom with all three, so you can just imagine how that was. Plus I had to wear all their hand-me-downs, and I inherited all their used bikes and toys. They even ruined Christmas—they told me when I was eight years old that Santa was really our parents, and I went to my mom crying. She grounded my brothers for two weeks for that one."

"Well, maybe now I'm glad I was an only child."

"I think there are good and bad things about having siblings or being an only child. My brothers and I are close, but we still wrestle and mess around when I see them. They all still live in the Northeast, so I see them every few weeks or so when I go home. John's the only one who's married, and his wife Lindsay is the coolest person you'll ever meet."

"That's awesome. It's great you are all close."

"Do you see your mom often? I'll bet she misses you."

"Every few weeks. Why do you say that?"

Greg pictured Kate in his head. Her shiny auburn hair. Those tiny freckles on her face. Her deep chocolate brown eyes. "I'll just bet she does. Now, it's really your turn this time. Talk to me."

Kate got up to close the window, and when she walked by her mantel, she saw the picture of her as a little girl with her mom. She picked it up, her fingers tracing her mom's smile and then her little pink ballerina costume. "I used to be in ballet with my friend Jen when we were little. We were inseparable ever since grade school. We ate lunch together every day and played after school and did our homework together. I actually used to go on summer vacations with her family to Sea Isle City." Kate sat back down on the couch and picked up a cube frame containing photos of her and Jen. The one on top was from their high school graduation. Their gowns hung down to the floor, and each held their diploma in their left hand, their other arm extended while holding out their caps and tassels. She turned the cube to see the two of them at a tap dance recital wearing red-and-black costumes and smiles so wide they looked painful. In another, she and Jen were bundled up in snowsuits making snow angels on her front lawn. "We would always decorate our Christmas trees together too. I forgot about that." She put the cube beside her on the couch and pulled her hair up into a ponytail but let it fall back down over her shoulders.

"Jen from CHOP, right?"

"She's the one. She always loved working with kids so the Children's Hospital is really the best place for her. And of course it's the best one in Philadelphia."

"That's good. Does she live downtown?"

"No, she's over in Manayunk. We talked about being roommates but the timing didn't work out. Maybe someday." Kate rolled the cube in her hand and saw herself and Jen at the beach wearing matching pink and green polka dot swimsuits when they were about ten. She remembered that trip, could still smell the vanilla fudge that Jen's mom bought on the boardwalk and the taste of salt water when she was running through the ocean surf and fell down, opening her mouth just as she hit the water. "So, Greg, I think it's your turn again."

Greg took a long swallow of Coke. "Changing the subject back to me, are we?"

"Is it that obvious?" Greg thought she was avoiding talking about herself and her childhood.

"Well, you know I'm a Phillies fan."

"You don't say," Kate joked.

"Ha-ha, very funny. Anyway, my dad used to take us to games at the Vet … you know, when he wasn't driving a thousand miles to take us to a pool. I would always bring my mitt because I just knew I would eventually catch a foul ball. And one year my dad splurged for lower level brown seats on the third base line for John's birthday. So there I was with my glove, and Bobby Abreu is up to bat, and hits one down the line. I think my eyes nearly came out of my head. I jumped out of my seat, and it bounced up in the stands and went right into my glove." Greg smiled and plucked the ball from his bookcase. "I felt like a star that day." He rolled the ball around in his hand and then quickly put it back before Rocky thought he was finally going to get it.

"That's pretty cool, Greg. Not many people can say they caught a foul ball from Bobby Abreu."

"Not a lot of eight-year-olds, anyway. I think that's what made me want to play outfield. But sometimes I played shortstop too."

"You'll have to show me pictures sometime." Kate thought of him in a tight baseball uniform. She glanced down at her ring and it was the color of a sparkling emerald.

"Anything for you." He would show her his high school yearbook, tucked away on his bookshelf.

"Did you play other sports?"

"A little basketball with my brothers when I was younger. We still get together to play once in a while. I run a little too but nothing competitive, just a few miles around the city. Did you play sports growing up?"

"I danced when I was young: ballet and tap. I didn't play sports in high school. Actually no, I was on the tennis team for two years, but I wasn't very good. Now I just like to work out at the gym or walk. I jog sometimes—like you, nothing competitive."

"Maybe we can jog together sometime then?"

"Sure, I'd like that." Kate twisted her hair in her fingers. She was enjoying talking to Greg. It felt familiar and easy, and she couldn't believe she had only just met him.

"So tell me more about you. I want to know."

Kate blushed and picked a piece of lint from her couch. "More about me ... there isn't much to tell. I'm close with my mom, and she's always been extremely supportive of me. She's a really strong woman. She used to work two jobs when I was young to pay for my dance lessons and costumes."

"Well, she raised a beautiful daughter."

Kate felt her face go red again. "Thanks. She was always there for me. Always took me to my lessons, always sat in the front row at my recitals, always helped me with my homework."

Greg almost asked about her father but decided to wait until she brought him up.

"When I got my first job out of college, I saved up and bought her tickets for a cruise so she could go with one of her friends. My mom used to travel a lot when she was younger, but after she got married, she just didn't have time anymore. She was so happy, but I think it made me even happier to be able to do that for her."

"You are the perfect daughter. She is lucky to have you."

"Aw, you are making me blush. You're sweet."

"So I've been told."

"Okay, don't start getting an ego on me now!" Kate joked.

Greg laughed. "Never, Kate. Not with you anyway." He balanced the phone between his ear and shoulder, thinking about the past week and a half. They spent about six hours on the phone and countless hours messaging online. She laughed at his stories. Greg could picture her sweet face, and several times wanted to crawl through the phone line just so he could see her. He reasoned that the worst she could say was no if he asked her on a date, and then at least he could heal his wounds in the privacy of his own apartment, Rocky by his side.

Kate was glad Greg couldn't see her, blushing to her heart's content, a big smile on her face. "Sure, I would love to go."

"Great. How about Friday night? I can pick you up."

Kate tucked a strand of hair behind her ear. "Friday sounds perfect."

CHAPTER 4

"Where are you taking me?"

Greg had called her one more time at work to confirm their plans and ask her to dress casually. She was wearing lightweight Capri pants, a pink top, and sandals that showed off her matching pink toenails. Her hair was pulled back in a barrette, and small silver earrings dangled as she walked. Her ring matched the color of the summer sky at dusk.

"It's a surprise," Greg said, a mischievous grin on his face.

"Well, it had better be good." Kate softly nudged him on the arm.

They walked side by side for a couple of blocks. The humidity had dropped, and a cool breeze rustled the trees. It was still light out, but the sun would be slowly going down over the next hour. Near the corner of Tenth and Chestnut, they came upon a homeless man sitting on the sidewalk, holding a cardboard sign that told passersby he was a Vietnam veteran. Greg looked at him, his face streaked with dirt, wearing a ratty T-shirt and jeans that were at least fifteen years old and had as many owners. He stopped and pulled a five-dollar bill from his wallet and put it in the man's cup. He and Greg nodded to each other. Kate smiled and then reached over to touch the back of Greg's hand. He gently took her hand, and they walked with fingers intertwined for six more blocks, taking in the sounds of the city: a street musician playing jazz on the corner, horns honking, car tires screeching, a city bus grumbling by, people talking on their cell phones. Yet despite the sounds and people rushing about, they felt like they were the only two people in Philadelphia.

"Here we are," Greg announced. They stood in front of his favorite local pub. Kate gazed up at the small wooden sign above the door that read "Bottoms Up." In the windows were lighted signs for Budweiser and Coors beer as well as banners for the Phillies, Flyers, Sixers, and Eagles.

Greg pulled the door open and led her in, his hand on the small of her back. Kate took in its rustic appearance, worn wooden floor lightly covered in peanut shells, and old jukebox in the corner. There was a rack filled with the *City Paper* and *Philadelphia Weekly* next to a vending machine selling mints and gum. She saw two older men in jeans sitting at the bar with half-empty glasses. At the bar she could see liquor bottles lined up on the shelf and a row of beer mugs and shot glasses. A very beat-up dartboard hung on the wall next to a couple of lighted signs heralding all four Philadelphia sports teams. This clearly wasn't the type of bar where you went for happy hour to have a cosmopolitan or strawberry daiquiri. Rick, the bartender, shouted hello to Greg, and Greg nodded. Kate nudged Greg on the arm. "You really know where to take a woman."

"This is a classic pub, Kate. Any woman should be so lucky."

"Well," Kate said as she glanced at two broken bar stools in the corner, "if you say so."

Greg walked over to the bar and ordered two beers from Rick. When he came back, he handed Kate a glass and a bottle of Miller. They sat down at one of the wooden tables in the corner, a bowl of peanuts in the center.

"This," Kate whispered, glancing around the bar, "is a real dive."

Greg laughed. "I'm glad you like it."

Kate started laughing and took a sip of her beer straight from the bottle. They smiled at each other, as if reading the other's thoughts. There was something about him, his easygoing nature, his sense of humor, the fact he didn't take himself too seriously. She was enjoying being around him and had a sneaking suspicion he felt the same. Greg tossed a few peanuts in his mouth. He motioned to Kate to take some, but she shook her head. Greg shrugged and popped some more peanuts in his mouth while leaving the shells in a small pile next to the bowl on their table.

Greg took a short swallow of beer and smiled at Kate in a way that made her feel that she was special to him.

"Hey, is that the same ring you had on when we met?" Greg moved his head closer to squint at the ring.

Kate glanced down and held her fingers out straight. "Yeah."

Greg wrinkled his brow. "But wasn't it blue?"

"Oh, it's actually a mood ring."

"A mood ring." Greg put his fingers on Kate's hand and leaned in closer to look at the stone. He took in the sea green color of the ring.

"I got it in New Orleans. Have you ever been there?"

Greg shook his head.

"Oh, you should definitely go sometime."

"I know. My buddies are always talking about going to Mardi Gras. Maybe next year."

"I went for work. It's wild year-round, Mardi Gras or not."

"I'll keep that in mind." Greg winked at Kate.

"Do you want to hear the story? About the ring." She took a sip of beer.

"Yes, of course." Greg pushed the peanut shells a little more out of the way.

"I was window shopping on Bourbon Street and went into this little store. It had candles and incense and all kinds of beads and jewelry and lotions. The woman who owned it was a clairvoyant or a modern-day witch. Her name was Mystic, but it must have been a stage name. Anyway, she had this small table with two chairs in the corner where she sold her services: palm readings, astrology, tarot cards, Ouija board, and a magic crystal ball. You should have seen her—she wore a long black and purple robe, and her hair was super long and covered by a black silk scarf. There was an eerie feeling about her, and just as I was about to leave the store, she came over to me, took my hand, and placed the ring in my palm. I was thinking, *What is this crazy woman doing?* Then she closed my palm and held my hands in hers."

"She said the ring had real powers, that it was not an ordinary mood ring. Then she closed her eyes and chanted a prayer. I thought she was crazy and just trying to make a sale to a naive tourist, but the look in her eye … it was like she really did have a sixth sense. So I ended up buying it, not only because I thought it was real but because I was afraid if I didn't, she would cast a spell on me." She glanced at the ring. "I've had it now for almost two years and let me tell you, she was right. This ring really works. My friends have never seen anything like it. And Jen is so jealous because her mood ring never changes from a sky-blue color. But this is the real deal. See, look now. It's only this color when I'm really happy."

Greg looked at the ring to see it had changed from sea green to a deep indigo-blue color, like the waters in the Caribbean. "That is amazing."

"I know. I watched it for hours that first day, and it didn't change colors until nighttime. When I bought it, it was the color of the sun mixed with orange specs, and about six hours later, it turned to emerald green, violet, pink, and then shimmering blue. That is when I knew there was something special about this ring."

"Is there any color it hasn't been?"

"Yes. Not once has it turned black."

"I'm impressed, Kate. I studied gemstones, minerals, and rocks when I was a kid, but this is much different than any stone I've ever seen."

"I'm glad you like it." Kate reached out and touched Greg's hand for just a second.

They both took short swallows of beer and put their bottles back down at the exact same time.

"Do you want to hear some music?" Greg motioned toward the jukebox.

"Sure."

"Anything specific?"

Kate thought about it for a minute. "Anything but rap."

"I think that can be arranged."

"Oh, and nothing country or heavy metal. And no sappy love songs or boy bands. Nothing too old either."

"So, pretty open-minded when it comes to music, then?" Greg had a huge smile on his face.

"Ha-ha, very funny."

"So what do you like, then?"

"Regular groups, some slow stuff, but not those whiny love songs. I mean, don't get me wrong. I like love songs. But there's a time and a place for them, and," she glanced around the bar, "this is neither the time nor the place."

"Gotcha." Greg stood and walked over to the jukebox. Kate was a unique girl, he thought as he pulled a few dollars out and inserted them in the machine. She was someone who could be a good friend and at the same time, someone he was attracted to and wanted to date. A woman who would look equally as good in jeans, T-shirt, and a baseball cap or dressed up for a black tie event. Someone he could confide in with his deepest thoughts, fears, and dreams but also someone he could pal around with.

He would be proud to bring her home to his family. And even though this was their first official date, he could imagine sleeping beside her at night. She wasn't the type of girl who would hog the covers either; she was too considerate for that.

She didn't seem like the type of girl who would fight over petty things or hold grudges. And without a doubt, she didn't sweat the small stuff. This much he could tell just in the first few hours of knowing her. He stopped flipping through the pages and glanced over at her. She was facing away from him, and he noticed the comfortable way she sat, her hair falling to the middle of her back. He turned back to the jukebox and continued flipping through the pages of the song listings before finally settling on a few songs he thought Kate would like.

Greg picked up two more beers on his way back and joined Kate at the table. The first song, "Brown-Eyed Girl," started, and as Greg watched Kate, there was a gleam in her eyes.

"I thought this was a good choice, especially with those beautiful eyes of yours. And not only that; the jukebox is so old there isn't any music from this century."

Kate laughed. "I like this song. My mom always listened to those older bands when I was a kid. You know, Hall & Oates, Journey, Chicago, REO Speedwagon. I know most of their songs just because I heard them so much growing up. But I've always liked Van Morrison too. And this song will never be out of style."

"Has your ring changed color again?"

She glanced down at her finger. "Nope. Still happy at ocean blue."

Greg looked away, hiding his smile, and took a swallow of his second beer. Kate had just about finished her first. She had never been a big drinker, and with that came a low tolerance for alcohol. There were several times in college when she went over her limit and had to spend the next day in bed fighting dry heaves and bed spins. She decided then and there that even that relaxed, happy buzz feeling was not worth the price of losing even one precious day. Kate loved life and lived every day with the kind of vigor and excitement of a child discovering the world for the very first time. She was charmed by Greg. He was unlike any other guy she had known. Most of the guys she met in college were either immature or not dating material for one reason or another. Greg was different. He was down-to-earth, and she felt relaxed with him; he wasn't the type to judge others. The fact that he had a dog said a lot about him too. She felt any single guy who had a dog knew responsibilities and commitment. He knew how to take care of others and knew how to recognize others' needs and wants. A dog needed a lot of attention, and after seeing him with Rocky, she knew without a doubt that someday Greg would be a great father.

"Do you play pool?" Greg motioned toward the pool table.

"It's actually been a while."

"How long's a while?"

"Probably three years"

Greg's eyebrows shot up.

Kate took a sip of beer and confirmed with a slight nod.

Greg put his hands on the table. "Do you feel you're up for a game?"

Kate looked over her shoulder at the broken-down pool table.

Greg nudged her on the arm. "What, are we afraid of a little challenge?"

Kate gasped. "No way! Bring it on!"

They stood up and walked over to the table. The green felt was worn in some spots, making the table polka-dotted with white patches. The balls, scattered around the table, were scuffed and scratched, having been hit one too many times. The wood frame was nicked and indented where people had carved secret messages. She looked closer and noticed someone had carved "I Love PJ" in one corner, and next to it there was a shockingly good picture of a mermaid with long flowing hair and about one hundred little scales on her tail. This reminded Kate of Ariel from *The Little Mermaid*. Next to that was WMMR with the number twenty-five after it. Of course that was for the popular Philadelphia radio station. She looked on the other side and saw a red heart with "M" carved inside and next to that was a realistic carving of the Phillie Phanatic. Walking a few more steps, she saw the words "Black Velvet." Kate smiled, wondering who had made each carving and what everything meant. Greg picked up a cue stick from the wall rack and reached across for a cube of chalk. "So, what do you want to bet?"

"We have to make a real bet?"

"It wouldn't be a real game if we didn't make a bet."

"Okay." Kate put her right forefinger on her lips and appeared to be deep in thought. "A kiss," she said simply.

Greg smiled. "Well, I think that can be arranged. But I should pick something too, just on the off chance you don't win."

She turned to putty for a brief moment as a chill went down her spine at the sight of his chin dimple. "Of course. I wouldn't have it any other way."

Greg thought for a second. He noticed the bartender pouring liquor into shot glasses and two people hovering over the jukebox. He had to pick something good. His brother John taught him to play pool years ago and he rarely lost. Dinner, a movie, a concert, Hershey Park, a baseball game. No, none of those were right. It had to be something good where they could talk and relax and get to know each other better. He looked to the ceiling while Kate leaned on the side of the pool table, awaiting his choice. "A day down the shore." He envisioned Kate in a bikini with taut tummy, shapely legs, auburn curls cascading down her back, wearing a bright smile on her face.

Kate's dimples appeared, her smile infectious to Greg. She didn't say a word. *A day down the shore*, she thought as she racked up the solid and striped balls. She pictured them walking hand in hand down the boardwalk and watching the waves roll in over the shoreline. She got her cue stick ready, and since Greg insisted that she break, she leaned back and sent the balls all over the table without any going in a pocket.

"Tough one." Greg walked over and surveyed the table. He decided to go for the green number six, which seemed to be an easy shot. He leaned back, aimed, and the ball rolled right in the corner pocket.

"Lucky shot."

"No luck involved here; this is all about skill."

Kate smiled and rolled her eyes for him to see.

Greg went again, sending the five ball into the side pocket.

"Well, I think you'd better get your bikini ready."

"Just you wait; I'm getting warmed up. I'm going to win this kiss."

Greg took his next shot and missed. "Well my talent seems to be taking a short commercial break. Please stand by. We apologize for the interruption."

"Whatever you say there, Greg." Kate smiled and got ready to see if she could win her first kiss. She sank two striped balls in a row and then it was Greg's turn.

Another fifteen minutes went by until Greg sank the eight ball to take the win. He tried not to gloat because normally he would have let her win. But his mind was on Kate in a bikini and he wouldn't be able to settle for just one kiss.

"So, you really are good at pool. Do you want to try to make these last five shots for me?"

Greg tried to contain his smile, but it was no use. He was feeling things for this girl he hadn't felt in years. Greg had a hard time taking his eyes off of her, especially when she blushed. There was an endearing quality about her that he couldn't resist.

"Sure, but let me show you some insider tips." Greg walked around the table and scoped out each possible shot. "Okay, Kate. Are you ready?"

"As I'll ever be." Kate took a deep breath and exhaled slowly.

"Okay, we're going to make a bank shot with number eleven. See how it's lined up? We can't make the shot without hitting it off the rail, so I'm going to show you how to do it. First take the cue in your hand like this." Greg demonstrated, and then Kate took the stick in her hand. He stood side by side with her to demonstrate. "Now, let's determine where the ball will have to hit the rail in order to deflect into the pocket. I think the far pocket is our best bet."

Kate put one finger on her lips and scanned the table, looking for the best spot. Her heartbeat pulsed in her ears, and she felt Greg's shallow breaths on her neck. His chest moved up and down with each breath and she noticed a trace of earthy cologne, even over the raw smell of the bar. She suddenly pointed to a spot across from where they stood, and Greg said that was the exact spot he would have picked. Greg lined up the tip and handle, and Kate took hold in front, leaned forward, and let the cue connect with the ball at just the right angle. It hit the exact spot they wanted, and the red-striped number eleven sunk in the side pocket as planned.

Kate took a step back and gasped. "That was awesome!"

Greg wore a satisfied grin.

Greg helped Kate finish sinking the four remaining striped balls, and once they were finished, Greg went to the bar and ordered another beer. They sat and talked for another two hours before calling it a night.

On the walk home, Greg took Kate's hand in his. They walked slowly down the nearly empty sidewalk, swinging their arms gently back and forth. Neither spoke as they enjoyed the cool summer night together. When they reached Kate's apartment, she pulled her hand from his and reached into her purse for her keys.

"Thank you for a fun night. I had a great time."

"Me too. You're welcome. Thanks for coming with me."

Kate held her keys without making a sound. "Well, good night. Thanks for walking me home too."

Greg looked down at his feet and then met Kate's eyes. "And don't forget about the shore. A bet is a bet, you know."

"Trust me. I'll be insisting that you hold up your end of the bargain."

"So, next Saturday then?"

"Next Saturday is perfect."

They stood next to each other under the moonlight for another minute until Greg stepped toward her, gently placed his hand on her cheek, and softly pressed his lips against hers. Kate felt tingles radiate down her body as she closed her eyes and kissed him back. It was a peck at first, and then they broke apart before quickly coming together again, their lips meeting as they began to kiss passionately, tongues intertwined as their arms enveloped each other. They kissed for several minutes, taking in the other's scent and basking in their budding new love. When they finally came apart, Kate's face was flushed and Greg put his hand on the back of his neck. Kate looked down at the ground and then back up at Greg. They were both smiling as they whispered good night. Kate slowly walked up the stairs to her apartment, aware that Greg was following her with his eyes. She waved once more before turning the key in her door. Once inside, she stood smiling with her back to the door to steady her weak knees, flashes of fireworks blinking from her eyes. As he watched her disappear to her apartment, Greg could only think of two things—that kiss and next Saturday down the shore.

CHAPTER 5

Greg and Kate headed south on their way to Ocean City, New Jersey. Greg had picked her up in his Toyota RAV4, and they were off. She was wearing white denim shorts, a lavender top adorned with little white flowers, and sandals. Her wavy curls were held back by a pair of sunglasses, and her only jewelry was her mood ring and little stud earrings. Greg got goose bumps thinking of her in her swimsuit and secretly hoped she asked him to put suntan lotion on her back. He had dodged the traffic after crossing the Ben Franklin Bridge and they were on a straight shot down the Atlantic City Expressway.

During the drive, they talked about their childhoods, college, and life in the city. They had texted a little bit each day at work, and on the two nights they were each home, they had talked on the phone until both of them nearly fell asleep. Kate kept their kiss in the back of her mind all week and found herself smiling for no reason, remembering the way he lightly caressed her face and how his lips ever so gently met hers. She had not expected to see fireworks or be weak in the knees from one kiss, but it had happened. She could close her eyes and see the bright flashes of red and orange, green and purple in the sky. She could still feel how her knees buckled as she walked up to her apartment. She remembered standing there for a moment, her back to the door, trying to steady herself before getting ready for bed. That kiss was most definitely not as simple as she thought it would be. It was emotional and moving, and if she was really going to speak the truth, life changing. She had never experienced a kiss so deep that she felt it all the way to her toes. As she lay in bed that night, replaying it in her mind, she knew beyond any doubt that that kiss would be one that she would hold dear for the rest of her life.

Greg was focusing on the road but envisioning the two of them relaxing on the beach, talking and laughing and sharing more stories. He loved that Kate enjoyed listening to his childhood stories and hearing about his life at Drexel. Greg felt a special twitch in his heart that she seemed to genuinely like Rocky and not just because Rocky was his dog. He knew she had a good heart and felt drawn to her, like a writer to their manuscript. He was trying not to let all of his thoughts be consumed by her, especially at work, but each day that went by, little by little, she was taking up more and more space in his heart.

"Do you mind if I change the station? I didn't bring music with me and I don't want to use my phone." Kate interrupted his thoughts as they drove down the Atlantic City Expressway.

"Not at all."

Kate started flipping through his preset buttons: commercial, news talk, bad song, commercial, weather, traffic reports.

Greg shrugged. "I have some old CDs in that box on the floor if you want. I never listen to them anymore." Greg pointed down by her feet. "Or I have my iPod with a decent playlist you might like."

"CDs should work." She picked up the box and started looking through it. "So you like U2, I take it." Kate tried to hide her amusement.

Greg smiled. "They are hand-me-downs from my family. I grew up listening to them because of my brothers. It just stuck."

Kate slid *The Joshua Tree* in and put the box back down on the floor. Greg adjusted himself in his seat as "Where the Streets Have No Name" started playing. Kate sat back and relaxed as they made their way closer to the shore. She watched out the window as they passed other vehicles: minivans loaded with kids and beach gear, SUVs with bicycles mounted to the back, trailers hitched up to trucks to be set up at local campgrounds. Greg felt a twinge in his stomach at the opening chorus of the second song, and when he glanced at Kate, she just gazed into his eyes but didn't say a word. "I Still Haven't Found What I'm Looking For." Greg shook his head slightly as if trying to release the feeling and watched the hundreds of other cars on the road, all heading in the same direction. The northbound side was practically deserted, which was no surprise to Greg, especially with the heat and humidity expected to be close to one hundred degrees in the city. As Kate listened to the song lyrics, she felt a pang in her heart and watched the color of her ring go from a sparkling apple green to burnt orange. *Nerves.* She twisted the ring on her finger 180 degrees and twirled a strand of hair behind her ear. Greg took one hand and rubbed the back of his neck for a second and then cleared his throat. He tried to concentrate on driving and tune out the music, but once "With or Without You" started, he noticed his palms start to sweat and turned the dial for the air conditioning up to medium. Kate squirmed a little in her seat listening to Bono's powerful lyrics and instinctively turned around to grab her bag and began to root through it. She looked for nothing specific and ended up pulling out a tube of lip gloss. When she put the bag back down, they both sighed at the same time and glanced at each other with a smile. Maybe they had both found what they were looking for. Maybe being without each other wasn't an option for them. It sounded surreal, but could it really be this easy? They had only met a few weeks ago. They hadn't met each other's friends or family or coworkers. But they had a unique, undeniable chemistry and connection that neither one could put their finger on. Greg thought about his three years with Heather and realized it was never this easy with her. Even in the beginning, he never felt this unquestionable connection. He didn't joke around like he did with Kate; he didn't share his most favorite childhood stories; he didn't take her to Bottoms Up, not one time in three years, because he knew she would judge and would never understand how that could be his favorite bar. She would never appreciate the down-to-earth feel of it or the comfortableness he felt watching a game and having a beer.

Kate didn't know what it should feel like to meet *the one*. Even though they were still getting to know each other, she felt protected and safe with him. He was someone she felt would never hurt her, and she needed that in a guy. The more she thought about Greg, the more her feelings were getting tangled up. She was trying hard to maintain an emotional distance, but it clearly was not working. Her heart gravitated toward the kiss and the strong connection she felt. Her spirit latched on to his sense of humor, friendliness, and good looks. It was overriding her levelheaded brain, which kept telling her to take things slow and not let herself get hurt.

As soon as "With or Without You" winded down, Greg cleared his throat. "Do you mind if we change the music?"

"I was just going to ask you the same question." Kate ejected the CD and put the radio back on. Katy Perry. Much better.

Traffic was moving well, and Greg only sporadically had to touch his brakes for delays or congestion. It was a good day to head to the shore, where they could enjoy cooler temperatures and less humidity than the city. Kate watched the trees pass by in a blur as she looked up at the sky speckled with wispy clouds. She envisioned Greg taking her hand in his and strolling down the boardwalk. She could see herself with his arms wrapped around her as they watched an orange-and-pink shimmering sunset. He would kiss her softly on the cheek, and she would turn slowly toward him, embracing in a tender kiss while the sun slowly merged with the ocean.

"What are you thinking about?"

His words jolted her back to reality. "Just daydreaming." She turned toward Greg as he held the wheel lightly with one hand. She could see the muscle definition in his arms under his T-shirt, and for the briefest moment, envisioned him in just his swim trunks.

They drove for another half hour before opening the windows and taking in the familiar, fresh salt-water scent they both loved. Greg scoped out parking and found a lot right away. They grabbed their belongings and walked toward the boardwalk. They weren't holding hands but were walking close enough that every few steps, their arms would graze against each other. Seagulls fluttered throughout the sky, and the breeze coming off the water was a refreshing change from the thick, muggy air in Philadelphia. They reached the boardwalk, which was overflowing with people: parents pushing children in strollers, groups of friends laughing and walking, couples with their arms around each other, all enjoying a carefree summer day. They walked over to gaze at the ocean to find white waves pouring in over the sand as sun worshipers lay out in a quest for the perfect tan. Children hauling buckets of water sculpted sand castles that unfortunately would be eaten alive by the surf in a matter of seconds. Some were shading themselves under umbrellas while others were playing a game of beach volleyball. Kate noticed a couple of guys playing Frisbee, and there was a small group of children who looked like they were playing tag. Kate and Greg both heard ice cream and hot dog vendors trying to sell their products as they traipsed through the sand.

"I'm so glad you asked me to come." She turned toward him. "Thank you."

"You're welcome. But I think I should be the one thanking you for sucking at pool."

Kate laughed and gently punched him in the arm. Greg turned and wrapped his arms around her, and they held each other for just a minute, savoring the closeness. Upon coming apart, they noticed an older couple on a bench watching them with a look of longing and remembrance. Kate smiled at them, noticing their hands were intertwined, and hoped she would have that kind of love when she was their age.

They began walking down the boardwalk hand in hand, passing T-shirt and souvenir shops, restaurants, jewelry stores, and salt-water taffy shops. They walked through Gillian's Wonderland Pier, where kids were screaming in delight on the rides and parents were helping their kids win giant stuffed animals. They walked slowly, ignoring the crowds and savoring the fun atmosphere of the boardwalk.

"Hey look at that!" Kate pointed to a little store called Timeless Treasures, where people could get their picture taken using different backdrops and wearing costumes from various time periods. "I did that with my mom when I was little. Have you ever done it?"

Greg eyed the store and then looked at Kate without saying anything.

"Can we? Please …"

Greg caved at the sight of her big, brown pleading eyes and let Kate lead him into the store. Greg had a sudden moment of déjà vu when he saw the backdrop that looked like a scene from his childhood days spent camping. "You know, I have done this before." Greg stared at the huge, deep blue river surrounded by trees and snowcapped mountains. "When I was a kid, my dad brought me and my brothers to a place like this on one of our vacations and we dressed up like old-time fisherman." Greg looked to the ceiling. "We had fishing rods and tackle boxes, overalls, and hats with pins. My brothers and I got to hold giant fake fish like we had just caught them. I know I have that picture at home somewhere. I'll have to dig it out and show it to you."

"I'd like that."

"How did you and your mom dress up?"

"Hula dancers. The whole nine yards: green grass skirts and leis around our necks. Big, bright flowers in our hair. I can show you sometime."

Bernie, a tall, thin man in his fifties, with curly black hair and sunbaked skin, interrupted their conversation to welcome them and share various picture options: Wild West, the jungle, Australia, Grand Canyon, Rocky Mountains, Paris, Hollywood, and New York City. Bernie showed them a slew of different costumes to go along with each theme: cowboys and cowgirls, gangsters, animal tamers, hikers and rock climbers, movie stars, French pastry chefs, runway models, Wall Street tycoons, policemen and firemen. Kate and Greg thumbed through the racks of costumes and then looked again at the various backdrops.

"Let's pick something we each like, even if it's not the same theme, we can just take separate pictures." Greg said.

"Deal. As long as the next time, we agree on the same backdrop," Kate said.

"I'm going to hold you to that, Kate."

Greg and Kate looked through the options a little more before making a decision.

"I'm going with Hollywood," Kate said. She studied the background with the famous Hollywood sign, a picture of Sunset Boulevard, movie cameras, and a star from the Hollywood Walk of Fame in the upper right-hand corner. Kate examined the costumes more closely and after a few minutes, she picked up a glamorous silver floor-length dress with spaghetti straps. "What do you think?"

"Wow." Greg's heart thumped a little in his chest.

"What are you going with?"

Greg looked through the backdrops one final time before settling on the Wild West. He gathered up a fringe brown suede jacket, cowboy hat, blue button-down shirt, dark blue jeans, and brown leather cowboy boots.

With costumes in hand, they each entered a dressing room to change. Greg changed quickly and was grateful the store was air-conditioned. He came out hoping Kate would be there, but she was still in her dressing room. He roamed around and waited, tried his hat in a couple of different positions in front of the mirror, and returned to the fitting room area.

"How do I look?"

Greg was taken aback. She looked like she should be strolling down the red carpet instead of the Ocean City boardwalk. The shimmering fabric accentuated her figure and hugged her perfect curves, which were in all the right places. Her bouncy curls were pulled up while loose tendrils framed her face. Her earrings matched the dress well, and he noticed her mood ring was a bright iridescent blue. On her feet were strappy silver heels that gave her at least a three-inch jump in height. "You, you look gorgeous. Radiant." Greg felt the words getting caught in his throat as he tried to sound normal. He realized at that moment he wanted nothing more in the world than to be with Kate. Luckily she was oblivious to the way he was feeling.

"Thanks. You don't look so bad yourself. Like you're ready to walk into a saloon, drink a shot of bourbon, and play a game of poker with a bunch of gold miners."

"Maybe that will be our next betting game, Kate."

Kate smiled, and then Bernie escorted her over to the Hollywood backdrop which he had set up while she was in the fitting room. There were various options for her to sit on a tall bar stool or chair, stand, or pretend she was at a photo shoot. She asked him to take one of each, and he was more than happy to do so. Greg watched, noticing the radiance she exuded as she smiled for the camera. She felt a little embarrassed about pretending she was modeling for a photo shoot but did it anyway "You're a very photogenic young lady."

"Thank you, Bernie."

He continued taking a few more shots, and once Kate was finished, Bernie got the Wild West backdrop ready for Greg. He moved into position and held a lasso in one hand. Then Greg was in the saloon scene followed by a train robbery setting. Kate watched, noticing Greg's sexy jawline as he pretended to be a serious cowboy. Once Bernie was finished, Greg and Kate headed to their dressing rooms to change back into their own clothes.

Greg paid for all of the pictures, which included white cardboard frames that said "Timeless Treasures, Ocean City, New Jersey." He asked for a second copy of Kate's photos, and Bernie smiled, knowing that Greg was lucky to be in the company of such a pretty young woman. He put all the photos in a bag, and Kate and Greg headed back to the boardwalk.

"Thank you, Greg. That really meant a lot to me. And it was fun." She reached out and gently touched his shoulder.

"Not a problem. It was fun, and I'm glad you had a good time."

After another half hour of walking, they decided to get iced coffees and go on the beach. They changed in the restrooms, and Kate came out wearing a two-piece emerald green swimsuit with little white hearts and her white shorts. Greg was shirtless in blue-and-yellow swim trunks. They walked down the beach, scoped out a quiet spot, and set out their towels. Kate took off her shorts and applied more suntan lotion to her arms and legs.

She asked Greg if he could get her back. As he massaged lotion onto her back and shoulders, he thought that life couldn't get any better than this. Kate then offered to get his back, and once their skin was shiny and protected from the sun, they laid down on their towels to relax.

"Do you come down the shore a lot?"

"Maybe a dozen times or so each summer. It's a nice break from the city, don't you think?"

"What do you do with Rocky?"

"He's usually okay at home if it's just for the day, but Brian is coming to take him out and give him dinner later. I can always bring him to one of my brothers or my parents, but sometimes I bring him down if my friends are getting a house, and then we all split it. They all like Rocky so it's not a big deal."

Kate nodded and gazed at the ocean as gentle waves rose up the beach. She smiled listening to the happy squeals of children who were standing near the water's edge as it came up and splashed over their feet. "It's almost like a mini vacation, even just coming down for the day."

"We're lucky we live close." Greg smiled and stared out into the ocean. He looked up where a helicopter was flying, trailing a long sign for a real estate company renting vacation units by the week or longer. "What's your dream vacation? If you could pick anywhere in the world, where would you go?"

Kate thought about his question. She had only been on vacation in the United States, mainly to local places: Maryland, Virginia, New England, of course the Jersey Shore, and her high school senior trip to Orlando. If she could pick anywhere to travel, hands down it would be Europe. "Italy."

"Italy is probably the best choice for Europe." Greg took a drink of his coffee. "I know you'll get there someday. Good things happen to good people. I don't know how true that is, but it's what they say."

"I hope so. What about you?"

Greg thought about all the vacations he had ever been on: the trip to Disney World and other vacations with his family. He had also gone to Cancun for spring break his senior year of college. Then his mind flashed to the vacation he and Heather took to Jamaica last summer. They had stayed in a hotel that Greg felt was fine, but Heather thought it wasn't as nice as they made it out to be on their website. She had wanted to switch hotels, but they couldn't find anything else available, and she ended up sulking for much of the trip. They were still able to have a relatively good time, but the experience had left a bitter taste in his mouth. He always liked adventure and the outdoors and was low maintenance, preferring camping over a four-star hotel. Greg sat up on his towel and turned toward Kate. "I think it would be incredible to go on an African safari. Don't you wonder what life is like away from civilization?"

"Sure, as long as the animals aren't eating you alive."

Greg laughed. "Well, we could rough it in the jungle first and then live it up in a swanky hotel in Venice. Gondola rides, homemade gelato, museums, speaking Italian with a Philly accent. They would love us there!"

Kate gasped for a split second and questioned in her mind what he had just said. *We could. Us? He was probably just saying that as a hypothetical or maybe it slipped out by accident. He couldn't possibly be talking about going on vacation together halfway across the world. Could he?* She looked out to the ocean and tried to come up with something to say but couldn't think of anything, so she changed the subject.

"What was the happiest or proudest day in your life?"

Greg thought for a minute about the moment he first saw Rocky, the day he graduated from Drexel, and the phone call that said he got the job. While each of those moments was special, it was not the defining moment for him. "I was six years old, and one of the kids at school teased me about my clothes and because I had a lisp. I remember sitting by myself at recess, hiding from the other kids so they wouldn't see me cry. After school I told my brothers what happened, and they took me down the street to the playground. There was no one else there, so we sat down on the grass near the swings, and they talked to me as if I were older, much more mature than I was. They told me not to pay attention to anyone who is mean to me and not to care what other people think. They said I was smart and good and that anyone who makes fun of me is not a friend. They said to be proud of myself and remember the three of them will always be there to help me, support me, and love me. They said I could grow up and be anything I want." Greg glanced toward the ocean. "They were so proud of me, as their brother, and I felt like the luckiest kid on earth to have them. I know we had our differences growing up, but this is what I like to remember most: the three of them coming to my rescue on a really bad day. And I have kept their words with me and always will." Greg smiled. "What about you? What is your proudest moment?"

"That is a great story, Greg. I want to meet your brothers."

"You will, for sure. They will love you."

Kate thought about her childhood, her mom, and her best friend, Jen. "When I was about nine, they had a father-daughter event for Girl Scouts. I was upset and refused to make the craft that the leader planned. I didn't tell my mom about the event, but she found out and said she would go with me. That made me feel even worse so I told her I wasn't going. Then Jen came over after school and was so excited to tell me that her dad was going to take both of us, that she and I were as close as sisters so he could be my dad too. I remember crying because I was so happy, and my mom helped me make a special craft for him. We got to the event, and one by one our leader called up each girl to share what was most special about her dad. When it was my turn, I said that Mr. Delvina was such a special dad because he chose me to be his second daughter since Jen and I were like sisters. Ever since that night, he has always been so good to me, as if I was his real daughter." Kate smiled thinking about the memory.

"That is great. I'm so happy for you that you have Jen in your life, and her father." Greg wondered again about Kate's biological father but refused to ask. *Maybe he died when she was young,* he thought.

After a few more hours of lounging on the warm sand, Greg and Kate packed up their towels, photos, and belongings; changed out of their swimsuits; and headed back to the car to drop everything off. Afterward, they grabbed pizza for dinner and then walked the boardwalk. They hit an arcade along the way and played Skee ball, pinball, and air hockey. They laughed and joked around and didn't care that they only earned enough points to get a hot pink, oddly shaped plastic cup that said OC NJ. Greg then tried his luck at the crane game in hopes of plucking a stuffed animal. After four tries, the crane latched onto a polar bear, which he proudly handed to Kate. As they were exiting the arcade, they saw a large wooden box called the Love Tester, which claimed to measure your sex appeal. The game sat right by the entryway, and there was a picture of a genie on the front. The genie had a seductive smile and was holding a traditional gold genie bottle. Her eyes appeared to be staring right at Greg and Kate. They both stopped walking and smiled at each other.

"Are you game?" Greg's eyebrows were raised and he jingled a few quarters in his hand.

"Absolutely."

They read the degrees of love silently: Ice Cold, Luke Warm, Bashful, Secret Admirer, Jealous, Flirtatious, Lovable, Amorous, Romeo, and Red-Hot Lover.

"Oh, you go first, Greg."

Greg put in a quarter, squeezed the handle, and as the bulbs flashed, Kate hoped he didn't land on Ice Cold. "Flirtatious. That's pretty good, right?"

"I would say that is right on target."

Greg dropped in a quarter for Kate, and the bulbs lit up in the same way, flashing quickly before stopping on Lovable.

"Not bad, Kate. That machine is right on the money. I think it's even better than your mood ring."

"Let's not go that far now." Kate smiled and glanced at her ring, which was a heavenly shade of blue.

As the sun started to fade, they made their way back down the boardwalk and stopped for soft serve vanilla ice cream cones. They ate slowly as they walked until the ice cream started dripping on their hands and they had to throw the rest away. They smiled, feeling like little kids, and each went to a restroom to wash their hands. Back on the boardwalk, they found an empty bench overlooking the ocean and claimed it as their own. Kate could feel herself falling for him as he put his arm around her. Despite her brain telling her over and over, "Do not let yourself fall for him," goose bumps formed on her arms as he inched closer and took his right hand in hers. As they watched the scalding orange sun slowly merge with the ocean in front of a hazy pink and purple sky, they didn't realize they were thinking the exact same thing: that being together felt more natural and right than they could have ever imagined.

CHAPTER 6

Heather knew something was wrong. She had been feeling queasy on and off for the past two weeks, no doubt because of Greg. She lost at least five pounds, not that she needed to, and was starting to worry she was really coming down with something. Her mood was becoming so out of character that her roommate even told her to just call Greg and get it over with. Twice her boss had come into her office to ask her a question about the upcoming "wedding of the year," as he called it, and she had completely flaked. She didn't care that the bride wanted an ice sculpture in the shape of a dove or a six-course, sit-down dinner. She didn't want to share her recommendation on whether cattleya orchids or peonies would look best as floral centerpieces. And she certainly did not care about the meaning of each flower and if one of their four hundred guests would read into the meaning and criticize the bride for making a bad choice. She had no interest in providing her expertise on which type, style, and color of Chiavari chair would be the most elegant. She didn't want to share her thoughts on whether the pesto arugula wraps or the pear and blue-cheese pastry triangles would look best on silver trays. And it was making her nauseous to discuss the bride's sickeningly sweet choices of gum paste roses, royal icing hearts, and fondant sugar pearls for her six-tier, multi-flavor wedding cake.

She sat at her desk, legs crossed, her skirt feeling too loose in the waist. She moved aside the thick wedding binder, opened her laptop, and checked her Facebook account. Great, bridezilla had friended her. She sighed and accepted the request, knowing this girl would now never leave her alone. And the wedding wasn't for another sixteen months! She quickly scanned some posts and liked a couple of random pictures from friends. But from now until the wedding, bridezilla would be filling her Timeline with useless wedding information. Great. She closed her laptop in a huff and stared outside. She had a view of the parkway and could see cars rushing past and flags blowing in the breeze. It wasn't humid, but even with the cold central air in the hotel, she felt unusually warm. She already knew she'd be a pile of sweat by the time she walked home tonight. Heather glanced around her office and tried to think of something, anything other than Greg. It wasn't like she didn't have a lot on her plate. There was the wedding of the year of course, a black-tie fundraiser to benefit pediatric cancer in two months, and a baby shower to plan with an overly controlling soon-to-be grandmother. To make matters worse, she had to work three events this weekend even though she wasn't the main event planner. She couldn't even remember what two of the events were despite having the team meeting yesterday. Was she losing her mind? Why on earth could she remember what that flaky, buttery croissant filled with fresh strawberries and lightly dusted with powdered sugar had tasted like when it hit her tongue and not recall the details of the meeting?

Her coworkers were laughing down the hall, and something about the high-pitched sound irritated her, like nails going down a chalkboard. She got up and closed her office door. Maybe she just needed quiet to think. She sat back down, picked up her cell phone, and opened it to photos … right to the selfie of her and Greg from three months ago. Their faces were touching, and they had goofy smiles, their eyes bright. Happy. They were happy. She knew she could bring him back from whatever this was. This break. That she initiated. She wanted to kick herself, but it was too late. Or was it? Of course he wasn't perfect, but who was? She loved him, was in love with him, at that was all that mattered. She learned to tolerate his dog. And his incessant need to watch as many Phillies games as humanly possible. She loved that he was intelligent and funny, and let's face it, she was attracted to him from that very first night at the bar. She loved that he was always clean-shaven, his face smooth to the touch. On the night they met, she was taken by his smile and cleft chin. And he had called her right away, which made her even more smitten. But if things ended, she would get over him and move on. She was always good about leaving the past in the past, especially when it came to relationships. She didn't keep in touch with a single ex. The only thing was, she didn't want her relationship with Greg to end. She wanted to marry him. Deep down in her heart, she knew she wanted to spend the rest of her life with him. And this made everything that much harder.

She threw her phone in her purse and put her head down on her desk. She was unusually tired lately and could fall asleep right here in her office. She knew the reason for this, of course. She wasn't sleeping well at night. It was not quite insomnia but more like restless sleep, night after night. She let herself close her eyes and really think … about Greg and what the outcome could be. Her heart breaking. Sharing their first dance at their wedding. Seeing his photo with another woman in the Sunday engagement section. Lazy Sunday mornings in bed with two adorable kids; one boy and one girl spaced two years apart. He would be the doting father and she would be the mom who did it all. The two of them, old and gray, playing with their grandchildren, her baking in the kitchen with their granddaughter and him playing catch on the front lawn with their grandson. From one to the next, each hypothetical situation started to jumble together until she finally stopped, sat up, and gave her cheeks a gentle slap to snap out of it. Twenty minutes had gone by before she came to the conclusion that she could not predict the future no matter how much she wanted to. She'd have to leave it to fate. And with that, she told herself to try not to think about him anymore today. Of course tomorrow would come and this vicious cycle would start all over again. But she would try. She would try to just let things happen the way they were meant to.

She thought about her own life and family. After her mom had ditched her when she was a preschooler, Aunt Clara had stepped in to save her. Aunt Clara, her mom's older sister by ten years, took her in and cared for her as if she was her own daughter. A single woman working as an elementary school teacher, Clara clothed her, fed her, planned her birthday parties, read her bedtime stories, chaperoned her school field trips, made homemade Halloween costumes, taught her how to sew and bake homemade bread, and explained what was happening to her body when she became a teenager. Aunt Clara was Santa, the Tooth Fairy, and the Easter Bunny all in one. Heather only had one memory of her own mother. She was three or four years old, hungry as usual, and playing with her Goodwill doll that was missing one arm and didn't have any hair. She was hugging the doll, telling her that she would take care of her and cut her own hair to tape to the doll's head. She told the doll she would share her dinner, if there was any that night, and put the doll to bed next to her when it was time to sleep. Her mother had come charging through her door, demanding to know if she had taken a necklace from her jewelry box. Heather said no, that she never took anything from her mom's room, but her mom didn't believe her and spanked Heather for lying. Her mother left in a huff, slammed the front door, and drove away. Heather curled up in her bed, crying and hugging her doll for dear life. Many years later, she learned that her mother was a drug addict and had pawned all of her jewelry for drug money, along with other possessions. Clara was awarded legal guardianship and her mother's rights were terminated. To this day, Heather was not sure if her mother was dead or alive. Her mother didn't know who Heather's father was, and that line was left blank on her birth certificate. Aunt Clara always told Heather that she was the daughter she was meant to have. She said Heather was the best thing to ever happen to her and that she loved her unconditionally and always would.

Heather opened her computer and searched her mother's name on Google and Anywho.com websites. She did this several times a year just to see if anything came up. It never did. She should stop looking. She loved Clara as if she was her own mother. She didn't need someone in her life that had treated her so badly ... her own mother neglecting and abusing her own flesh and blood.

Heather closed the window on her computer and decided to just try to concentrate on work for the rest of the afternoon. She texted her coworker so they could talk about the three weekend events again. She was happy to have work this weekend to keep her mind off of Greg. Her coworker came down to her office a few minutes later, and they began going through each event. Heather sat there, nodding and taking notes, with just a small portion of her mind thinking about him.

CHAPTER 7

"Tell me about your day." Kate was lounging on her sofa in baby pink summer pajamas, cradling a glass of lemonade. The sun had set about an hour ago, and even though it was still a little humid, her ceiling fan made her feel relaxed and cool.

"I finally fixed this glitch in an app that I had been working on since last week. There was an error in the coding that was making the program freeze up whenever the user tried to hit backspace. It was odd but it's all good now."

"Such a hard worker you are! That's great."

"It was a relief to resolve it. And as a bonus my boss gave me our company's Phillies tickets for next week's game against the San Francisco Giants." Greg had the Phillies game on with the sound muted. The Phillies were up by three runs, but Greg wasn't paying too much attention. Rocky was curled up lying next to him on the couch.

"Cool, a great perk for you."

"It is. That's about all we have though ... nothing like the perks you get. Speaking of which, what did you do at work today, little Miss PR? Go on a long lunch at another potential restaurant client?"

"You know we only do that on Fridays!" Kate laughed. She felt comfortable joking around with Greg and knew he felt the same. "Anyway, today we came up with an exciting campaign for this new trendy restaurant in Ardmore. We already have five events booked to attract media attention and generate interest from the Main Line."

"Fun." Greg took a gulp of his Gatorade and turned to see that Rocky had fallen asleep.

"It was! Plus the owners have been in the business for over twenty years so it's guaranteed to be successful. It's actually upscale fondue so I'm sure it'll be fun too."

"Well maybe I'll have to take you to dinner at this hip new fondue place."

"Greg Janera, are you asking me on a real date?" Kate smiled into the phone.

"The bar and shore weren't real dates?"

"You know what I mean, silly. A date where you get all dressed up."

"Ah. And what would you wear to this fancy fondue restaurant?"

"A dress and heels. Or a skirt and heels. Pretty much the opposite of what I wore to Bottoms Up and the shore."

"Oh, well I think we will have to go there soon. Far be it from me to keep you from wearing heels."

"It would be fun, and I could learn a lot more about you."

"What do you want to know?"

Kate sighed into the phone. "There's still so much."

"Like what?"

"For starters, when's your birthday?"

"December third. You?"

"March twentieth. And what about Rocky?"

Greg patted Rocky on the head, and the dog woke up and licked his arm. "June sixth."

"Okay, good."

"Good?"

"Yes. What are your favorite types of movies?"

"Action and adventure, superhero, thrillers, horror." He paused. "You probably hate those, right?"

"I like thrillers and some scary movies if they're done well. But I love drama, comedy, chick flicks, and romance."

Greg got up and grabbed a bottle of water from his fridge. He still hadn't cleaned it out completely even though he was able to get rid of the mold smell. He went back to the couch, with Rocky resting comfortably on one end. He sat down and petted his dog's soft coat. Rocky yawned and stretched his legs out before getting up, walking in three circles, and lying down again.

"I know you love to read. Do you have a favorite book?"

Kate set her lemonade on her coffee table and grabbed a light blanket from the back of her sofa. She thought for a moment as all the books she had ever read flashed before her eyes. It was impossible to pick just one; she loved them all: the classics, the contemporaries, memoirs, drama, chick lit, mystery, romance.

"I can't pick one. I love them all."

Greg laughed. "Okay, I'll let that one slide."

Greg paused for a few seconds to collect his thoughts. He didn't want to hang up just yet. "Can you believe this dog? Right now he's camped out on the couch, snoring louder than a bear. I guess he had a tougher day than both of us combined."

"Tough day from what? Sleeping?"

"Apparently. That and barking at the mailman. And walking back and forth to the kitchen. Poor Rocky. If only everyone had the life of a dog." Greg ran his hand down Rocky's coat but he didn't even move a muscle.

Kate laughed and took a sip of her lemonade.

Greg shook his head. "You know, Kate, in my next life, I think I'll come back as a dog. Get to eat and sleep and play all day. Sounds great, doesn't it?"

"It doesn't sound bad."

"What would you come back as in another life?"

Kate thought for a minute and looked at her ceiling. "Well if I had to pick something, I would have to go with a kitten."

"A kitten?"

"Sure. They're super soft and they get to cuddle up with their owners."

"Do you think they would ever cuddle up with a dog?"

Kate smiled knowing exactly what he meant. "Maybe. Plus they're cute and small."

"You're already cute and small."

"Thanks." Kate blushed, grateful they were on the phone.

"Well, you do know that eventually you'd turn into a cat, right?"

"Nah, I think I would just stay a kitten."

They were both quiet for a few seconds. Greg took a gulp of his drink and glanced at the clock. He grinned into the phone. "I want to kiss you good night."

"You do?" Kate said in a sweet but sexy voice.

Greg sat forward on the couch and rested his elbow on his knee. "Do you think you can help me out with that?"

"I might be able to."

"You don't say?"

"But first you're going to have to get up off the couch."

"Really?"

"Yup. And then you're going to have to put your sneakers on."

"My sneakers are on."

"That's a good start."

"And I'm off the couch." Greg stood in his living room, staring at the door.

"Even better."

"And then you're going to have to go for a walk."

"Where?"

"Old City I guess."

"I see."

"And you're going to need to grab your keys."

"They're in my hand."

"I guess that's the last thing to do."

"I think it is."

"Oh, hey, Greg, I have to go now because my friend is coming over and I'm not dressed."

"Is that right?"

"I wouldn't lie about something like that."

"Well, in that case, I'm running."

CHAPTER 8

There were indentations in the carpet from where Greg paced back and forth. Rocky watched him from the couch, his eyes following his every step as he walked from the front door through the living room and to the kitchen. He walked past the smattering of *Sports Illustrated* and *Men's Fitness* magazines littering his coffee table. His shoes were strewn near the front door and there were more than a few dirty dishes in the kitchen sink. Then he turned and went back and turned again in a never-ending vicious cycle as his mind flip-flopped between Heather and Kate, Kate and Heather, Heather and Kate. He wasn't sure what he would say and how he would say it, but time was running out. Today was the deadline he gave himself to call Heather. It was already ten o'clock and he still hadn't picked up the phone. He sat down on the couch and asked Rocky what he should do. When the dog simply tilted his head to the side, Greg knew he would just have to deal with it on his own and get it over with. He went into the kitchen, grabbed his cell from the counter, and waited another minute before calling her number.

"Hi." Greg sat at his kitchen table, doodling Kate's name on a piece of paper as the phone rested between his shoulder and ear.

"I'm glad you called. We need to talk." Heather was also sitting at her kitchen table but was nursing a cup of herbal tea.

"That's actually why I'm calling too."

"Can you come over tomorrow night, around eight?"

"Yeah, eight o'clock works."

"Okay. I'll see you then."

Greg said bye, clicked the phone off, and drew a heart around Kate's name. The call wasn't nearly as bad as he'd imagined, but he knew the call wasn't the tough part. That would be tomorrow night at eight. He ran his hand over his face and opened a bottle of beer.

Greg and Heather had been dating for three years, and while most of that time was good, the break Heather initiated in May was a relief to Greg. It was a chance for them to see if they were really meant to be or if they should end their relationship and move on. Over the past month, Greg started developing strong feelings for Kate. Kate. His Kate. He decided after he officially ended things with Heather, he and Kate would go out and celebrate. He would take her to that new fondue place and then to that show she wanted to see at the Academy of Music. They would have a wonderful night, he would confess his feelings, and they would start a real relationship. He visualized the evening in his head: he would wrap his arms around her, holding her tight and whispering in her ear that she was everything he ever wanted in a woman. They hadn't discussed it, but in his heart, he knew Kate felt the same about him. He would tell Kate that he loved her. He would tell her he was falling in love with her. He would tell her because it was the truth.

He thought about seeing Heather and wondered how he would break up with her. The easiest thing to tell her was that they both had changed. They drifted apart and no longer wanted the same things. Heather wanted to get married, buy a house in the suburbs, and raise a family. Greg wanted these things too but not yet. He wasn't ready for marriage, a mortgage, or kids. He wasn't ready for them with Heather and wasn't sure that he ever would be. He now looked to the future and saw Kate—he and Kate saying, "I do," in front of family and friends; he and Kate moving into their first home together; he and Kate welcoming children into the world. He would tell Heather he'd like to stay friends but knew in time that would fade. But he also didn't want to hurt her in any way. He used to think he and Heather would end up together—until Kate came walking into his life. And something about Kate set his heart on fire. He couldn't even put his finger on it. Probably because it was a combination of chemistry and connection and also so many of her qualities: sense of humor, ease with herself, caring nature, beauty, thoughtfulness, playfulness. The list could go on and on.

Greg would be honest and up-front, but he didn't feel he necessarily had to tell Heather about Kate. It might cause Heather to become upset for no reason, and no good could come out of it. He wondered to himself if he would still end things with Heather if he had never met Kate. But that was not possible to answer, as he could not imagine his life without Kate. In such a short time, she was becoming one of the most important people in his life.

Heather wasn't sure how she was going to tell him. She hadn't told anyone yet, not even her roommate, Sara. What were her options? Some might say she had plenty, but in her heart, she only had one. Her mind was made up, and no one could say anything to change it. She was going to be a mother, and she was determined to be a good one. She was already following her doctor's orders: eating right, exercising lightly, staying hydrated, staying away from secondhand smoke, not drinking alcohol, getting extra sleep, and taking her prenatal vitamins. She was hell bent on not letting her child be treated as her mother had treated her. There would be no spanking or yelling, and there would always be plenty of food. Her child would always have a clean, warm bed to sleep in and wouldn't have to wear tattered hand-me-downs or play with used, beat-up toys from Goodwill. She would not be like her mother. She thanked God for Aunt Clara, knowing she would be a wonderful grandmother. Maybe Aunt Clara could come down and stay for a couple of weeks in the beginning to help and also form a bond with the baby. Heather would be a loving and attentive mother and would always give her child unconditional love, support, and encouragement. She would put her child first, always, no questions asked. She placed her hands on her belly, and although she couldn't feel a bump yet, she made a promise to the baby she was carrying that he or she would have a safe and happy life with two loving parents. Her baby would feel loved and cared for and would grow up with the necessary values to become a responsible member of society. She was sure of this.

She knew it wouldn't be easy, but with Greg by her side, the two of them could accomplish anything. Together they would be happy, they would make it work, and a baby would bring them closer than they'd ever been before. This baby would mend the rough patch they'd been going through and unite them as a family. They would go back to what they were like in the beginning. They would do things together as a family: outings to the Please Touch Museum, Sesame Place, and Philadelphia Zoo. But they would also concentrate on themselves as a couple and go out on date nights, make love when the baby was sleeping, and recapture whatever they had lost. They would communicate and tell each other how they were feeling and what they needed; they would stay on the same page. She wouldn't pressure him about marriage; she promised herself that the minute the line turned pink on her pregnancy test. But she was sure it would eventually happen and knew they would have a committed and happy marriage. Greg would be an amazing father, the way he was with her and Rocky: loving and kind and caring. He took care of that dog as if it was his own child, making sure to play with him every day, walk him several times a day no matter the weather, and give him only the best organic pet food and those expensive squeaky toys from the specialty pet stores. He even spoke to Rocky as if he were human. She laughed remembering the story he told her about when he first got Rocky and buckled him in a dog seat belt harness for the drive to his apartment at Drexel. Rocky had wriggled out of it after five minutes so Greg drove extra cautiously so he wouldn't get into an accident for fear that the dog would get hurt. Ever since then, he always made sure the harness was secure and that Rocky was buckled in the car. As Rocky got older, he got used to staying in his seat belt harness, which gave Greg a sense of relief. She never even heard of someone who put a seat belt around their dog.

She thought about the time Greg took care of her when she had a weeklong bout of the flu. He brought her soup, tissues, and medicine, and came over after work each day to be with her. He did her dishes, sorted her mail, and even brought her books, magazines, and crossword puzzles. Heather was positive he would show the same love, the same kindness to their child. She looked down at her belly and placed both hands on it. "Everything is going to be okay. I love you and I know your daddy does too," she whispered.

It had rained throughout the day, and the temperature had dropped to an unseasonably cool and breezy fifty-six degrees. Greg threw on jeans after a quick workout and shower, and grabbed a slice of pizza for dinner. As he walked toward Heather's apartment, he rehearsed his speech in his head. He passed Bottoms Up and smiled, thinking about him and Kate shooting pool and their first kiss. His mind wandered to their trip to Ocean City, and he got a chill down his spine. He knew the talk with Heather would be painful, but he was determined to do it quickly, like ripping off a Band-Aid. It would sting, but the pain would be over soon, and he and Heather would be able to move on with their lives. She would meet someone new, get married, and have the family she always wanted. She deserved to be happy, and Greg knew he was not the right guy for her. *Not anymore.* He belonged with Kate, and the feeling was so intense that he felt it in his core. He reached Heather's apartment and took a deep breath. As he walked up, he thought about the conversation and wiped a bead of sweat from his forehead. He cleared his throat, wiped his hands across his jeans, and rang the doorbell. A minute later, Heather opened the door wearing a thick terry cloth blue bathrobe. Her dirty blonde hair was in a haphazard ponytail, and she didn't have on a stitch of makeup.

"Are you okay?" Greg's mouth fell open when he saw her. He wondered how he was going to break up with her while she was sick. He figured worst case, he could wait another day. Maybe two.

"No, actually I'm not. Come in. We can talk in the kitchen. Sara's not here."

Greg got a sick feeling in his stomach as they walked through the hallway to the kitchen he knew so well. They had made dinner for each other over the years in that kitchen, and he remembered lots of good times. On their six-month anniversary, Greg took her out to celebrate with dinner and drinks at her favorite restaurant. After coming back, they headed straight for the kitchen, laughing and talking over a bottle of wine. He recalled making her breakfast in bed for her twenty-seventh birthday: waffles with strawberries and whipped cream. He gave her a silver locket necklace that year, and he remembered how much she loved it.

He knew this visit would not be nearly as enjoyable as times past. In fact it would be downright difficult, but he had to do it. Maybe they both realized things were going to change by the slow steps they were taking. But once they reached the kitchen, Heather gave a small smile and motioned for him to take a seat.

"Do you want a drink?"

"No, thanks. I'm okay."

Heather poured herself a glass of ginger ale and sat beside him. He didn't know if she was sick or if she was angry. Maybe she found out about Kate. Or maybe she had the flu. He ran his hands down the front of his jeans and told himself to wait and hear what she had to say. Heather didn't say anything for several minutes. Greg looked at her and then looked around the room, wondering if he should start. In his mind he wanted to tell her they would be better off ending things now. They could each start over, they deserved that much. Greg looked up and their eyes met. Heather's eyes were twinkling with the look of both fear and excitement. She folded the napkin on the table and bent her straw from side to side.

"What is it?"

Heather made a crooked smile and cleared her throat. She took a sip of soda and then looked him in the eye and said the words she had been hiding from everyone for the past four weeks. Greg dropped his head, and in that instant, he knew his life was changed forever.

* * *

A week later, Greg went with Heather to her doctor's appointment. Her vitals were normal, and Heather was doing fine despite morning sickness and fatigue. At work she had to keep saltines and ginger ale at her desk just to make it through the day. She was typically in bed by nine o'clock, sleeping straight through until seven except for waking two or three times a night to use the bathroom. Dr. Farrell said the nausea and fatigue should quell after the first trimester, and Heather gave a sigh of relief, hoping she was right. Despite her morning sickness, she was also hungrier than usual but could only eat small amounts of food at a time. Everything tasted different too. Fruit that she normally loved was too sweet and tomato juice that she used to hate, now she couldn't get enough of. One day she wanted salad with Thousand Island dressing; the next day is was all about salmon and mashed potatoes.

"As long as you take care of yourself, you'll be just fine. And it is very important to drink plenty of water so your body stays hydrated. Especially in this summer heat."

The words drifted in and out of Greg's ears as he was still trying to grasp the fact she was pregnant. He had a nervous twitch in his side, and he absently cracked his neck back and forth. Greg was aware of his face going pale while Dr. Farrell told them what would be happening over the next thirty-some weeks. However, these words seemed to be meant for someone else. It was as if he were floating above himself and looking down at a stranger. It wasn't he who needed to be her coach during the delivery. It wasn't he who should attend Lamaze or breastfeeding classes with her. It wasn't he who needed to help around the house when she didn't feel well or run to the store in the middle of the night to pacify her cravings. He was lost in thought as Heather sat beside him in the office. He turned his head slightly and saw her smiling, both hands on her baby bump. He felt warm all of a sudden and noticed his shirt was slightly damp from sweat that had just formed on his back. Heather reached over, took Greg's hand in hers, and gave it a small squeeze. Then Greg looked up and shook his head gently upon hearing the doctor say that on or around February sixth, he would become a father.

CHAPTER 9

"I have no idea, Jen. I mean, I just don't understand it."

"He's a guy, Kate. What's to understand? They lose and gain interest quicker than they change their underwear. I would give it another week or two and then call him again." Jen rubbed lotion into her hands and threw the bottle back in her purse. They were at Dunkin' Donuts, sitting at a table away from most of the patrons. Each had ordered an iced coffee, but Kate could barely touch hers.

"I guess. Maybe you're right. We did have a great time down the shore and the bar so maybe he's just busy or something. And he did come over a few weeks ago just for a good night kiss. It was so sweet, Jen. We were on the phone and all of a sudden he says he wants to kiss me good night." Kate blushed and then stared at her coffee and picked it up. She held it in her hands and then put it right back down. She picked up two sugar packets and put them back on the table.

"Are you sure that's all he wanted?" Jen's eyebrows were practically at her hair line.

Kate's mouth fell open. "Jen!"

"Well I'm just saying. Think about it, Kate. Don't you think it's odd that pretty much right after the night he comes over and all he gets is a kiss, you barely hear from him again?" She tossed her hair over her shoulder and turned at the sound of her name but realized it was directed at someone else.

Kate mulled this over in her head. "No, it can't be that. I mean, Greg isn't like that. He's been so sweet ever since we met, and when he came over that night, we kissed for a little while and then he left. He is such a good kisser and we have this ridiculous strong connection. I honestly see fireworks, Jen. And he's all about holding my hand and hugging me. I just, no, that can't be it. And you know what, if that was really all he wanted, he'd realize by now he picked the wrong girl."

"Exactly." Jen sipped her iced coffee and turned to check out a Philadelphia police officer who had just walked in. Her eyes darted over his uniform and a chill ran up her spine. He looked to be six foot tall with a shaved head and crystal-blue eyes. "That is what I need, Kate." Jen gestured with her eyes to the officer, who was facing away from them at the counter.

Kate rolled her eyes. "No, Jen, that's not it. I mean, why would he bother listening to stories about my childhood and college and about our friendship? Why would he tell me all about his family? You know he even asked me to go to his parents' house for dinner. He said his mom was planning a family dinner and he wanted me to come and meet them."

"When?"

"I don't know. I don't think his mom has picked a date yet."

"Uh-huh. Sure." She gazed toward the officer again.

"Jen!"

"Okay, okay. You're right. I'm sorry for saying that. It just seems a little too convenient if you ask me." Jennifer twirled her necklace and looked in her friend's eyes. They looked sad. The gleam was gone from the previous month. Kate's ring was also permanently going back and forth from deep orange to slate gray to mud brown. "Well maybe he's just having some other family issues or something."

"I don't think anything's wrong with his family."

"Well, maybe it's his work. Some guys get totally wrapped up in work and can't even focus on anything else."

"I don't think that's it either. He always tells me about the projects he works on. He does really well there." Kate sighed. "This is just not like him. Something must have happened."

"Not like him? You guys just met, what, two months ago?"

Kate nodded.

"And since you've barely talked to him for what, nearly three weeks, you really don't know him at all. I mean how do you know someone well enough in four weeks to start analyzing them?"

"Okay, Miss. Cynicism. I get your point. I'm not going to worry about it anymore. If he calls, he calls, and if he doesn't, he doesn't. End of story. I'm not going to let some guy come in and break my heart." *Again.*

"Now that's my girl. You know, I've been friends with you since kindergarten, and you are finally seeing the light." Jen sat up a little straighter in her seat and nodded.

Kate stirred her coffee with her straw, watched the officer walk out the door with four cups in a holder, turned, and gave a weak smile to her best friend.

Jennifer looked at Kate's ring and saw it was murky brown. She knew her friend well. Their friendship began over twenty years ago when Kate was Katie and Jennifer was Jenny. One day, Jenny asked Katie to play on the swing set during recess, and from that moment on, they were joined at the hip. Throughout elementary and middle school, they had sleepovers, shared lunches, and spent hours on the phone. They passed notes folded into origami during classes and stayed up late talking about boys and giggling into the early morning hours. Each summer, Jennifer's parents took Kate with them to Sea Isle City, where they spent a week at the beach, going on boardwalk rides and eating ice cream and salt-water taffy until they were sick.

On one particular summer day when they were about ten years old, they sat outside in Jennifer's backyard under the shade of a weeping willow tree and planned their weddings. Katie would wear a gown like Cinderella and style her hair in an updo with a sparkly tiara. She would dance all night with her Prince Charming to music played by a live band. The June celebration would have an outdoor ceremony and reception under a big white tent filled with all the people she loved. Secretly she hoped her dad would come back to walk her down the aisle as was the tradition, but even at her young age, she was starting to lose hope about that. But her mom, she knew her mom or even Mr. Delvina would be the one to walk her down the aisle. She would have a five-tiered round cake with strawberry frosting and different colored flowers decorating each tier. The next day, her and her prince would leave for an exotic two-week honeymoon to Hawaii, where she would return pregnant with their first child and would live happily ever after.

Jenny's dream wedding was a black and white ball in January where snowflakes would decorate the ballroom at the fanciest hotel in Philadelphia. She would be adorned in a white mermaid gown, and her black hair would be in curls tumbling down her back. Her four-tier vanilla and chocolate cake would sit next to a snowflake-shaped ice sculpture. Afterward, Jen and her new husband would escape the cold for a luxurious two-week honeymoon in Tahiti. They would wait two years to have kids and then would have a boy and then a girl, exactly two years apart. Weddings, marriage, and children were the dream of many little girls, and Katie and Jenny were no different.

"Do you want to do something this weekend?" Jen twirled her hair. "Surprisingly enough, I have off Saturday night and all day Sunday. We could have a girl's night out—hit Delaware Ave and then spend Sunday lounging by a pool drinking margaritas and checking out hot single guys."

"A pool? We haven't gone swimming all summer and now you come up with a pool?"

"Well, not yet. But if you say yes, I'll find us a pool."

"I don't know."

"Whaddya mean you don't know? What's not to know? Drinks. Wearing our bikinis and getting a sun-kissed glow. Hot, single guys. You can even read one of your novels. Let me repeat: Hot. Single. Guys. It's pretty simple, if you ask me."

"C'mon, Jen. I'm really not interested in meeting anyone else right now."

"I think it's time you got back in the game."

Kate rolled her eyes. "You know, if you weren't my best friend ..."

Jen cut her off. "You'd have a pretty boring life?"

Kate laughed. "Okay, I'll go. Are you happy now?"

"Don't sound so enthusiastic about it."

"Sorry, Jen. It sounds great, I swear. See?" Kate gave a wide smile to appease Jen but was still at a loss over Greg. She knew something was wrong. She felt in her gut he'd changed. He didn't return her texts, and the one time she did get him on the phone, he was absent-minded and distant, asking her to repeat what she'd said. She had asked him what was wrong, but he held steadfast that it was nothing and not to worry. But she was worried; how could she not be? Each dream she had of her and Greg was slowly fading from a crystal-clear image to a foggy mist of nothingness. It was slipping away from her just when she had been so close ... so close to finding *the one.*

CHAPTER 10

"Pregnant?" Tom said, more as a statement than a question. He had both hands on the table and sat up straighter after he spoke. He met Greg's eyes and then glanced away for a second. He took one hand and rubbed the back of his neck before cracking it from side to side. "Pregnant," he said again, softer this time, as if trying to let the news sink into his brain. Tom and Greg had been buddies since freshman year, both of them with similar interests in sports. They met the first semester at a University City bar during a Phillies playoff game. They played indoor basketball that fall and winter in a Philly league and then baseball in the spring. The next three years were more of the same: watching sports on TV and in person, playing sports, going to local bars to catch a band, or just going out and enjoying the unique venues and events the city had to offer. Tom had come to Drexel from upstate New York and, after graduating, landed a counseling job at a large hospital. They footed his tuition at Villanova University, where he recently graduated with a Master's in Psychology. The two were at Bottoms Up with a pitcher of beer and bowl of peanuts in front of them. The bar wasn't crowded, which made the music from the jukebox and the noise from the Phillies game seem louder than it should have been.

Greg shook his head. "She's about three months now." He rubbed his arms and looked down at the table. "I have no idea what to do. I don't even think it's really hit me yet." Greg cracked his knuckles and then picked up his beer, put it down without drinking, and pushed his glass away. He crossed his arms and turned to the TV, not caring in the least who was winning. For that matter, he didn't even know who the Phillies were playing today.

Tom looked at his friend. The happiness of his time with Kate was nowhere to be found. Instead there was a worn out face staring back at him: eyes with faint, dark circles, sallow skin, and stubble on his cheeks and chin. "What does Heather want to do?"

"She's scared but excited. She doesn't know I was going to break it off. She said this is the perfect way for us to get back on track: have a baby together. She didn't say it but I know she expects to get married." Greg met Tom's eyes. "She doesn't know about Kate. And it's not like I planned on meeting her. It just happened, and she's pretty much taken me by surprise. She's amazing and I …" Greg trailed off. He picked up his beer but put it down without taking a drink. "I don't know what to do."

Tom took a long pull of beer. He rubbed his hands down the front of his jeans and then absently over his shaved head. He was quiet for a minute as he considered his psychology and counseling background. He wanted to help his friend and tried to focus on what he would tell a client in this situation. Most of his clients were young adults dealing with the after effects of childhood trauma: abuse, neglect, addiction, death, bullying. Tom treated every client as if they were his only one and took phone calls from them off hours if they needed to talk. He dug deep into his clients' minds to get to the root of the issue and came up with an action plan that enabled each one to heal in the best way possible. He took accurate and complete notes during each session and would refer to online resources and text books if he needed help deciphering the problem and creating a course of treatment. He regarded each case differently, depending on the person, even if they had the same exact childhood trauma. This matter with Greg was much different, not only because he was his good friend for over six years but because a child would soon be involved.

Tom was a one-woman man and he treated his girlfriend as a princess. He grew up with a father who was emotionally and mentally abusive towards his mother, and she unfortunately accepted it. He realized as a child of seven years that he would never treat a woman the way his father did. His mother was his rock, and to this day he did not understand how his father could have done that to her. But despite that, Tom was the last person on earth who would ever judge someone, no matter the circumstances. He prided himself on giving honest, relevant advice. Tom took a long pull of beer. "You've been with Heather for what, four years now?"

"Three."

Tom sat up straighter in his chair and pretended he was in his office and Greg was resting on the comfy blue couch. Pale blue walls surrounded them with tranquil pictures of the beach and ocean. "So you are in a three-year relationship and realize that maybe she isn't the one and you meet Kate." Greg gave a small smile at the sound of Kate's name. "And now Heather is pregnant and thinks you two will be riding off into the sunset together." Tom poured more beer in his glass.

"Thanks for the recap, man." Greg reached for his beer then put the glass down again before taking a drink. "I never thought I would become a father this soon."

"I need to talk it out; it is easier for me to give you advice. But I need to ask you some questions first."

"Fire away."

"How do you feel about Heather? Do you love her?"

Greg didn't say anything. He looked at his beer and then back to Tom.

"Okay … how do you feel about Kate?"

Tom noticed a tiny twinkle in his eye. "Kate." Greg looked at the ceiling for a moment. "I feel very strongly for Kate." *I love her.* "I still care for Heather, but it is different now."

"This might be hard to answer, but how do you feel about becoming a father?"

Greg exhaled the breath he was holding. "I don't know. I mean, I know being a parent is a lot of responsibility and I will do my best to be there for my child. I want to be involved in his or her life and be that person they can depend on. I know I need to support the baby, not just financially but be there. Be a good dad."

Tom pushed his near empty glass across the table. "And Heather? On being a mother?"

"Heather didn't come out and say this, but she wants us to be a happy little family. What would you do if this was you and Danielle?"

"I would marry her, or at least get engaged. But then again, living together is practically being married, without the ring. And after four years of dating and two years living together, I'm starting to think it's time to make things legal anyway. Danielle's definitely been hinting about it, especially since she's in one of her friend's weddings next year."

Greg nodded. "But you love her. You're in love with her, right?"

"Yeah, I'm in love with her. I didn't realize there was a difference between loving someone and being in love. Danielle taught me the difference." Tom brushed away some peanut shells. "Okay, just for a minute, forget Heather is pregnant. What would you do?"

"Hands down I would have ended things with Heather. I want to be with Kate."

"Okay, now put the baby back into the equation. What would you do now?" Tom looked directly into Greg's eyes.

"I don't know. How can I choose between my child and the woman I …" Greg said.

"Hold up. You love her? You're in love with Kate, aren't you?"

Greg cracked his knuckles again and adjusted himself in his chair. He reached for his beer and this time took a drink. "I just don't know how it can possibly work."

"Stop for a minute and let's think about this."

Greg sat back in the chair and clasped his hands behind his head. He looked at Tom to continue.

Tom took a deep breath and rested his elbows on the table, bringing his hands together. "Have you thought about what will happen if you stay with Kate? You could file for joint custody and pay child support. But if you stay with Heather, then no more Kate. Can you see Heather as a single mom or can you see you and her together with the baby? Or can you see yourself with Kate and having joint custody?"

If Tom wasn't so good at his job, Greg would have been sorry he asked him to hang out today. "It makes sense to talk this out, but it's already getting too complicated. I can't see any of it. Can't see myself as a dad, can't see Heather and me together with a kid but can't see her as a single mom either. I can see myself with Kate but not with partial custody of a kid. I just wish she wasn't pregnant. I know that sounds horrible since it's my kid and all, but it ties me to Heather for basically the rest of my life. And what is Kate going to think? She might not even want to be with me once she finds out."

"Give Kate a little credit, Greg."

"You're right, you're right. Kate isn't like that. But what would she think of a new father who deserts his own child?"

"C'mon, you wouldn't be deserting your child. There are plenty of people who share custody. Look at all the divorced people in the world with kids. Actually one of our neighbors got divorced last year and they have two kids. He said it's hard but he makes it work, for the sake of the kids. He and his wife were making each other miserable and they just couldn't work things out, finally realizing they would be better off getting a divorce. But you have to think about what you really want and who you want to be with. And you have to think about what is best for the child. You're the only one who can make that decision. Just make sure that you really think about it, talk things out. You know I'm here to talk anytime."

Noticing his cell phone vibrating on the table with Kate's name lit up, Greg gave a small smile. Tom raised his eyebrows, and Greg stared at the phone until the vibrations stopped. Greg took a gulp of beer and pushed the glass away. "Thank you, Tom. I can't tell anyone else right now. I know I have some big decisions to make."

"Anytime, Greg. I know you'll make the right decision."

"I wish it were that easy. I really do."

Tom patted Greg on the back and tried to reassure him that everything would work out in the end. He suggested walking down the street to the pizza place to get some dinner, but Greg wasn't hungry. He even turned down going over to South Philly to get a cheesesteak. He could only think about impending fatherhood and with that, possibly losing Kate.

By the time Greg got home, he was spent. *Pregnant.* The word resonated in his ear like song lyrics you can't get out of your head. What should he do? What could he do? Why did this happen, especially now? This was more than life throwing him a curve ball. This was life throwing him a missile. He sat down on the couch, resting his elbows on his knees and put his hands to his face. Rocky followed him and sat at his feet. He didn't even know how he felt about Heather anymore. The mother of his child. He cleared his throat, trying to be strong, but a few tears spilled from his eyes. Rocky jumped up and licked his arm, his tail wagging as if trying to tell him that things would be okay. Greg petted Rocky's head as tears continued to roll down his cheeks. Rocky licked his hand and whimpered, circled a couple of times, and laid down, his head resting on Greg's thigh. Greg turned off the light and lay down too. "You really are my best friend, Rocky." Greg ran his hand down the dog's thick, dark coat. "I love you, and no matter what, I'll always be there for you." Greg and Rocky would sleep on the couch that night, Greg fully dressed and Rocky never leaving his side.

CHAPTER 11

Kate sat on the couch, clutching her stuffed polar bear while reading her novel, hoping that tonight was the night she and Greg would finally talk. She read the book, gauging the time by each chapter instead of looking at a clock. She sensed it was getting late since the sun had set when she was on chapter four and now she was almost to chapter nine. Maybe Jen was right. What they had was a very short summer fling, albeit with no sex. She didn't want to call it a fling, since that implied it was like a one night stand. She and Greg had undeniable chemistry, and she got butterflies in her belly just thinking about him. They shared easygoing conversation and electric kisses. It couldn't be over, could it? She put her book down, wondering if what started out as a promising relationship was simply ending for no apparent reason.

She should just call Greg and ask how he was, what was going on, and find out the reason he'd been so distant. She considered his possible excuses: he met someone else, was no longer interested, afraid of a commitment, moved away, became a priest. She laughed at herself, hoping none of those were true, especially the last one. She remembered the way he looked straight into her eyes when he spoke and held her gaze a little longer than necessary. He was the only guy who ever made her weak in the knees. That had to mean something, didn't it? She felt it in her heart and soul that he was *the one*. When she was a teenager, she would ask her mom's married female friends how they knew it when they'd found their soul mate. They told her, "When it's right, you'll know it. You'll just know, and you won't question it." She never understood what that meant until now. Greg was absolutely *the one* for her. She was as sure of that as the sky was blue. But if he was *the one*, why did he seem to suddenly vanish from her life? Did he not think Kate was *the one* for him?

She put down the polar bear and picked up the phone. She stared at it for several minutes before calling Greg's number and then hanging up abruptly before the call went through. She wrote up a text and then deleted it without sending. Holding the phone in her hand, she could feel it get moist from perspiration on her palms. She didn't want to seem desperate. She didn't want to appear needy. If he was interested, he would call; it was as simple as that. Guys called when they wanted to talk to you. They moved mountains to see someone if they truly wanted to. They found a way even if there were a million other things going on. She put the phone down and sat back on the couch, clutching the polar bear in her arms, thinking of that beautiful day down the shore when he'd won it for her.

Greg was behind at work in resolving yet another software glitch. He slacked on keeping up with e-mails and missed two client meetings. His apartment needed vacuuming, his laundry overflowed in his hamper, and he hadn't taken out the trash in two weeks. He wasn't even taking Rocky on his usual long walks in the park, and the dog could feel the sadness that his owner was holding deep inside. The pressure was building for him to grow up and take responsibility for his child, be there for Heather, and make things right. Greg never imagined himself in this situation, and even though he was old enough to be a responsible and devoted father, he couldn't make a decision lately to save his life. His heart yearned to be with Kate, and he knew without a doubt that he loved her. But he had a child to consider now, an innocent child who deserved his love and attention. A child who needed a full-time father, not every other weekend, one day during the week, and the occasional holiday. A father who would hold his hand when he took his first steps. A father who would play catch with him in the yard and teach him to ride a bike.

But what if it was a girl? He guessed he would do similar things except maybe include having tea parties with her and her dolls. These thoughts made Greg smile despite his heart being torn in different directions. Maybe he should just focus on the baby and not worry about his relationship with Kate or Heather. Wasn't that what being a dad meant … being selfless? But what about his happiness? If not right now, then in the future. Could he really be happy for the next eighteen years without being in any relationship? Did his happiness no longer matter because he was going to be a dad? He considered three scenarios: no relationship, a relationship with Kate, or a relationship with Heather. If there was no relationship, he would just focus solely on the baby and his work. If a relationship with Kate could work, maybe he and Heather could work out child care on their own and he could spend equal time with the baby. It would be difficult, yes, but they could make it work. Kate would understand if she truly loved him. Kate would support him no matter what. And Heather would have to understand too. As long as he was a good dad to the baby and helped her, he didn't think it would be an issue. They were on a break for a reason, after all.

He considered his third scenario of mending his relationship with Heather. Should he propose and marry her? Could he fall in love with Heather or would his love for Kate thwart that from ever happening? What if they broke up again down the road? Would he always be thinking of Kate and wishing he was with her? Would it be better or worse for the baby to have two parents who stayed together for the sake of living under the same roof, even if they weren't happy? What if he and Heather eventually became miserable living together? He would never want a child to grow up in an unhappy home. But what if this was years from now and Heather insisted on staying together and working out their issues? She would remind him of how happy they were in the past and how, with a little effort, they could be happy again. If they stayed together for the wrong reasons, would the baby grow up thinking it was his fault? Greg didn't know what to do, but he was sure that he wanted everyone to be happy, especially his child, even though he realized he couldn't play God with people's lives.

Heather started browsing baby stores for nursery furniture and baby clothes, receiving blankets and bibs. She would pick up little stuffed animals and smile, picturing her baby holding it, hugging it, and loving it. After a week of researching a multitude of cribs, swings, car seats, and strollers, she placed her hands on her belly and tried to feel a kick even though she knew it was a little too early. She had walked through the stores with her head held high, up and down the aisles, determined to give her baby the best start in life. She also shopped at maternity stores buying clothes she now needed. Her jeans and skirts no longer fit in the belly, and maybe it was her imagination, but her feet seemed swollen. It was okay though; she was excited to be a mom and knew she would lose the weight after the baby was born. She read nursing helps moms lose weight faster. She would nurse her baby for sure, and not just for the weight loss; she had read it was healthier for the baby. She also read breast milk was easier to digest than formula; and let's face it: raising a baby was going to be expensive and breast milk was free. Let's not forget that it would help her get back to her original size!

But even if it didn't, she knew Greg would still be attracted to her; he wasn't the type to obsess about her weight. Anyway, how could he not be attracted to the mother of his child? Her skin already radiated the natural glow of pregnancy, which felt as if sunbeams were shining through her skin. Being pregnant made her feel closer to Greg, even though they hadn't made love since May. She was carrying his child, his firstborn, a child they created out of their love. They would dissolve any issues and pick up where they'd left off. She couldn't even remember why they'd taken a break in the first place. She loved Greg unconditionally. What more could he want?

Raising a child would be difficult between working full-time jobs and mending their relationship. But she and Greg would be a team; she didn't doubt that for one second. He would step up to the plate and be the father she knew he could be: caring and attentive, loving and loyal. He would move in, and the three of them would create a happy, loving family. They would share the bills, and with both of their salaries, they would be okay. She pictured the three of them having family dinners during the week and sharing Sunday mornings in bed with the baby. Saturday nights would be their date night, and even though they might have to scale back to two date nights a month, she knew she could count on a friend or one of Greg's relatives to watch the baby for a few hours while they went out to dinner or to a movie. It would be important to their relationship and their sanity. Everything would work out in the end. They would have a baby to love and take care of. Everything would work out. It just had to.

CHAPTER 12

Arriving five minutes late, Heather grabbed *Fit Pregnancy* and *American Baby* magazines from the waiting room. The examination room had a sterile feel to it: stark white walls without any art or medical diplomas. It simply had a chrome sink and counter, two chairs, and an examination table. Heather always dreaded going to the doctor, but being pregnant made it different. A level of excitement took over; eliminating her typical fears of doctors since she knew this was par for the course. She sat on the table flipping through *Fit Pregnancy* and read about some safe, low-impact exercises she could do at home. She analyzed the pictures of pregnant women doing special yoga and low weight-bearing strength training, and decided she would try it tomorrow. Even though the last thing she felt like doing was working out, she wanted to stay in good shape throughout her pregnancy. This would make it easier to deliver and also to lose the weight afterward. A few minutes later she opened *American Baby* and started turning the pages but was interrupted when the door swung open.

"Hi, Heather. How are you doing today?" Nurse Judy Wexler walked in, placing Heather's chart on the countertop. She was in her thirties, with long bleached-blonde hair, a perfect French manicure, mesmerizing green eyes, and a body that said she never missed a day at the gym. Heather felt a brief pang of jealousy. She put her hand on her stomach and wished and prayed for no stretch marks.

"Some morning sickness, cravings, and sore boobs, but otherwise fine. I started showing a few weeks ago."

She opened up her chart. "The doctor can speak with you about your nausea. Cravings and sore breasts are normal. You can try wearing a sports bra or sleep bra for more support. It might help. I see you are now twelve weeks along so you may notice your nausea start to subside. I'm just going to take your vitals and then you'll have an ultrasound."

Heather nodded and stood up to get her weight checked. Nurse Wexler then took her blood pressure and heart rate. She wrote down the results on her chart and told Heather everything was normal. She asked if Heather was consuming alcohol or smoking, and Heather said absolutely not.

The nurse escorted her to another room for the ultrasound. Once inside, Heather reached for *American Baby* again and turned to an article on the prevention of SIDS. She read about half of the article before a good-looking guy with chiseled features and dark hair entered and closed the door. He didn't even look old enough to be a college student. Still, his white lab coat meant he'd gone through some kind of medical training to become an ultrasound technician.

"Hi, Heather. I'm Adam, and I'll be doing your ultrasound today." He reached out to shake her hand.

"Great. Thank you. Before I forget, I don't want to find out the gender. I want it to be a surprise when he or she is born."

"Okay, thank you for telling me. Now, I'll need you to lift your shirt, and then I'm going to squirt some warm gel on your abdomen. Then we can take a look."

Heather took a deep breath and slowly breathed in and out. The room was dark, and when she looked at the ceiling, she wondered if she was going to have a girl or a boy. She had started thinking of nursery colors and decided she'd probably go with pale yellow or light green, something neutral. She wanted to have a decorating theme, and bounced around ideas like Winnie the Pooh, Dr. Seuss, or Beatrix Potter. She was excited to be a mother and knew in her heart that the baby would help mend the rift between her and Greg. He was clearly nervous about the baby; all first-time fathers were nervous. She wanted to give him the time and space he needed to let reality sink in.

Adam held the transducer on Heather's gel-covered abdomen and swept it fluidly across her belly. He looked back and forth between the screen and the transducer while Heather continued breathing in and out in a rhythmic pattern. Heather looked at the screen as well but couldn't see anything clear enough to decipher the image of her baby. Adam mumbled something and then looked intently into the screen without moving. He held his gaze for at least twenty seconds before turning his head to the right and then to the left. Finally he looked at Heather with a smile on his face.

"Okay. I'll have Dr. Farrell go over the results with you."

"Is everything okay?"

"Dr. Farrell will go over everything."

"Is something wrong, Adam?"

"No, nothing is wrong. You can get dressed and go back to the examination room."

After Adam left, she wiped the remaining gel from her belly, dressed, and walked back to the other room. She took a seat on the table and nervously flipped through *Fit Pregnancy* again. She absently turned back page after page without reading a single word until the door opened once again.

"Hi, Heather. Sorry to keep you waiting. How are you feeling today?" Dr. Diane Farrell held Kate's chart and took a pen out of her coat pocket. Her hair, dark as a permanent black Sharpie, was meticulously cut in a bob framing her heart-shaped face.

Heather put the magazine down beside her. "Well, I'm a little nervous after the ultrasound, but I'm hoping everything is okay."

"Take a deep breath, Heather. Everything is fine." She looked to the empty chair. "Is Greg not joining us today?" Dr. Farrell took a seat on the chair and wheeled over to Heather. She put her eyeglasses on and glanced at Heather's chart.

"No, he couldn't make it. I'm a little upset because I made this appointment around his schedule and then some meetings came up at work and he couldn't get out of them."

"Okay, well, don't be upset. Lots of mothers come in by themselves. And you'll be able to fill him in on everything that happened today and take home the ultrasound pictures so he'll feel like he's part of the entire pregnancy."

"Absolutely. He's my first call after I leave."

"Are you having any problems I should know about, or do you have any questions besides the ultrasound you'd like to ask before I start?"

"I've still been having some morning sickness but I guess that's just par for the course."

"Yes, nausea is normal. Ginger Ale, ginger tea, and crackers can help. It's important to always have food in your stomach, so eat something as soon as you wake up. I can also write a prescription for you in case that doesn't work."

"That would be great. Otherwise, everything seems to be in line with *What to Expect When You're Expecting*. Except … well if I could just eat and sleep for the next six months, I would be so happy."

Dr. Farrell laughed. "I was the same way when I was pregnant with my son, Tyler. And of course you are tired because the baby robs you of a lot of your energy. But as long as you're watching your diet and avoiding the no-nos, you'll be fine. It's healthy to gain between twenty-five and thirty-five pounds during pregnancy so don't worry about that too much. You started your pregnancy at a normal weight, and you don't have any health problems, which is good. And you're taking your prenatal supplements, right?"

"Yes. Thanks for the reassurance too."

"You're welcome. I'm always here to help. Any other questions that you'd like to ask?"

"No, just the results of the ultrasound."

"Okay, just let me know. Now let's take a look." Dr. Farrell scanned the ultrasound images on the screen. "Now let's see. There, I see ..." she trailed off. Something had caught her eye in the ultrasound image and she wanted to be one hundred percent sure before she said anything to her patient.

"See what? Is everything okay?" Heather's heart started racing and beads of sweat formed on her brow and the back of her neck. Her mind raced with thoughts of birth defects and abnormalities. Trying to push those thoughts away, she reached around and lifted her hair off of her neck, wishing she had a barrette or ponytail holder to keep it up. She sighed and let her hair fall back down.

"It's okay, Heather. Just give me a minute." Dr. Farrell peered closely, allowing her eyes to move back and forth over the images.

Heather put her head down and stared at the ceiling. She could feel her heart pounding in her chest as she gripped the side of the examining table.

"Well that explains it a little better."

"Explains what? Please, you're really starting to freak me out. Is something wrong with my baby?"

"No, Heather." She looked directly into her eyes and smiled. "Nothing's wrong with your *babies*." She accentuated the plural sound of the word.

Babies? Babies? She meant baby, right? Heather blinked three times in rapid succession and then laughed. "That's funny. I thought you just said *babies*. As in more than one."

Dr. Farrell turned serious as she held her gaze on Heather. "I did."

Heather's face drew a blank. "Excuse me?"

Dr. Farrell held her gaze on Heather.

"Wait, this is a joke, right?" Heather quivered and rubbed her palms on the paper lining of the examining table.

"There are two fetuses, Heather. You're carrying twins."

Heather sat still and silent for a minute and then shook her head. "Well that can't be. I can't be having two babies. I ..." The blood started draining from Heather's face until it slowly matched the white of the walls.

"It's going to be okay. Many women have perfectly healthy pregnancies with twins. Take a deep breath and slowly breathe in and out."

Heather tried to catch her breath and clutched the paper lining on the table.

"Let me get you a glass of water. I'll be right back."

Perspiration beaded up on her forehead, and she suddenly felt a bout of nausea coming on. She lifted her hair again and wiped her fingers across her forehead and the back of her neck. When Dr. Farrell came back in, she handed Heather the water and some saltine crackers. "I don't understand," was all she could muster.

"It'll be okay. Just try to relax; everything is going to be fine. I promise we'll take good care of you and your babies. I'm glad you came in today so now we know. Let me show you the ultrasound images."

Heather stared at the images without blinking. Twins? There was no way in hell she was pregnant with twins. She must have someone else's ultrasound. *Yes, that's it. Dr. Farrell is looking at someone else's results by mistake. This is just a big misunderstanding. A very big misunderstanding.*

"I think this is some sort of mistake. See, there is just no way I am pregnant with twins. I know I can't provide the most accurate family history, but I'm pretty sure there are no twins in my family. Or Greg's. So, this just can't be right. It just can't be." Heather shook her head and was firm in her tone.

"Heather, take a deep breath. Let me assure you these are in fact your ultrasound images. I know this is probably overwhelming for you right now, but the ultrasound is accurate."

Heather wiped her forehead but just continued to stare at Dr. Farrell and shake her head.

"Now, let me show you. Here is your name, so these are your images. Take a deep breath." Dr. Farrell paused as Heather closed her eyes and then slowly opened them again. "Do you see them? Right there, and see the other one right over there? The second one was hiding a little so I had to be sure before I said anything." Dr. Farrell pointed to the ultrasound image that showed two visible sacs. Two babies. Twins. "The fluid levels appear normal, and I can see two placentas. When you come into my office, we'll discuss everything you need to know about carrying twins, and I'll give you some information to take home. Everything's going to be fine, Heather. I assure you."

Heather forced her head to nod but had to keep her hands clutched to the paper lining for stability, support. This moment would go down in her memory along with the moment she heard the news the terrorists struck the World Trade Center on September eleventh. It would become a monumental moment in her life that she would never forget, no matter how old she was. She would probably still remember this moment even if someday she developed Alzheimer's or had amnesia. *Twins.* She kept saying the word over and over in her head. *Two babies.* She continued reminding herself like a mantra: *twins.* She said the word over and over again as she gathered her purse. And again and again as she washed her hands. *Twins.* But wait, maybe this was a dream. She closed her eyes and even clicked her heels three times, hoping she would wake up in her own bed to the sound of her cell phone alarm buzzing. When life was just handing her one baby. One baby. Not two. But when she opened her eyes, she was still standing in the examination room.

Heather gingerly walked into Dr. Farrell's office and practically collapsed into the chair. Dr. Farrell gave her a reassuring smile.

"Dr. Farrell, I'm having a hard time believing this. I mean, I hate to question your medical expertise but I just can't be pregnant with twins." Heather put her hand on her belly to see if she could feel two babies.

"Heather, I assure you one hundred percent, you are carrying twins."

Heather felt tears well up in her eyes, and Dr. Farrell handed her a tissue. She wiped her eyes and cleared her throat and in that instant, she knew this was no joke. "Okay, if you're right about this, are you sure it's just the two? I don't think I could handle another surprise at my next appointment."

"It's just two, Heather."

More tears fell as she heard Dr. Farrell confirm for the thousandth time she was carrying twins. *Only two,* Heather thought. Like raising twins was going to be a piece of cake.

CHAPTER 13

Heather had a list of errands to run after her doctor's appointment, but when she finally made it outside, she couldn't remember a single one. She walked slowly, carefully placing one foot in front of the other so she wouldn't faint on the sidewalk. She forced her mind to focus on remembering the direction to her apartment. *The way home.*

"Excuse me, can you tell me how to get to the Reading Terminal Market?" A woman in a long summer sundress spoke with a thick Southern drawl and spit on Heather when she talked as they waited for the light to change. Heather looked up to see the Fourth Street sign staring back at her and realized she had just walked four blocks in the wrong direction.

Heather, on a normal day, could walk to the Reading Terminal blindfolded from any part of the city. It was a popular spot for Philadelphians, and she and Greg had gone there often for brunch, to get a cup of coffee or just to browse the merchandise from the many shops. She stared at the woman, no expression on her face and eyes so glassy they could have been marbles. "Twins." When the woman heard her response, she mumbled something about this not being the City of Brotherly Love and stomped off. Heather turned around to walk the correct way to her apartment, saying, *Twins,* over and over in her mind, replaying the word as if it was skipping on an old vinyl record. When she finally reached her apartment, she fumbled with the key. Once she got in, she closed the door, leaving the mail exactly where the mail carrier delivered it.

Heather folded on the couch like a broken pretzel and stared at the wall as if it was going to change the fact she was pregnant with twins. That or she was looking at the wall to tell her what to do, give her advice, keep her safe. For the next three days, she ignored her phone, e-mail, and anything to do with work. In fact, she didn't even leave her apartment after coming home from the doctor's office. What difference did missing a few days at work make now anyway? She might have to stop working earlier than planned and would probably have to take a long leave of absence so she could stay home and take care of the babies. Day care for two infants would be astronomical, plus she wouldn't trust just anyone to care for her babies. It didn't matter than she earned a bachelor's degree in Hotel Restaurant Management with a minor in Business and graduated near the top of her class. Or that she worked her way from the ground up to become an event manager at the Four Seasons. She thought about the summers she worked in various hotel front desks, pacifying customers who were unhappy with their rooms or not satisfied with the housekeeping service. After college, her title of catering assistant seemed glamorous until she realized she was working around the clock, planning small events during the day and managing the onsite work on nights and weekends. Once she became event manager, she had her own assistant and it seemed like all her hard work had finally paid off. But she was not ready to stop now. She wanted to become a sales manager, bid on the larger city events and programs, and create winning contracts that her clients wouldn't be able to turn down, all the while earning substantial commission.

Now, all that would be flushed down the drain, at least until the twins were old enough that she felt safe sending them to day care. And after this three-year break to be a full-time mommy, would she have to start from the ground up all over again? Would anyone hire her to pick up where she left off after three years of breastfeeding, potty training, and watching *Sesame Street*? She placed her hands on her belly and looked to the ceiling. "Why did this happen to me—a single woman who is technically still on a break with her boyfriend?" One baby, okay. She and Greg could handle that no problem while still having time to mend their relationship. But twins? There would be no time to do anything else but take care of them. It would be double the work and double the expense. They could financially manage one baby. Heather could work part-time and just hire a nanny for twenty hours a week. But twins would make them a one-income household. Even if she did keep her job part-time, most of her salary would go to the nanny, and she would miss them too much. But that was taking for granted that Greg would move in and support all four of them. Speaking of Greg, how would he react? She could tell he was hesitant and nervous with just one baby, but now that there were two, would he bolt? No, she thought, Greg would never leave her and his children. But it was so much to ask. They weren't married and had yet to discuss it, and now they surely couldn't afford the wedding Heather had always wanted. But that didn't matter now. They would be parents to twins in about six months and that would be enough to worry about. She felt the emotional drain taking its toll on her body. Her shoulders felt heavy, her eyes hung low, and her energy was gone. She shook her head and walked back to her bedroom to take a nap.

Once Sara came home and realized Heather was using her third sick day in a row, she went into Heather's bedroom to find her sleeping with the comforter pulled up to her neck. Her winter drapes were down, making the room pitch dark despite it being sunny and eighty-five degrees outside. She left the room and closed the door gently, figuring Heather needed her sleep. Once the babies were born, she wouldn't be getting much.

Around eight o'clock, Heather woke up, but it took her several minutes to realize where she was. That was one thing about being pregnant, she thought. She went into such a deep sleep that she woke up discombobulated. Even after her eyes adjusted to the light, she couldn't place where she was despite it being the same bedroom she'd had for the past five years. Once she gently shook off the sleep and rolled over, she made her way to the bathroom and then walked into the kitchen, joking to herself that the babies were ready for their next feeding. And they hadn't even been born yet! Should she be eating for three? She didn't think so, but what difference did it make now? In a couple of months, she was going to be as big as a house. She shook her head and opened the freezer door, which blasted her with a wave of arctic air. She looked at the carton of strawberry ice cream and winced, opting instead to grab an orange and loaf of bread from the refrigerator. She threw two slices in the toaster and reached in the cabinet for a can of vegetable soup. After reaching for a plate and knife, she started peeling the orange and popped slices in her mouth until the toaster dinged and the soup was hot. Heather buttered the toast and carried the plate of toast, orange, and bowl of soup to the sofa and turned on the TV to a badly acted Lifetime movie. The warm soup soothed her and the crisp toast with melted butter comforted her belly. She was starting to feel slightly better, and after three days was getting used to the fact she was going to be a first-time mom to twins. She ate slowly, and after she finished half of her toast and half of her soup, she put down the plate and bowl to let everything digest.

Sara heard her up and about and joined her in the living room, plopping down on the couch wearing cut-off denim shorts and a hot pink tank top. Heather didn't know anyone who wore such bright colors, herself preferring more muted and pastel tones. Sara's silky blonde hair fell past her shoulders and her green eyes stared at Heather and her choice of food.

"What, no pickles and ice cream?"

Heather let out a low groan. "Contrary to what most people think are normal pregnant cravings, the very thought of anything salty or sugary is nauseating. But thanks for the mental image of the two together."

"Sorry."

Heather cleared her throat and put her feet up on the coffee table. "It's okay. I guess I'm used to it by now. You know, last week I realized I have an aversion to chicken salad. Someone at work had it for lunch, and I had to head straight for the bathroom. Now there's a mental image for you."

"Gee, thanks. I'll never be able to eat chicken again."

"Now it's my turn to say I'm sorry. You know, though, this is just the beginning. It's only going to get worse from here on out."

"Don't say that."

"Well then, do you have any words of wisdom, Dr. Lewis?" Heather rested her hands on her stomach.

"I don't have my PhD yet, mind you. But if I had to give you my guidance-counselor expert advice, you're going to be a fantastic mother. Even though it will probably be the hardest thing you ever do, I just know things are going to work out. You'll see."

Heather gave a half smile. "I'm just so nervous. Twins. Midnight feedings times two. Double the diapers. Double the terrible two tantrums. Double the laundry. Good lord,

Sara—double the stretch marks! Double the everything. Double the college tuition eighteen years from now."

"Calm down, Heather. Take a deep breath."

"You sound like Dr. Farrell."

"Heather, look. Everything will work out. You're a strong woman, and once they're born, you'll see; they will become the most important people in your life. You won't even remember what it was like before they were born. And Greg will be there." Sara paused. "Have you told him yet?"

Heather shrugged her shoulders and shook her head ever so lightly.

"What are you waiting for?"

Heather reached for a pillow and put it over her belly. "I don't know. He called twice to find out about the ultrasound, and I can't answer. What if …"

"Don't be crazy. Greg's a great guy, and he would never not be there for you and the babies. It might take him a little while to get used to it, but once he does, I'm sure he'll be happy about it."

"You think?"

"Yes, I really do."

"I hope you're right." Heather picked up the remote and muted the movie. "Sara? I just—well, there's something else."

Sara sat back down on the couch and looked at her roommate of five years.

"As long as you're right about Greg, which deep down is what I truly hope, he'll probably move in a little bit before the babies come and …" Heather looked toward the ceiling, searching for the right words to say, but then Sara cut her off.

"And you need me to move out. I understand, Heather, and honestly, I would have moved out even if you hadn't asked. I don't want to get in the way, and I'll need quiet to write my dissertation. And two babies crying at all hours—well, I know you understand."

"Thank you."

"I'll always be here for you whenever you need me, to babysit or just to talk or if you need a mom's night out!"

"I may take you up on the mom's night out. I'll need that for sure."

Heather and Sara shared a hug, each of them realizing their friendship would change, whether or not they wanted it to.

Sara stood up and walked to the kitchen. Heather sat up a little straighter, smiled, and, before she lost her nerve, grabbed the phone and called. As soon as she said the words, she felt the love and support seeping through the telephone line. She always knew she could count on Aunt Clara for anything. But it was the way Aunt Clara said she would immediately help with anything Heather needed that gave her a feeling of relief. Heather felt even better as she placed her hands on her belly and whispered that everything was going to be fine. She would tell Greg soon. *One down, one to go*, she thought. It wasn't like it was her fault she was pregnant with twins. He couldn't blame her or be mad or anything. She didn't get pregnant by herself, after all. So Greg would have no choice but to be supportive. He was the father and had an equal part in all of this, and as Sara pointed out, everything had a way of working itself out.

On that note, she finally relaxed and let herself smile, thinking of two little ones: two babies she would love unconditionally and who would love her just the same. Two babies she would introduce to the world. Two babies she would teach and love and care for. A game plan started forming in her head on how to tackle twins. Two cribs. Two car seats. Two high chairs. A double stroller. One changing table. One dresser. Two baby swings. Two mobiles. One glider and ottoman. Two Exersaucers. Two Jumperoos. One baby monitor. One breast pump. A lot of bottles. One big baby gym. Safety gates. One baby bathtub. Two sets of bedding, blankets, sheets, and towels. One huge diaper bag. Two baby carriers. Enough bibs, onesies, hats, socks, and pajamas to last at least five days without doing laundry. Toys, books, puzzles, and games. Diapers and wipes. A lot of diapers and wipes. And baby wash, shampoo, diaper rash cream, pacifiers, rattles, baby detergent, baby lotion, and …

CHAPTER 14

Kate sat on her sofa, hands planted on her stomach, trying to will away the knots. The polar bear sat beside her in its usual spot, but she didn't pick it up. Looking at her mood ring, she knew it was only this deep pumpkin color when she was anxious, nervous, or scared. She racked her brain all day but couldn't figure out why he wanted to talk to her tonight. *In person.* She grasped onto the notion that he missed her and wanted to start dating again, even though his actions told her this was not the case. They had spoken only a couple of times a month since August, and each conversation was shorter than the last. She remembered trying to listen for little clues in his voice that would explain what was happening, but he would contradict himself so much that she felt confused by even his most heartfelt words. He still deeply cared for her but had a lot going on. He missed her but never gave her the feeling he wanted to actually get together. He asked about her work and life as if he were truly interested, but when she asked him about his life, he was quick to dismiss her questions with brief answers and didn't elaborate on any topics she brought up.

Over the past few months, she tried to push him out of her mind and focus on her work. The restaurant opening for Three B was a smashing success. Taking place in mid-September, it was attended by hip young New Yorkers along with press, social media personnel, restaurant critics, and twenty of the biggest restaurant bloggers in New York City. Their eclectic menu, cozy atmosphere, new age decor, and personable staff got rave reviews, and they were well on their way to becoming the new *it* place. The Boston medical conference, another event led by Kate's firm, showed an increase in attendance by nearly twenty percent with doctors from all over the world. It attracted a great deal of press from the medical and scientific communities and was slated to be even bigger the following year in San Francisco. The conference was Kate's first trip to Boston, and she fell in the love with the charming city. Her coworkers had a rare two days free to explore the sights and went everywhere, from Harvard Square to Faneuil Hall to Newbury Street. She relished the walking city and especially enjoyed the Public Garden and North End. She made a mental note to go back and visit sometime during the summer and go to a Red Sox game and take a drive to the Cape. The West Chester car dealership was booming with sales and attracting car buyers from not only Chester County but Montgomery and Delaware Counties as well. She had biweekly meetings with the management and marketing teams and afterward would go visit her mom. They would sit and talk over a relaxing dinner and catch up on each other's lives. Kate was proud of her mom for getting a recent promotion at work and treated her to a gift certificate for a day at the spa. Ellen's new role was director of human resources. She had worked her way up in her company, starting as human resources assistant when Kate was in elementary school, moving up to benefits coordinator by the time Kate was in middle school, and becoming hiring director when Kate was in high school—and now her current role. Her mom loved being a part of her large transportation firm where she was one of the family, even giving Kate ten thousand dollars toward college when she graduated high school.

Kate and Jen also spent much-needed girlfriend time together, with Jen trying hard to get Kate back in the dating pool. Kate appeased her and went out on one blind date. Randy, a friend of one of her coworkers at CHOP, had just moved to Philadelphia from Tucson and wanted to meet new people. He took her to dinner on a crisp October evening. It started out well enough with normal conversation until he ordered beef soup at the restaurant. As he ate it, some of the soup landed in his beard and mustache, and he either didn't realize it or didn't care. It was hard for Kate to choke down her salad as she tried not to stare at the bits of beef and vegetables stuck on his hairy face. She told him she had an early-morning meeting the next day, and he walked her home right after leaving the restaurant. Randy had reached for her hand, but she quickly put both hands in her coat pockets, telling him she was cold. She shook his hand after saying good-bye and thanking him for dinner, escaping to her apartment before he had the chance to kiss her good night.

Kate and Jen also visited Jen's parents several times over the past few months. Jen's father, Troy Delvina, tried to get Kate to confide in him about what was bothering her. Although Kate loved Jen's dad, almost as much as a real father, she never felt comfortable enough to share her feelings about Greg. Kate almost shared her dilemma with Jen's mom, Nancy, but decided against it. She knew it was best to simply focus on living her life and put Greg out of her mind.

Today, however, Kate's mind was fixated on Greg since receiving his call that morning. He wouldn't go into any detail, simply asking if he could come over tonight to talk. She tried to relax in a bubble bath after work, but it hadn't done anything to wipe away the pang piercing her insides. She rested in the warm water, which was filled to the brim with vanilla-scented bubbles. She tuned out the music playing on Pandora and concocted all different scenarios: he was moving away or he couldn't live without her or he met someone else. But nothing seemed to make any sense! After she got out of the tub and got dressed, it was almost eight. With the knots growing as the minutes ticked by, she kept her hands on her belly and closed her eyes until suddenly there was a soft knock on her door.

"Hi." Greg stood at Kate's door, wiping his shoes on the doormat and shaking excess water from his jacket before taking it off. She moved to the right, and he stepped inside. It was a cold, steady rain but about fifteen degrees too high for snow. Kate took his jacket and hung it on the coat rack. Little beads of water on his hair and face fell onto his shirt, making small, dark, perfect circles on the blue fabric.

"Let me get you a towel."

"No, that's okay. Thanks." Greg stepped into Kate's apartment, and the two of them walked into her living room. Greg shivered slightly and blew into his hands to warm up. "Wow, do you sell poinsettias or something?"

"No, silly. I work in PR—remember? Don't tell me you've forgotten already." She regretted the flirtatious tone in her voice, but the words escaped as natural and clean as fresh sheets out of the dryer.

"I know that, but it's just, I've never seen this many poinsettias in someone's house before."

"I just like them. Especially at this time of the year."

"I'll say." Greg scanned the room, taking in the vibrant red and pink flowers and muted green leaves in pots lined with gold, red, and silver foil.

"I'll probably get some more next week. Don't you feel like they brighten things up and put you in the Christmas spirit?"

"If you say so. I mean, I guess so. It's just—wow, there are really a lot."

"Thanks. I'll take that as a compliment."

They stood for several seconds in silence, neither knowing what to say.

"Do you want to sit down?" Kate motioned toward the couch.

"Sure."

"Can I get you something to drink?"

"No, thanks. I'm okay." Greg settled on the couch and glanced at some magazines on her coffee table.

Kate smiled but didn't say anything. She wished she could go back to that night when he came over for a good-night kiss. She had opened the door, and they kissed immediately before her front door even closed. She felt so close to him; the way they kissed was magical. The connection she felt, she knew he felt it too. It was undeniable, raw and unique, something she had never felt before.

"How was your Thanksgiving?" Greg asked, breaking her thoughts.

"Thanksgiving?" Kate blinked her eyes, trying to return to the present. "It was good." She paused. "I spent the weekend at my mom's. We made dinner, watched the Macy's Parade, and did some Christmas shopping. How about you?"

Greg nodded. "It was fine; we all went to my parents' house."

They were sitting about six inches apart, facing each other. She knew he was stalling to discuss the real reason he was there, which had a whammy effect on her stomach as the knots did not dissipate. She looked down at her ring, and it looked like a well-cooked butternut squash. She twirled a strand of her hair. "So what else is new?"

He glanced at the poinsettias again and noticed the polar bear beside her on the couch. *That perfect day down the shore.* He wished they could go back to that day. Searching for the right words, he looked into her eyes, but nothing came out of his mouth.

"Greg?"

"Sorry. It's just … there's something I need to tell you."

"Okay." Kate put one leg under the other and repositioned herself on the couch so she was about two inches closer to him. She smiled and thought about all the things she loved about him. His kindness and sense of humor and good looks. His chin dimple, work ethic, and love of sports. The way he was with Rocky. His easygoing nature and love of adventure. She waited for him to say something, but there was just dead air between them. Kate swallowed. "You know you can be honest with me. If you don't want to see me anymore …" She paused. "I'll understand Greg, I mean …"

"No, Kate. That's not it." Greg looked away and then turned to meet her eyes. "That's not it at all."

"Okay, then what is it?"

"I need to tell you something."

"You said that. And that something is …" Kate inched forward on the couch and leaned her body another inch closer. Up close, she grasped the weariness he was carrying. His shoulders were hunched, an invisible heaviness leaning down on them.

Greg shook his head as if trying to shake the problem away.

"Are you in trouble?"

"No, not the kind you probably mean."

"Do you need my help?" She reached out to touch his arm.

"I'm sorry, Kate. I don't mean to scare you. It's just …" He trailed off. "It's just, this is really difficult."

"Are you sure you don't want a drink? I have some of your favorite beer in the fridge."

Greg gave Kate a small smile. "I'm sure. Thanks." Greg cleared his throat. *It's now or never*, he thought. "Remember when we first met?"

"Of course I remember."

"Well, I never told you but I was sort of coming out of a relationship."

"Okay. And?"

"We dated for three years."

"Oh, that's your big news? That I was your rebound? I really don't care about that." Kate laughed but abruptly stopped when she saw the serious look on Greg's face. "Lighten up, Greg. Whatever you need to tell me, unless someone died, it can't be that bad."

"Kate, I'm so sorry for what I'm about to say. I never meant for this to happen, and I never meant to hurt you."

Kate stared silently at Greg with a blank expression on her face, her heart now thudding in her chest. Her stomach dropped and a bead of sweat formed on her temple that she quickly wiped away.

Greg put his fingers on the bridge of his nose and took a deep breath. "Okay. I was dating someone for three years before we met. Her name is Heather. We were actually on a break when you and I met, so it wasn't like I was cheating on her or you or anything."

Kate nodded and felt more knots hitting her stomach like missiles.

"And things with you and me were going great. I mean, I've never felt this way before and ..." Greg trailed off and looked away. "There's something else now, and I thought we would be able to work it out since I wanted to officially end that relationship with her and be with you. But now, I just, I just don't think that it can work."

"Greg, what are you talking about?"

Greg took a deep breath and looked at the wall, searching for the best way to say it. He didn't know how except to be direct. "It's Heather. She's pregnant. With twins." Greg looked into Kate's eyes. "My twins."

Kate opened her mouth slightly. "Oh." Her head dropped, and she felt like she was going to pass out or throw up—one or the other. Twins? Greg was going to be the father of twins with his ex-girlfriend? She sat quietly, trying to absorb this information as Greg held his gaze on her. "Wow." She uncrossed her legs and sat forward on the couch, cementing her elbows to her knees. "I don't know what to say."

They sat in silence for several minutes as Kate took in the news. He would go back to Heather, and they would be a family. She could never compete with the mother of his children. It was over for them, and the realization came fast and furious.

"I'm so sorry, Kate."

Kate gave him a weak smile before turning her back to him. She sniffled, and as much as she did not want to, the tears came flowing down her cheeks, little drops of sadness.

"Please don't cry, Kate. I never meant for this to happen. I never wanted to hurt you in any way; you have to believe that. I need you to believe that."

Kate turned back around to face him. "I know." Kate wiped at her eyes. "So then, what does this mean for us?" she asked even though she already knew the answer. It would be over for them.

"I don't know." In his heart, he knew too. But how could he possibly say the words aloud to the woman he loved?

Greg and Kate sat on the couch in silence for about five minutes. Kate glanced down at her ring and watched as the orange color slowly melted away into a murky brown. She looked up and cleared her throat. She took off the ring and set it on the coffee table so Greg couldn't see. "When are they due?"

"February."

Kate nodded. "Well, I guess you'll be busy."

"Yeah."

"So …"

"I don't know, Kate. I mean, I didn't expect this. I hope that we can stay friends. I can't imagine us not being friends."

Kate swallowed hard while trying to hold back any more tears. "Of course we can be friends."

"I hope you mean that because your friendship means a lot to me."

"It means a lot to me too." Kate felt a lump in her throat as she forced the words out.

"Good."

Kate wiped a couple of new tears from her eyes and willed herself to stop crying.

They sat silently for a few more minutes, each of them trying to absorb the impact this would have on their relationship. They stared at each other, Kate feeling a chill in her bones and Greg feeling a sickening pit in his stomach.

Greg cleared his throat and stood up, feeling dizzy and putting his hands on the back of the couch to steady himself. He felt wiped out, as if he just worked out for two hours straight without a single sip of water. He hoped he would be okay to walk home. "I'm so sorry, Kate. I hope you believe me. This was never my intention. I never wanted to hurt you." Greg shook his head, and Kate got up from the couch.

"I know. I'm sorry too."

Greg walked over to get his coat, and Kate followed. Once they reached the door, he turned and wrapped his arms around her, and the tears fell from her eyes onto his shoulder. They held onto each other as if they did not want time to move forward. He kissed her on the forehead and the top of her head, and Kate gave him a soft kiss on the cheek.

"I'll call you," Greg said.

"Okay. Don't be a stranger."

Greg put on his coat with his back to Kate.

"And, Greg?"

He turned back around to face her.

"I'll always be here for you, no matter what."

Greg gave her a small smile. "Thank you."

Greg walked back down the stairs, Kate listening to each footstep. The rain had stopped, and it was eerily quiet. She stood in her doorway, replaying the conversation. Deep down she knew she should be happy for him. It wasn't as though she and Greg were in a long-term relationship. They had only met in June and he was her friend, despite the fact she was in love with him. She would have to put her feelings aside and be his friend or she might lose him altogether. Heather was going to be the mother of his children. How could she possibly compete with that? She couldn't. Ever. She loved him and wanted to believe that he loved her too, but that didn't matter anymore.

Kate shook her head and decided then and there that she would be his friend. She cared deeply for him and couldn't imagine not having him in her life. Swallowing hard, she told herself she would be a *real* friend, the type who would pick you up in the middle of the night if you had car trouble. Someone you could call twenty-four/seven to listen and offer advice to. The friend you would always feel close to even if months or years passed between phone calls or visits, and who would be supportive no matter what.

But what kind of friend doesn't even say congratulations when the impending birth of twins is announced? She should have said congratulations. That's what people say when a friend tells them they're going to have a baby. *Or babies.* Even if it hurts to say the words, that's what the other person would expect. A real friend would have offered congratulations.

"Hi, Greg. It's me, Kate. I forgot to tell you something." She hesitated to form the words in her mouth. "Congratulations. I'm sorry I didn't tell you before." Kate wiped her eyes as she spoke into his voice mail. "Congratulations, Greg. I know you're going to be a wonderful father."

CHAPTER 15

The twins arrived three weeks early at Bryn Mawr Hospital on a bitter cold January fifteenth. "Two baby boys, what could be more precious?" Heather had said as the sleeping bundles of joy lay in her arms in the hospital bed. Each was swaddled up tight in the traditional blue-and-pink-striped hospital blanket, soft little blue caps covering their heads. She cradled one in each arm and kissed them on the forehead while wearing the most content smile. Her smile never left her face despite the after pains she felt from the delivery.

She delivered her first son at nine o'clock in the evening, and fourteen minutes later, his younger brother arrived. The large team of doctors and nurses filled the room, which overwhelmed Heather, but she understood that is the way it had to be since all twin pregnancies were considered high risk. Each baby was whisked away for assessment, and it felt like an eternity until Heather was able to see them. Greg was by Heather's side from the moment her contractions started the night before: holding her hand, coaching her breathing, and reassuring her that everything was going to be okay. After the doctors and nurses completed their evaluation of the babies and got them cleaned up, Heather was finally allowed skin-on-skin bonding while she recovered in the birthing room. She breathed in their sweet newborn scent, closing her eyes and falling in love with her children. Despite being fraternal, they looked similar. Heather gazed at each of their little faces, memorizing their squished noses and plump little lips, one with his eyes tightly closed, the other one with a little slit open. Greg stood next to her, lightly touching their tiny fingers and toes. She could already tell them apart easily and not just because one had the tiniest freckle on his right cheek. She was their mother, and if anyone in the world needed to tell them apart, it was her.

While the hospital staff moved Heather to her private room, she anxiously awaited holding her babies again, her arms feeling empty without them. In the chaos of the birth and helping Heather recover, Greg took this opportunity to race to the maternity waiting room. There he found his parents and brothers as well as Aunt Clara, Sara, Tom, and Danielle. He walked in smiling, and everyone jumped out of their seats and hugged and kissed him. Then the questions came at rapid fire. Yes, Heather was doing great; the twins were perfect, both healthy and bald with great sets of lungs. The first one weighed four pounds thirteen ounces and was eighteen inches long, and his baby brother was four pounds nine ounces and seventeen and a quarter inches long. Heather would be able to have visitors in the morning. They didn't name them yet. He and Heather would tell everyone soon how they could help.

Wrapped gifts with giant bows, balloons, stuffed animals, and flowers sat on the plastic tables that filled the waiting room. After talking with everyone, Greg and Tom went to the downstairs lobby. Greg posted pictures on Facebook and made a few late calls to those who weren't there.

He left a message for his boss on voice mail to share the news and also that he would begin his paternity leave. Although he knew the next three weeks would be hectic, he was happy to help Heather as much as he could. He was excited to bond with his children, as Heather had told him that it was important in the first few weeks. He anticipated a lot of diaper changes and lack of sleep. That was okay; he figured that he would just drink stronger coffee.

As soon as Greg hung up the phone, Tom suggested going to the hospital cafeteria.

"How are you feeling?" Tom sat back in his chair and watched Greg dump a couple of sugar packets into his steaming paper cup.

Greg shook his head and took a gulp of coffee. "It hasn't hit me yet, even though I held both babies. It feels surreal."

"Give it a few days. Once you get home, I'm sure it'll feel real."

"No kidding. But we have a lot of family to help us out." Greg stretched his arms and cracked his back. "Things will work out. They kind of have to, you know?"

"Do I ask if you talked to Kate?"

Greg subconsciously looked at his cell phone lying on the table. "No, not since I was at her place last month. I can't call her right now." He rubbed his hand over his cheek, feeling little prickles of stubble. "She'll probably see it on Facebook, but I will talk to her soon. It's just … I'm not looking forward to that conversation." Greg took another big swig of coffee.

"Take your time. She'll understand. She cares about you; she wants you both to do what's right."

"That's the hard part, Tom." Greg ran his hands down the front of his jeans. "I know I need to be a father to my boys. I want them to grow up knowing I love them and that I'll always be there for them. But Kate … the way I feel about her is so different than how I feel about Heather." Greg stopped and looked around the near-empty cafeteria. "Even though the boys were just born, I kind of get it now. Being a father is selfless, and my kids need to come first."

Tom smiled. "You are growing up, my friend."

Greg gave a weak smile and stared at his cell phone again. "And remember Danielle and I can help too, with the babies."

"Thanks. I appreciate that."

Once Greg made it back to the nursery, he looked at the babies through the glass window, sleeping peacefully, all bundled up. Their scrunched faces and tiny fingers and toes were a miracle. He never knew he could love so deeply, and even though he was still nervous about being a father, he felt unconditional love when each little boy opened his eyes, looked straight at their father, and squeezed his pinky with their tiny hands. As he looked at his sons, he made a promise to them. He would be the best dad possible. Even though he would have to learn as he went along, Greg was committed one hundred percent to always being there for his children.

Greg walked back over to Heather's room, and the two sat together, enjoying a few moments of quiet before the nurses brought the babies in. A few minutes later, they were wheeled in, each still sleeping in the tiny bassinets. Heather could see their tiny pink faces, the rest of their bodies swaddled up nice and snug. She knew that life would never be any sweeter. "Hunter and Cole?" Heather peered up at Greg with her question. Greg kissed her forehead and brushed away the hair matted down on her face. "Sounds perfect." Greg smiled at Heather and then looked at his sons. "Hi there, Hunter and Cole," he whispered.

Heather was anxious to come home from the hospital and get the twins set up in their cute cream-colored Winnie the Pooh nursery. Six weeks after she digested the fact she was indeed having twins, she got to work making list after list of everything that needed to be purchased, cleaned, painted, organized, wallpapered, stenciled, and baby-proofed. She received quite a few gifts from her registry at her shower, and she and Greg bought the rest together. They worked to get everything ready before her thirtieth week: the cribs, mobiles, changing table, dressers, and comfy glider with ottoman where she would nurse and rock the babies to sleep.

One day in mid-December, Heather woke up at six o'clock in the morning with an overwhelming urge to clean her apartment from top to bottom. Since she couldn't bend down to tie her own shoes, she enlisted the help of Sara and Greg. When Aunt Clara came over that morning bearing more gifts, including extra crib sheets, blankets, and towels, she found Greg scrubbing the kitchen floor, Sara disinfecting the bathroom, and Heather with her huge belly lightly dusting the bookshelf. Clara laughed and told them this was simply nesting at its finest.

Just three short days after giving birth, Heather and Greg took their newborn twins home. Greg had moved in the month before and chose to sublet his apartment. Subconsciously, he wasn't quite ready to give it up despite being on a month-to-month lease. As the two of them walked into their apartment, each carrying one baby snuggled and buckled into his car seat, Heather couldn't recall a happier time in her entire life.

The next three weeks went by as if in slow motion. Each day was filled with constant activity, day and night blending together like steaming coffee and fresh cream. Greg and Heather were awake for what seemed like twenty-four hours a day as they tried and failed several times to get the boys on the same schedule. She tried her best to nurse them together, despite the challenge of holding one in each arm as they latched on and off in the early days before her milk fully came in. They each woke every couple of hours around the clock. Their diapers needed changing just as often but rarely at the same time. Heather quickly got used to five minute showers, not doing anything with her hair besides putting it in a haphazard ponytail, and wearing sweats day and night. The thought of getting a manicure was laughable, and the very last thing on her mind was how she looked. She tried her best to sleep while the babies slept, but sometimes she felt so over exhausted that she would just lie awake in bed, staring at the walls. She and Greg covered for each other in thirty-minute increments so they each had time to shower, check e-mail, make phone calls, and walk Rocky. Laundry piled up, and the trash cans were filled with dirty diapers, wipes, paper plates, cups, and plastic silverware. Fortunately, Aunt Clara and Greg's family were pitching in by bringing over home-cooked meals and helping with some of the cleaning and laundry. Heather nearly bowed down to kiss Greg's mom's feet one night when she showed up with a giant tray of lasagna to add to their refrigerator.

As the days went on, Hunter and Cole both nursed extremely well. Heather felt great that she was able to nourish her babies, but it also left her tired, dehydrated, and ravenous. In a sleep-deprived moment of exhaustion when Cole slept peacefully and Hunter screamed at the top of his lungs, Heather wondered if one of the babies was not really hers and the twins had been separated at the hospital. She couldn't fathom how Hunter cried so hard day and night while Cole was more or less content and happy. Even though their tiny faces looked similar, they were such different babies. She kept this thought to herself because she knew Greg would go barging into the hospital and demand to know if they in fact brought home the right children. Of course they were their beautiful perfect twin boys.

About two weeks after Heather came home, she was eating forkfuls of tuna casserole right from the serving dish standing over the sink at two o'clock in the morning. A large ice-cold bottle of water was next to her that she drank in mere minutes. Greg walked in wearing the same sweats he'd worn three days earlier, and as he approached her and opened his mouth, she put a forkful of casserole in. She started laughing uncontrollably. She was thinking back before the twins were born, and how she assumed that she and Greg would still be able to go out on date nights. The thought of getting ready for a date now was unfathomable; she didn't have the energy even if she could have a full-time nanny. She remembered back when she was pregnant, thinking she would be able to exercise while the babies slept and now realizing that breastfeeding was more of a workout than she ever could have imagined. She had to laugh or else she would cry. And when Greg started laughing too, they both went into hysterics in a matter of seconds. When both of them were doubled over in pain, they stopped abruptly, overcome with exhaustion. It was a rare quiet moment in their household, but when little Hunter started to cry a few minutes later; Heather raised her eyebrows at Greg and went to the nursery. Greg, alone in the kitchen, picked up the same fork Heather was using and shoveled some more casserole in his mouth, threw the plastic fork on top of the garbage can, and traced Heather's steps to help with their son.

These three weeks at home with the babies were unlike anything Greg had ever experienced. He wasn't sure what to expect, but he knew he was in over his head. He slept maybe four hours total each day, mostly on the couch, and didn't wear anything except sweats or old jeans. He didn't check sports scores, and his magazines and mail went virtually unread. He didn't have time for much of anything and noticed several occasions where Rocky's water bowl was completely dry. He subsisted on coffee, the large tin of chocolate chip cookies compliments of Sara, and whatever his mom or Clara cooked. His one salvation came during Rocky's walks, and even those were cut short to about ten minutes. Greg would have to drag Rocky back into the apartment with the dog staring at him, wondering why he wasn't getting his usual twenty-minute walks three times a day and especially wondering why he didn't get to run through the park anymore. Greg petted Rocky on the head and told him that once the boys were on a schedule, if they were ever on a schedule, he could take him on his usual long walks again. Rocky gazed up at him and tilted his head to the side and then jumped up on the couch, circled twice, and lay down to sleep. Greg stared at the dog, wishing Rocky could somehow help out around the house. He quickly shook his head, and when he heard Heather yell for him to grab a new package of diapers, Greg sighed, grabbed a pack from the closet, and brought it up to the nursery.

"Here you go." Greg opened the package and handed Heather a clean diaper. Heather undid each sticky seal on Cole's diaper and was immediately squirted.

"Shit! Damn it! I knew that was going to happen!" Heather reached for a baby wipe and dabbed at her shirt. Greg tried to hide his smile and went over to pick up Hunter. She shook her head and managed to get a new diaper on Cole before dressing him in a clean pair of pajamas. She took off her sweatshirt, revealing a nursing tank top.

"Heth, have you seen my Sixers sweatshirt?"

Heather turned around with Cole in her arms. "Yeah, I washed—oh shit!" Heather set Cole back in his crib and put her hands to her forehead.

"What?"

"It's still in the machine. Along with the full load of darks I washed three days ago."

"Oh. It's okay. I'll go run it through another load." Greg gently put Hunter down in his crib.

"It's probably all mildew now and, well, whatever."

"It'll be fine."

Heather looked down at the ground. "Greg?"

"Yeah?"

"Did you think it would be this hard?"

Greg shook his head. "No idea."

Heather swept her hand across her forehead and rubbed her temples. "Are we ... do you think we're going to be okay? You know, raising two boys? Twins? I just don't know—"

Greg put his hands on her shoulders and looked straight into Heather's eyes. "Yes. I do. I really do." Greg wrapped his arms around Heather because right now, a hug was top priority. It didn't matter about the laundry or the dishes or the dust bunnies under the coffee table. As she nestled in the groove of his neck, Heather realized this conversation, however brief, was the first one that did not have the word *diaper*, *feeding*, or *sleep* in it. "We're going to be fine," he breathed into her hair. Greg stroked her back up and down and felt a few of her tears fall on his shirt. Heather sniffled and wrapped her arms around him tighter, holding onto the comforting and secure feel of him. She felt cared for, protected, and reassured that everything would be okay. Greg would not let her down, and she loved him more for it.

Greg didn't want to admit to Heather that he was looking forward to going back to work. Three weeks cooped up in the apartment with newborn twins was more work than being at his office eighteen hours a day. Make that twenty. But his three weeks of paternity leave was up and it was time to return to his job. On his first day back, he kissed the twins before he left and then kissed Heather, telling her to call him if she needed anything. He gave her a long hug as he noticed sadness in her face that he wouldn't be there to help with the babies. Greg walked to work and as soon as he entered the office, his coworkers surrounded him, asking to see pictures. Greg smiled, pulled out his phone and after everyone oohed and aahed at the pictures of the babies, he retreated to his office with a large coffee in hand and closed the door. He sat in his chair and ran his hands across his smooth, clean desk. It was good to be back, he thought. Back to starting his day with a hot shower, dressing in clean work clothes, and walking to his office among a sea of grown-ups on the streets. His office was a refuge, a room with four walls where he could get peace and quiet to his heart's content. He never thought he'd say that about work, but after the last three weeks, it was true. He yawned viciously as he caught up on his twenty-seven voice mail messages and was half finished going through a few hundred e-mails when he looked up and noticed it was one o'clock. He wasn't hungry, since he was loaded up on caffeine, but knew he'd have to head out and grab some lunch. He called Heather to check in, and once he knew everything was as good as could be expected on the home front, he walked over to the window.

It was a gray, cloudy, blustery day, and he could see people below all bundled up in heavy winter gear walking to and from lunch, running errands or heading to appointments. Greg stared glassy eyed and allowed his thoughts to turn to Kate. He wondered if she was in her office or out and about at a client meeting or restaurant. He shook his head, realizing he still hadn't told her about the birth of the twins despite the fact she had to have seen it on Facebook. He knew in his heart he was procrastinating about talking to her about it because how do you tell the woman you love you are officially a dad. A dad who has children with another woman. He couldn't blame her if she never wanted to talk to him again. Kate was an innocent victim, and Greg had never wanted to hurt her. But that is precisely what he did.

After returning from a quick walk to grab a sandwich, he sat back down at his desk and opened his e-mail to find a screen full of new messages, but the one that stuck out was from Kate Shuster. His heart stopped for a second at the same time his finger clicked the mouse to reveal a short paragraph. He read it quickly, and upon hitting reply, he closed his eyes and began to type.

* * *

Kate had a lump in her throat when Greg's e-mail came back. She had been slowly torturing herself for weeks, looking at his Facebook post over and over: the pictures of his babies … sweet, innocent baby boys who deserved a full-time father. The moment she saw that post, her heart dropped to her stomach, but she could not stop herself from looking at it over and over again. She promised herself she wouldn't contact him. She knew he would be incredibly busy and honestly didn't know if he would want to hear from her. But on this cold, blustery February day, her heart ached for some form of contact with him. For weeks, she had curled up in bed at night, telling herself over and over that she needed to give him time and space. Her heart hurt as she listened to sad love songs on Pandora. She tried to convince herself that nothing was ever going to happen with him. It was over. Over before they even really began. On nights like that, she would sleep with a box of tissues beside her and the polar bear in her arms. She clicked open the e-mail, her heart beating in her ears. She read his words and slumped in her chair like a fallen soufflé. He was busy with the babies. He needed to stay with Heather. She was very dear to him, and he treasured their friendship. He hoped she was doing well. There it was in black and white, and she knew she would never be able to compete with the mother of his twin sons. Kate replied with a simple congratulation and that she understood. Then she deleted his reply, as if trying to erase it from her mind. In that instant, she picked up the phone.

"Fifth floor. Nurse Delvina. How can I help you?"

"Jen, it's me. Okay, I'll go."

"Really?" Jen turned around at the nurse's station, the phone to her ear.

"Yeah, now go set it up before I change my mind."

"Okay. I saw him this morning. How's Saturday night?"

Kate smiled crookedly and forced the word out. "Perfect."

"Ooh and I ran into another lab tech who just so happens to be suddenly single just in case it doesn't work out with Ben. He's a hottie too. Should I set you up with him?" Jen was smiling mischievously into the phone.

"Don't press your luck. But thanks for trying. I'll give you an A for effort."

"Hey, what are friends for if not trying to make their best friend happy?"

Kate usually had a nice time on her blind dates, (although some were as enjoyable as watching paint dry or as awful as the bearded guy); however, they never went beyond the first date. Was she picky? Maybe. Was she comparing each date to Greg? Probably. Was she still in love with another man? Definitely.

Thanks to Jen, Kate dated on and off like this for about a year and a half. Kate never realized there were so many different career options at the hospital, and she seemed to have gone out with everyone from a doctor to an orderly to guys who worked in the back office. But it started getting old when each date was more of the same. Dinner or drinks or coffee or a movie. While she sat across from her date in a restaurant or coffee house, politely nodding along, she pretended to listen and actually be interested in their stories of college or childhood or work or travel. Her mind was always elsewhere, and with that, she sometimes accidentally called her date by the wrong name. Once, she and radiologist Sebastian were walking downtown and just passed Bottoms Up. He asked her to name her favorite vacation spot; she smiled wistfully and replied, "You already know that, Greg." She caught her mistake when she heard his name in her own ears and apologized, making an excuse that Greg was a coworker she had been working with on a new project. He nodded as if he understood, but a few minutes later he excused himself to make a quick call and then suddenly got paged to go into work. She ended up walking home alone, went upstairs to her apartment, put on sappy love songs, and curled up on her couch clutching her polar bear. She grabbed a pad of paper and a pen and wrote a to-do list while listening to "Jar of Hearts" by Christina Perri.

1. *Stop going on blind dates.*
2. *Focus on your career.*
3. *Get over Greg.*

She knew she would have no trouble conquering the first two. Simply tell Jen she was finished with dating and not to set her up with anyone else. She would then go into work early each day and stay late each night and not let her thoughts wander to anything other than work. Number three, though, was going to take some hard work. She held the polar bear tighter and then suddenly released it, got up, and put the stuffed animal in back of several shoeboxes at the top of her closet. She wiped her hands and turned off the music. She hadn't felt that good, since … she felt the thought coming to the forefront of her memory. She thought it was long buried, but it came creeping back like a ghost that haunts you from the grave. She hadn't felt that good since their first date at Bottoms Up. And as she looked down at her ring, she realized that just the thought of that night turned her ring to fuchsia pink in a matter of seconds. Her eyes glazed over the ring before she took it off and put it at the top of her closet next to the bear. *Push everything away, and maybe I will forget*, she thought, hoping it could really be that easy.

CHAPTER 16

The twins turned two-and-a-half years old, and Greg and Heather had settled into a comfortable routine. After feeling the financial pinch of raising twins, Heather went back to work three days a week to her same position at the hotel. On her work days, Greg took the twins to day care in the morning, and Heather picked them up on her way home. Heather would get them settled, feed them dinner, and play with them—usually with building toys, puzzles, cars, trucks, and trains. Greg usually got home by six thirty, and both parents would give them a bath and get them ready for bed. Greg would curl up with the boys and read bedtime stories, and once they were tucked in, Greg and Heather would have dinner together, talk about their day, pay bills, discuss what needed to be done, make weekend plans, and usually fall asleep in bed watching TV, reading a book, or going online. On Heather's days off, she would take the boys to the park, zoo, museums or library, or let them play at home while she caught up on laundry, cooking, and cleaning. On weekends, they would do activities as a family as much as possible. Greg would also watch them while Heather went grocery shopping, ran errands, or worked onsite at an event. Their new typical Friday and Saturday nights consisted of ordering takeout and watching a movie on Netflix.

As challenging as it was, Heather relished her role as a mom. She loved being called Mommy and looking into her children's eyes to find innocence and love. She treasured watching the boys take their first steps and say their first words. She loved seeing their faces light up with wonder when they saw the different animals at the zoo or the diverse colorful fish at the aquarium. She remembered the gleam in their eyes when they saw Santa and the twinkling Christmas lights in the city. She watched them grow from tiny newborns to strong, healthy, and active toddlers with more energy than an entire football team. And although the terrible twos were a little rough at the start, she and Greg had survived thus far, ready to tackle age three.

Greg had changed quite a bit since moving in with Heather. His life no longer revolved around sports; he simply didn't have the time and had to settle for catching the highlights on ESPN or getting the scores on his phone. And although he still loved Rocky dearly and always would, the dog was no longer number one in his life. He didn't have all day Saturday to spend with him at the park or take him to the dog run for leisurely workouts. He had people depending on him now, and he would be damned if he ever let his children down. He would walk through fire to protect them and would give his life in a heartbeat. Right from their birth, his boys became the most important people in his life.

Greg's work improved after the twins finally got on a regular schedule at six months old and then when they started sleeping through the night right after their first birthday. He worked harder and smarter, forgoing long lunches, office chatter, and coffee breaks. His colleagues noticed a difference in him, a new determination that was not there before. Greg wanted to focus on his family when he was at home and keep his work solely at the office. The highlight of his workday was coming home at night to Hunter and Cole squealing, "Daddy, Daddy!" and running to him, climbing on his leg with outstretched arms to be picked up. Greg would pick them up together and envelop them with hugs and kisses. He already made them little Phillies fans and bought them tiny logo shirts and hats. Greg took them to their first Phillies game when they were eighteen months old, and although they seemed to enjoy the noise and crowd, they cried and screamed upon seeing the Phillie Phanatic up close. But now that the boys were older, they giggled as they watched the popular mascot acting silly and running around the field. When Greg took a photo of the boys with the Phanatic last month, they hugged him and didn't want to leave his arms.

On weekends, sometimes with Heather and sometimes without, Greg would take the boys to Penn's Landing, Franklin Square, Please Touch Museum and various other city attractions. He already had plans when they were a little older to teach them to ride a bike, take them camping, and teach them how to swim. Greg's parents were doting grandparents to their first two grandsons, and his brothers defined the word *uncle*. They were lucky little boys. Greg and Heather took them to the Fourth of July parades, organized their own little Easter egg hunts in the park, and held them up high so they could hang ornaments on the tree while singing Christmas carols. They spent Thanksgivings at his parents, Christmas Eve with Aunt Clara, and reserved Christmas Day at their apartment, which started their own holiday tradition as a family. After pancakes for breakfast, Heather and Greg sipped hot cocoa and relished watching the boys play with their new toys and games.

Kate held steadfast to her plan to focus on work. She landed a new job at the Brooke Allison Agency and was eyeing even better opportunities that seemed to be lurking around every corner. Although she didn't love the type of clients in this new job, which were mainly financial institutions, insurance agencies, and credit card companies, she was grateful to gain the experience and knowledge. She dreamed of one day moving to New York or Los Angeles and getting into one of the big PR firms that were always in the media. She pictured herself on television, speaking out on her client's behalf on the morning news shows or writing an article or online post that would go viral. Sometimes she would dream even larger. She would walk to work, a bounce in her step, and envision what it would be like to one day open her own PR firm. She would make all the decisions: the type of clients to target, the media and PR campaigns to manage, the employees to hire. She even considered opening the agency right in Old City and eventually purchasing a house nearby.

Kate was content with her social life, which consisted mainly of hanging out with Jen and some coworkers. In her free time, she worked out at the gym, walked the city, and read as many books as she could get her hands on. Books served as an escape, both from life and reality. It was a way to live vicariously through a fictional character, a way to forget her pathetic love life. Because when it came down to it, she was still in love with Greg. The more she thought about it, the more pathetic it seemed. He lived with Heather and his children; Kate had no place in his life anymore. Why couldn't she accept the plain and simple fact that it was never going to work?

She wondered why she couldn't get over Greg and move on. How hard could it be? Obviously harder than she thought because whatever she did or didn't do, nothing seemed to work. She knew why. Deep in her heart she knew the reason she could not get over him. Maybe she never would. But she kept trying regardless. She would pinch herself whenever she thought about him, hoping that would help her stop. In actuality, it only made her arms blotchy. She stopped listening to sappy love songs. She stopped looking at the photo of him and Rocky atop the art museum steps. She stopped looking at his Facebook page.

She considered seeing a counselor, but couldn't bear the thought of talking about Greg with a stranger. She knew there wasn't a counselor in the world that could help her get over Greg. One night the realization came crashing down. She was reading *The Notebook* for the hundredth time and grasped that if Allie had gone back to Lon, Noah would have never gotten over her. Because Noah knew that Allie was *the one* for him. It just wasn't possible to get over *the one* you were supposed to marry, the person you were meant to share your life with, your soul mate. Kate would just have to learn to live with it and maybe, just maybe in time, she could learn to love someone else, even though she couldn't fathom truly falling in love again, not even close to how it was with Greg.

CHAPTER 17

Kate settled into her third new job as PR associate at the Morgan Kline Agency. The timing was perfect. At age twenty-eight, she was deathly bored of working for the financial industry and just finished revamping her resume. Then magically, her college internship boss called to steal her away for the position. She interviewed once and was hired the following week with a substantial increase in salary. She went out with Jen to celebrate, updated her wardrobe, started wearing her mood ring again, and told anyone who would listen about this new exciting position in a well-established yet young firm located in the Northern Liberties section of Philadelphia.

One of her first assignments was to work onsite at the national Web and App Design Conference and Expo for which her firm was heading up all public relations. There were seven others from the firm going, and once she heard the event was in Chicago, she volunteered to take the last spot. She had never been there and had heard so many wonderful things about the city. Even though she was assured the days would be long, she was determined to work in some free time, even if it meant she had to skimp on sleep. Michigan Avenue, Millennium Park, Navy Pier, Rush Street, Lincoln Park, shopping—yes, she could get by on less sleep in order to see as much as possible.

Working onsite for fourteen hour days in power suits and heels too high to comfortably walk in, Kate was on top of her game. By day two, she knew this was her niche: managing public relations, providing media assistance, and coordinating interviews at large conferences and tradeshows. Kate's colleagues were already singing her praises and admiring the talent of the new girl. She raced around accommodating reporters and writers, editors and photographers, making sure everyone had all the information they needed. She had a continuous smile on her face. The business at hand was an adrenaline rush for her, and she didn't want to stop.

"You're making the rest of us look like slackers," her colleague Tammy joked. She was taking a break with feet up on the table, latte in hand, and phone plugged into the charging station kiosk. Kate simply shrugged and walked away to add some more media kits and press photos to the table.

The next three days were more of the same. Up at five in the morning, showered, dressed, and at McCormick Place by six thirty. Opening the press room by seven with media personnel already lined up outside the door, Kate made it her responsibility to straighten up the room and replenish press kits and media photographs as well as make sure the coffee, tea, and pastries were delivered and set up. The days were busy, with Kate mainly working the press room but also going back and forth to the expo and talking with exhibitors, attendees, and customers. She was gathering important information and feedback to help improve next year's conference and make it the best it could be. She would finally make it back to her hotel by nine or ten at night after a business dinner meeting or group dinner with colleagues. Collapsing into bed, it would be just hours before she started all over again.

"So, c'mon, Kate. We're all going to dinner since tomorrow is the last day of the conference, and you can't not go." Her coworker, Ashley, had just walked back into the press room after a brief client meeting.

Kate frowned. "I'm just really tired, Ash. I'm so disappointed I didn't get to see as much as I wanted to, but I could fall asleep on the floor right now. I was looking forward to just going back and taking a bubble bath." Kate sat down, took off her shoes, and began to massage her right foot.

"Did I mention we're going to House of Blues?" Ashley raised her eyebrows and ran her fingers through her silky red straight hair. Her navy-blue suit looked as if it was specially tailored for her body. Ashley collected paperwork, sat at a desk, and opened her laptop to start writing a report.

"I don't care if you are going out with Oprah. I am beat. I'll be surprised if I make it through to the end of the day."

"All right, but there's a really good band playing tonight. It would be a shame to miss it and just have to hear the wild stories tomorrow."

Kate gave a half smile and tilted her head.

"Just saying. But promise me you'll think about it and text me later if you change your mind." Ashley stood to get some other files from the tradeshow office and put her hands on her hips.

"Okay, but it's not likely." Kate switched feet and began to massage her left. She could feel the blisters as well as the knotted-up muscles in her neck. She made a mental note to book a massage and pedicure when she got home. After Ashley left, there was no one in the press room, so she took a moment to stretch her neck, now wanting that bubble bath more than ever. A quick glance at her watch confirmed she would be at her hotel in three more hours. She put her head down for just a minute and rubbed her temples. *Just breathe and relax,* she told herself. Fifteen minutes later, with renewed vigor and cup of coffee working its way through her body, she got up to head back to the exhibit hall. The conference corridor was crowded with attendees rushing to and from sessions as well as the expo, and she dodged people as she walked.

"Kate?"

She stopped in her tracks, looking to see where that familiar voice was coming from. It was noisy and she couldn't decipher if it was a reporter, writer, or someone who had a question on a press kit or needed more information. People rushed all around her as she looked to the right and then to the left and then spun around. Her mouth formed a perfect O and she felt her makeup evaporate into thin air as her face turned white. The two of them stood in the middle of the traffic as if they were the only people in McCormick Place.

"Oh my God! What are you doing here?"

"I should be asking you the same question." Greg shuffled his laptop bag to his other shoulder and smoothed his shirt.

Kate stood silent for a moment, not believing who she was seeing. Greg? Here in Chicago at the same conference? It just couldn't be. She did not notice the throngs of people walking by, the noise, or the cell phone conversations. She met his eyes, still not believing he was standing there, but then he smiled and that chin dimple came out, and her knees nearly buckled.

"I switched jobs." She took a breath and tried to stand straight. "And my new firm handled the PR for this conference so ..."

"Oh. Well, congratulations on your new job."

"Thanks." Kate looked away and then back at Greg. He hadn't changed a bit, and she had to put her hand on her stomach to quiet the flutter of butterflies. "And you?"

"Oh, right. I'm here for work too. I got into web design over the last year, and my boss wanted me to attend."

"That's great. I remember you wanted to design websites. Congratulations on going after it."

Greg smiled. "Thank you."

There was a natural pause as they gazed at each other. Greg had never seen Kate in a suit before and was taken aback by her classic professional style with heels that made her look at least four inches taller. Kate tried hard not to stare. But Greg was smiling and just the sight of him made her stomach quiver. After everything that happened, how could he still do that to her?

Greg broke the silence when he heard an announcement on the intercom. "So did you get to do anything fun since you've been here?"

"I shopped a little on Michigan Ave, and we went to dinner on Navy Pier even though it was freezing out. I want to come back sometime when it's warm and I don't have to work. What about you?"

"I haven't been able to do too much, except we went to dinner on Rush Street twice."

We? We? Are Heather and the twins with him? "Um, are you … here with …" Kate trailed off and glanced down, spotting a deep egg yolk color on her mood ring.

Greg cleared his throat. "No. A couple of guys from the office came too. But other than that, I'm here by myself."

Kate released the breath she was holding. "Me too. I mean except for my seven colleagues. Are you going home tomorrow night?"

"My flight's at six. You?"

"I have to stay till the day after. We still have a lot of work after the conference."

Greg nodded and looked across the corridor. There were only a few stragglers left walking around, as the second to last session of the day was just getting underway. He shuffled his laptop bag again to the other shoulder. "Are you doing anything tonight?"

"No." She tucked her hair behind her ear. "I mean, I don't think so. My coworkers are going to the House of Blues, but I wasn't planning on it."

"Oh."

"Are you doing anything?"

"No."

Kate looked into his eyes, eyes she used to know so well. Was she dreaming or imagining what she was seeing? That spark was still there, an attraction like electricity, undeniable chemistry. *Magic.*

"Well, maybe since neither of us has plans, we could hang out? As friends. It'd be fun to spend some time together and catch up."

Kate got a pit in her stomach, telling her this was not a good idea. It could be dangerous, the way she still felt for him. But she was an adult, and adults can put their feelings aside for the greater good. She wouldn't do anything to cause either one to be uncomfortable. When would she get this chance again? She wouldn't. With that thought, a smile graced Kate's face. "I'd like that."

They decided to meet at seven o'clock in the lobby of Kate's hotel, the Sheraton Grand Chicago, and grab drinks and some dinner. As Kate showered and dressed, the butterflies came back with a vengeance. She had to steady herself as the water ran over her body, washing away the scent of stale convention center air. She pictured Greg showering at the exact same time and wondered if he was as nervous and excited as she was. She didn't know it at the time, but Greg was wishing away butterflies of his own.

Kate came down to the lobby five minutes early to find Greg standing off to the side, gazing at nothing in particular. She stopped for a moment to look at him and realized how deeply she had missed him. Her heart felt lonely without him in her life, and some nights she dreamt that they were together, doing everything from vacationing in the Greek Islands to everyday things like grocery shopping. In her dreams, they are incredibly happy together; they snuggle and watch movies, they go out to bars and see new bands, they kiss for hours, they take Rocky on long walks, they watch sports, they go away on occasional weekends to a bed and breakfast, they make dinner together after work …

"Kate. Hi. Are you okay?" Greg spotted her and walked over. "You look like you're a million miles away."

"Hi. No, I'm fine. I was just thinking about something." Kate smiled. She put her hand to her cheek and could feel the heat from blushing. She tried to will it away.

"I found a bunch of restaurants within a few blocks. We can walk or take a cab."

"Let's walk. I'm up for anything."

* * *

Their tiny table for two had a clear view of the most pristine snowflakes falling on Michigan Avenue. The lampposts reflected the glistening coating of new snow, making it appear to be a winter wonderland. There were people walking up and down this truly Magnificent Mile, wrapped up in pretty colorful scarves and hats. It seemed so quiet and peaceful outside that a feeling of calm overcame Kate and she got lost in a dreamy moment.

"This is gorgeous, Greg."

"It doesn't seem this peaceful at home when it's snowing."

Kate tucked her hair behind her ear. "So how are your boys? They must be getting so big."

Greg smiled. "They're good. Thanks. They actually just turned three." Greg reached into his pocket, pulled out his cell phone and showed her some pictures.

Kate stared at the picture of the two boys on Santa's lap and remembered the night Greg told her about them. She was shocked then and realized it was still hard for her to believe he had twin sons. "Oh, they're precious. Look how cute they are." Greg detected sadness in her tone even though she was smiling.

"Thanks. They're a handful, but what do you expect. My little men." Greg laughed as he put his phone back.

"And how is Rocky?"

Greg cleared his throat. "He's good. I can't believe he's almost ten though." Greg shook his head.

"Well he still has some years left. He's such a good dog."

"That he is. He's just slower these days, not as active as you remember him." Greg noticed the waitress out of the corner of his eye with tablet in hand. He opened the menu and began to scan the entrees. "We need another minute." Greg nodded and smiled at the waitress, who walked away after a slight sigh.

They talked for ten more minutes about their jobs, the books Kate was reading, and Philly sports Greg was following until the waitress came back and they had to place their order.

After a relaxing dinner of filet mignon for Greg, sea bass for Kate, and red wine for both, they walked down Michigan Avenue as the snow fell lightly all around them. It was so quiet and peaceful that Kate could hardly believe they were in the middle of the city. They shared easy conversation and walked close, the sleeves of their coats grazing each other's. They felt the same nervous anticipation as when Greg walked her home after their first date at Bottoms Up.

They made their way back to Kate's hotel, and she tried to gauge what Greg was thinking when they entered the lobby. Was this good night or just the beginning of their night? She shook off the winter chill and removed her coat, catching Greg's eyes locked on her face. She felt the pit in her stomach come back, hard and knotted. It was her love for him: undeniable, raw, pure. She put her hand on the back of a sofa to steady herself, her legs weak.

"So."

"So."

"Do you want to stay for a little bit and talk some more?" Kate looked across the lobby and spotted a loveseat in the corner, away from the main commotion of people coming and going.

Greg's eyes followed hers and he smiled, his chin dimple making Kate melt all over again. He put his hand on the small of her back and led her over to the sofa, where they both sat down, close enough that their legs were touching. Kate crossed her legs and then uncrossed them. They each detected a noticeable tension but didn't mention it. They started talking some more about what they had been doing over the past couple of years. Their hands touched accidentally when Kate shifted on the sofa, and when they looked into each other's eyes, Kate had to gasp for a breath. She looked down at her lap and crossed her legs again, unsure of what to do. When she looked at Greg, she could see he was thinking the same thing: *Do you want to come up?* Neither could come out and say the words but it was understood between them, as if they were reading each other's secret thoughts. Greg looked her in the eye, and Kate simply smiled. They stood up simultaneously, and Greg reached out for her hand. He led her to the elevator, holding her hand until they got inside. He put his arm around her after she pushed the button, and she nuzzled up to his chest. They went right up to Kate's floor, and walked down the hall until they were standing outside of room 2404.

Kate turned to face him, and Greg enveloped her in a tight but soft hug. They pulled back slightly and looked in each other's eyes. Ever so gently, they let their lips come together, softly at first and then with a wanting and urgency that neither expected.

They kissed, greedily and hungrily, for several minutes before coming apart and taking in much needed air.

"Your kisses are like nothing else I know." Kate tried to regulate her breath. "I can't even put the feeling into words because I've never been kissed the way you kiss me. I've never felt this before, except with you." She felt magic when Greg kissed her. The earth stopped moving, time stood still, and fireworks lit up the sky in a rainbow of colors and loud clashes.

Her words sounded sweet to Greg, and he took Kate in his arms, holding her tight for a long time. They breathed in the other's scent: Greg's earthy masculine cologne and Kate's sensuous perfume coupled with a hint of coconut from her shampoo. They were standing in the same spot, just outside Kate's hotel room, very much aware of where this could lead. Kate pulled back and looked deep into Greg's eyes. *I love you,* Kate said silently but couldn't bring herself to say aloud. There was too much at stake, and she understood the circumstances even though she couldn't fully accept them, even after three years. She knew though at that moment, there was nothing she wanted more than to be one with Greg, to feel all of him and be with him in the most intimate way a woman can be with a man whom she loves unconditionally. It was a love she felt deep in her soul.

Greg was thinking the same thing. He loved Kate as much as she loved him, and fervently wished for the circumstances to be different. But he did not regret his boys and would never give them up. Although Heather was an excellent mother, he knew he was living a lie. He was in love with someone else. Kate. His Kate. No matter what happened in the future, she would always be His Kate.

Greg's hand lightly caressed the side of Kate's face, and she allowed herself a small smile. She placed one hand on his shoulder and leisurely moved her hand down his arm, feeling the strong muscles under his shirt. He brushed his hand down her cheek with a feather touch, and she leaned into him until their arms were wrapped around each other. He brought his lips to hers and began to kiss her again, softly and innocently at first, but soon they became passionate kisses; their lips and tongues moved in rhythm with one another. Kate let her hands gently coast up and down his back. Greg held her in his arms, mesmerized by her kisses, hungry for more.

"Do you want to come in?" Kate whispered in between kisses while trying to catch her breath. She was sure Greg could feel her heart thumping as their bodies pressed against each other.

"Are you sure?" Greg gently pulled back. They stared at each other for what felt like an eternity until Kate nodded her head.

Kate fumbled with the key card twice as red lights blinked back at her before a little green light appeared and the door clicked open. They walked into the darkness and put their coats down on the luggage rack while Kate's purse slipped to the floor. Small shards of city lights seeped through the drapes as snow continued to fall, soft and peaceful. Kate walked over and turned on the radio to the only station that came in clearly. "Look at that, Chicago in Chicago. See, silly, I told you there was a time and place for slow, sappy love songs."

Greg walked over and took her in his arms. They hugged, enveloping each other until they slowly started dancing. It wasn't dancing as much as it was slowly swaying back and forth to the music, holding each other and breathing in the moment.

"Mmm, what's the name of it?"

Kate hesitated and held him tighter. "Will You Still Love Me?"

Greg stopped moving, leaned back slightly, and met her eyes. For several seconds neither one moved, their eyes focused on each other, unspoken words between them wanting to be released.

"It's just the name of the song. I wasn't asking or ..." Kate lowered her head and rested it on his chest.

Greg ran his fingers through her hair and then placed two fingers on her chin so softly she barely felt it. He raised her head gently to meet his eyes. "You know you can ask me anything. You do know that, right?"

Kate's heart pounded so loud she could barely hear the music. Her insides trembled, and when her lips parted, no words came out. Greg's eyes held tight on hers, and she knew what she wanted to say but the words stuck hopelessly in her throat. Why couldn't she ask him? She wanted to kick herself silly. Instead she put her head back on his chest and squeezed him a little tighter. They swayed together ever so softly until the song ended.

Kate felt a tingling throughout her body after they came apart. She mustered up a little courage, leaned up, and whispered in his ear, "How is it possible that I miss you and we've never been together?"

Greg felt his blood racing through his veins. "I don't know, but I feel the same way." he murmured back.

Greg let his hands wander down to her hips while Kate explored his chest and back. Kate kissed him on the shoulder and looked up. He brought his head down to her level, their lips met, and they kissed passionately without reserve. Greg caressed her shoulders, and Kate clasped her hands onto the sides of his face. Greg then surprised her but he held her so tight that she wrapped her legs around him.

"You're strong."

"You're light."

Kate smiled. "Flattery will get you everywhere, Mr. Janera."

Greg repositioned her, scooping her into his arms, cradling her as if he was going to carry her across the threshold. He walked her over to the bed and carefully placed her down.

"Are you sure? I ..."

Greg caressed her cheek with the back of his hand. "I've never been so sure about anything in my life."

"I just need to know that ... that this will be okay," Kate whispered. For a second Kate let herself think of Heather, but deep down she wanted to believe that Greg was only with her because of his kids. The last thing she wanted to do was split up a family, especially since his boys needed and deserved a good father who was there for them each and every day. She knew in her heart Greg was an excellent father and didn't want to negatively affect his children.

Greg put his fingers lightly to her mouth. "Shhh." Greg looked away and then back at Kate. "It'll be okay because I ..."

Greg sat down beside her on the bed. He pushed thoughts of guilt out of his mind and concentrated on the here and now. He loved Kate, in the most pure sense. He slowly kissed her, and before they knew it, they were laying next to each other on the king-sized bed, kissing passionately. Small shadows of light from the city reflected on the walls, and tiny snowflakes brightened up the cold, dark sky. As they kissed, they let their hands explore each other, gently. She smiled at him, and Greg got a quiver up his spine at the sight of her dimples. Kate reached up and started unbuttoning his shirt until she was able to peel it off. She let her hands roam down his bare chest, thinking it felt just the way she'd imagined it. Greg rolled Kate's sweater up and over her head, exposing a baby pink bra. They began kissing again as Greg reached around and gently unhooked her bra, allowing it to fall off naturally. He eased himself down on the bed so they lay on their sides, chest to chest. Kate took a shallow breath, unbuttoned his jeans, and gently slid the zipper down. Greg inhaled sharply and pushed his jeans and socks off, letting them fall to the floor. Kate's hands roamed his body as if trying to memorize every square inch, every freckle, every muscle. She sensed he was holding back, so she unbuttoned her jeans and gently slipped them off. Greg raised his eyebrows when he let his hands roam down her back to her legs, and Kate simply shrugged. Greg laughed and kissed her on the lips, then the neck, and then the lips again. Kate slid off his briefs, grazing his thigh. Greg cleared his throat, and as he looked her in the eye, he used one hand to carefully take off her matching baby pink thong. He looked deep into her eyes as if he were looking into her soul, and she returned his gaze and kissed him without any hesitation. He slowly rolled so he was covering her body, and when she wrapped her legs around him, he let his deep love and passion for her take over. They became one, right there on the twenty-fourth floor of the Sheraton Grand Chicago.

"I don't think I'll ever get enough of you, Greg. If we did this every day, it still wouldn't be enough."

Greg rolled over to his side. "Mmm, what am I going to do with you?" Greg winked and ran his hands through her auburn curls.

Kate laughed. "I don't know, but I'm sure you'll think of something."

Greg spooned her, and Kate held his hands. He quivered a couple of times and she brought his hands up to kiss them. They snuggled comfortably; legs intertwined, and lightly kissed every couple of minutes.

She rolled back so her body was facing him. "If you and I were together, I would get a tattoo with your name right here." Kate rolled down the sheet and placed her fingertips two inches below her belly button. "In blue, your favorite color." *That's how much I love you,* she wanted to tell him. She had to nearly bite her tongue so the words wouldn't come out.

Greg gulped. "Now you're just being cruel. You do realize you're driving me completely crazy, don't you?" Greg's smile lit up the room.

"I am?" Her voice was sweet yet seductive, and Greg could not resist this woman if his life depended on it.

Greg placed his arm around her naked waist and began kissing her zealously as he gently caressed her breasts. Their lips made passionate harmony, and before they knew it, they were one again, taking each other in and feeling the deep strength of love. A love that was electric.

"I could stay like this forever, in your arms." Kate rested her head on Greg's chest listening to the steady rhythm of his heartbeat. She was putty in his hands.

Greg didn't say anything, but he squeezed her tighter and never wanted to let go. She was *the one* for him. *The love of his life.* He knew that with certainty, deep in his soul that he yearned to let out but knew he never could.

She kissed his chest and placed one hand on his stomach, wanting to remember every single detail of this night as long as she lived. She memorized a few freckles on the right side of his chest and a small scar on his left shoulder. Kate would never forget the curve of his biceps and triceps muscles and the strength in his back. She closed her eyes and memorized the ruggedness of his skin next to hers and took in a deep breath of his earthy scent. When she opened her eyes, he was gazing at her. She had never felt so sexy in her life.

"Ooh, I have an idea," Kate said.

Greg smiled and raised his eyebrows.

"You'll like it. I promise." Kate winked at him as she jumped out of bed. Greg watched her walk, graceful and confident, toward the bathroom.

Ten minutes later, they were lounging in the tub surrounded by fluffy white bubbles scented with vanilla and lavender. Kate had her back to his chest, and his arms covered her body. The hot water swirled back and forth around them, creating steam and vanilla-lavender bliss.

"I can't believe this."

"So you like?"

"I wouldn't mind doing this every day." *With you.*

You can, Kate thought to herself. *We can be together. We can make it work. We would figure it out. Maybe it wouldn't always be easy, but I love you.* The words were caught in her throat, and she had to swallow twice to make them go down. Would she ever be able to tell him? Come out and say how she really felt? Would it make a difference if he knew?

Instead, she would live in the moment. She turned her head and kissed him. The water swirled, caressing their bodies, and it felt like being on a cloud in heaven. She was with the man she loved, someone she'd waited to be with for over three years, and she knew that whatever happened in the future, no one could ever take this night away from her. She would cherish and hold it close to her for the rest of her life.

"Kate, you are absolutely irresistible."

"Well, at least I perfected something."

They both laughed and kissed again as the water gently swayed back and forth throughout the tub. Some of the bubbles overflowed onto the bath mat, but they didn't care; they were living in the here and now. It was warm and wet, and Kate felt incredibly sexy being naked next to the man she loved. They relaxed in the sudsy water while Greg started to give her a massage, and Kate let her hands rest on his thighs.

"So I guess this week was stressful for you? Your neck feels tight." He leaned in and gave her a soft kiss.

"If I was, I'm not anymore, not here with you."

He kept massaging her neck and shoulders, and when he was able to work out the knots, he wrapped his arms around her, and she interlaced her fingers in his. Greg kissed the top of her head intermittently, and when he did, Kate squeezed his hands just a little bit tighter.

"You are beautiful." Greg breathed into her hair and slowly exhaled.

"You can stop with the flattery, really. And besides …" Kate laughed.

"No, Kate, that wasn't flattery. You are beautiful." He leaned in and kissed her. Their skin felt slick, soapy, and slippery on each other.

Kate quivered and felt tingling down to her toes. She let her thumb trace circles on his hand.

When the water cooled, they let the tub drain. They stood and rinsed off under a steady stream of hot water while kissing, letting their hands roam wherever they wanted. "You are so sexy," Greg whispered while nibbling on her ear, "I just," he mumbled, trying to catch his breath, "have to have you." He turned off the water and wrapped her in a fluffy white towel and then wrapped a towel around his waist. Kate squeezed some excess water from her hair before he picked her up and carried her to the bed, where they made love again, passionately, with a hunger for one another. Their bodies created passionate energy from their deep mutual connection. The deep yearning left them to wonder why it had taken them so long to be intimate. Greg felt a surge of raw adrenaline coursing through his body that he'd never experienced before. Kate was captivated by Greg and the love she felt for him. Once they came apart, they regulated their breathing and simply got lost in each other's eyes. After several minutes, Greg adjusted the sheets so they could get under them and snuggle in together. They lay there in comfortable silence, holding hands until exhaustion overcame them and they drifted off to sleep. When they awoke about four hours later with the February sunlight peeking through the curtains, they were in the same exact position. They kissed. It was a feeling that was so perfectly natural and comfortable that it felt as if they did it every day.

"Good morning, sleepyhead."

"Mmm, good morning, Greg."

They kissed again and rubbed the sleep from their eyes.

They each felt what the other was thinking but didn't say a word. They loved each other to the core, but neither could say the words aloud. There was too much at stake, too much to risk, too much to lose. They just lay in the comfort and peace of each other's arms for the next hour until they were forced to get up and go back to reality.

CHAPTER 18

Jen was drumming her fingers on the kitchen table as she stared at her best friend. She adjusted herself on the chair and crossed her legs. "Well?"

"Well what?"

"C'mon, Kate. I know you better than anyone. You've been acting funny ever since you got back. I know something happened, so there's no point in trying to deny it." Jen stood up and put her hands on her hips. She took two steps until she was inches from Kate.

"Nothing happened." She tried to hide her ring, which was a strange mix of violet and tangerine.

"Oh really? I'm not buying it." Jen walked back, sat down, and started drumming her fingers on the table again. Kate twisted her neck from side to side and picked up an apple from a bowl on the table.

They sat for several minutes. Kate put the apple back and ran her fingers through her hair. She took a long swallow of wine. Jen watched her, waiting. They were sitting in Jen's kitchen, a cozy, bright yellow room filled with sunflowers, pictures, candles, and fresh flowers. Kate always enjoyed spending time at Jen's apartment and then walking up and down Main Street, going to bars, restaurants, and different shops.

"Okay. Of course I was going to tell you, but you have to promise not to tell anyone. We made a pact, and I don't want him to find out."

"Him? Who?"

Kate tilted her head to the side and smiled.

Jen raised her eyebrows as everything clicked into place all at once. "Oh my God! What the hell was he doing in Chicago?"

Kate exhaled the breath she was holding. "Surprise!" Kate shrugged her shoulders. "You can only imagine my reaction. He was at the conference. Small world, huh?"

"Sure, whatever, small world. So did you guys go out or what?"

"We went out all right," she mumbled under her breath.

"What?" Jen leaned forward on her chair and put her elbows on the table. "Are you saying … that you and Greg hooked up?"

Kate picked a piece of lint from her jeans. She took another gulp of wine. *Truth serum; liquid courage*, she thought. "It was a onetime thing, Jen. I swear."

"Oh my God! This is huge!"

"Well …"

"I think I'm actually speechless. This is the last thing I expected. Wow. You and Greg. In the sack." Jen shook her head and stared at Kate.

"I guess I like surprising people."

"How did this happen? I mean, I know how it happened, but how did … I mean, what the hell happened out there?"

"It was just one of those things." The wine started taking effect, and it culminated between her heart and her head. "A little wine, some dinner, snow falling, soft music on the radio, and once he kissed me, that was it. You know how I feel about him." Kate shook her head and looked into her near-empty glass.

Jen picked up the bottle of wine and added some more to each of their glasses. "Did you tell him?"

"No, and he didn't say it either."

"Okay, well I guess that's good, right?"

"I guess. I have no regrets, Jen. I could not have planned that night if I tried."

Jen took a gulp of wine and smiled. "So, since I already know, I guess there's no harm in sharing some details, right? I mean, what are friends for?"

Kate smiled and looked at her friend. "It was the most amazing, unbelievable, perfect night. He was so romantic and tender and loving." She looked at the ceiling and then back at Jen. "Honestly, it was like how I imagine a wedding night."

"Wow, that good."

"It was. I'm only sorry that was it. We still can't be together and ..."

"Well at least you had the chance to be with him. Even if it was only one night."

"I know. I keep trying to tell myself that. But it doesn't make it right. For God sakes, he's practically married, but ..." She looked directly at Jen. "Honestly, I wouldn't have changed one thing about that night. It was perfect, he was perfect and if I died today, I would die happy."

"Don't regret it. And if it was that amazing, consider yourself lucky. I've never been with a guy where it felt like a wedding night." Jen put her hand on Kate's hand and squeezed.

"I don't want to say this out loud, but I'm going to anyway. I really love him, truly from the bottom of my heart. And not only do I love him; I'm in love with him, and that is the part that makes this so unbelievably hard. Because I can't have him. We're just friends. That's all we'll ever be, and basically it sucks."

"I have news for you. Life in general sucks. Welcome to the club."

Kate turned her head to the side. "Thanks."

"I'm sorry, I'm sorry. I don't know why I said that. Life doesn't suck; it's really specific situations that suck. You know?"

"I know. All too well."

"So, what are you going to do?"

"What can I do? Nothing. I think it's best if Greg and I don't talk for a little while until everything blows over. If enough time passes, it'll be like it never happened."

"He's a guy, Kate. I don't think he'll ever forget that it happened."

"We'll just pretend, then. We have to for the sake of our friendship."

"Are you really going to be okay just being friends?"

Kate thought about this for a minute. "I don't know. I can't imagine us not being friends, so I don't really have a choice."

"There's always a choice."

"I love him too much to walk away and not talk anymore just because it might be a little awkward. It'll all be forgotten eventually. He's back now to his happy house, and I'll be the last thing on his mind."

"I doubt that. But even though I know you won't like this, you really should try to get over him so you can move on and meet someone who is available. You deserve to be happy, and I hate seeing you waste so much time on this guy you can't have."

"Easier said than done." Kate looked away toward the kitchen window. It was another cold February day; clouds filled the sky and remnants of snow lingered on the sidewalk and trees along Main Street.

"I know. But at least think about it, okay? I know you want to get married and have kids someday, and being emotionally attached to Greg isn't going to help you at all."

"I know. I hate to admit this, but I don't even know how to begin to get over him. I never had a problem before, getting over past boyfriends. But Greg is different. He's *the one* or at least he should be. That is just how I feel. I feel so strongly for him that I can't even imagine being with someone else." Kate shook her head. "How do you get over the person who you are meant to share your life with?"

Jen put her hand on Kate's shoulder. "That's the million-dollar question. If you solve it, you've uncovered one of life's most complex problems. About love, anyway. And what's life without love? Nothing."

* * *

"Here, you need this more than me." Tom poured the remaining beer into Greg's glass. He took a long swallow and pushed the glass away before brushing some peanut shells on the floor and wiping his hands on his jeans.

"You think it was wrong, don't you?"

"If I did that to Danielle … I wouldn't even have a chance to be in the doghouse because she'd be throwing my clothes out the window."

"But it's different with Heather and me, you know that."

"I know, but … you know what, it really doesn't matter what I think."

Greg shook his head. He tuned out the Flyers game as well as the bar chatter, cell phone conversations, and jukebox music. He could only hear Tom's words.

"Remember what I said about having your cake and eating it too. It's like that now. You can't have them both. And if you think you can, you're kidding yourself." Tom let Greg think about that and got up to get another pitcher of beer.

Greg stared at the table with no expression on his face. He was at a loss about what to do, what to think, and how to act. Could he honestly stay friends with Kate after what happened in Chicago? Their friendship had changed, and they couldn't go back to the way it was. Could he still be with Heather and pretend he hadn't slept with another woman? A woman he loved and knew he should be with? Could he stay with a woman for the sake of his kids? He knew it was wrong but that is exactly what he was thinking. In the same breath, could he leave his boys and their mother for another woman? No, because how could he instill values in his kids if he just up and left them? He was stuck. There was no use denying it now. He was one hundred percent in love with Kate. He wanted to call her that instant from Bottoms Up and tell her. He always envisioned he would tell her in person, but the urge to get the words off his chest was so strong that he didn't care if it was on the phone or not. He loved her from deep in his soul, with his entire being. He loved Heather too, but in a different way. They were friends, partners, and parents, sharing the responsibility of raising two young sons. He loved her as a friend, as the mother of his children, but he was not in love with her. He realized that years ago but let his love for his children determine his ultimate decision. He didn't regret it. When his boys snuggled with him at night to read books and ran to him when he came home from work, he knew he made the right choice. As hard as it was to admit, he did the right thing putting his children's happiness ahead of his own.

After Tom set the pitcher on the table, he patted Greg on the back. "She's really the one that got away, isn't she?"

Greg gave a half smile. "She is."

"I wish I knew what to tell you. What happened after? How did you leave things?"

"We didn't talk about what would happen. Just that we would talk after we got home."

"But you haven't talked to her yet, right?" Tom poured more beer in Greg's glass.

"Right. I'll text her soon."

Tom nodded. "I hate to say this, but you have to decide what you want. And also what Heather and Kate want."

Greg nodded and took a long drink. He had already made his decision. It was called being a selfless father, a responsible and caring parent. He could never leave his boys. It meant he would have to stay with a woman he wasn't in love with. It meant possibly breaking Kate's heart. Greg shook his head and felt the strain in his neck and shoulders as if he were carrying heavy sacks of potatoes strapped to his back. His neck cracked, and he reached up to try to loosen the knots with his fingertips.

"Do you think you'll tell Heather?"

"No. I don't know. Probably not. Do you think I should?"

"If you want to be honest, maybe you should. But only you can decide."

Greg felt the complexity of the situation and all its implications. If Heather found out, she could end everything, and then what would happen to his kids? He would get joint custody, maybe, and he didn't know if he could handle that. But what if Heather forgave him but wanted him to never talk to or see Kate again? He couldn't handle that either.

"I think I'm just going to wait it out. I know that sounds pretty bad, but I can't make any decisions right now."

Tom nodded and patted his friend on the back.

After their last pitcher of beer was emptied, Greg and Tom stood up and headed outside into the chilly February night air. There were stars gleaming in the sky, and when Greg looked up, he noticed a big dazzling one that appeared to be shining right over Old City. He closed his eyes and made a wish.

Greg and Tom parted ways, and as Greg walked home, he kept looking up at the sky toward the beautiful bright star, hoping Kate was seeing it too.

CHAPTER 19

Kate waited two months of not hearing a word from Greg before she reached the point where she couldn't handle the silence for one more second. But when she actually picked up the phone to call him, her fingers quivered as she punched in his number. She looked at the deep eggplant color of her mood ring and knew there was no turning back. It was easier to call him at work on his office line, when she knew he'd be alone and able to talk. She dreamt about him at night occasionally, smiling in her sleep to the comforting sound of his voice and the passionate luxury of his lips on hers. The intoxicating feel of skin on skin, the sexiness of his chin dimple, the mesmerizing moment they became one. But when she woke alone after each dream, she was crushed with the reminder that their beautiful, romantic night in Chicago was a one-time-only deal. To cheer herself up, she would tell herself there would always be a very small chance. As long as she loved him, there was always a chance. When there is love, there is always hope.

"Hello. Greg Janera."

Kate hesitated for a moment, surprised that he answered on the first ring. "Hi." She slid her chair closer to her desk and rested her elbows on top.

"Oh, hey." He stopped typing. "How are you?"

"Okay."

"I'm sorry I haven't called. It's just been hectic. I know that's no excuse though." He wheeled his chair around and faced the window.

"No, that's okay. I just wanted to say hi and see how you're doing." Kate cringed as she said the words. That was so not the reason she was calling.

He watched a flock of birds gracefully soar through the sky. *Stay free,* he thought. "I'm doing okay."

I'm not. I miss you. I love you. I'm a mess without you, she wanted to say. "Me too," is what came out of her mouth.

"So, how's work?"

"It's good, the same." Kate rolled her eyes because work was the last thing she wanted to talk about. She doodled a multitier heart in her notepad. She traced it over and over. Her ring all of a sudden looked like a monarch butterfly, with tiny shapes of orange and brown. She had no idea what that meant. "I actually wanted to see if we could talk sometime, maybe meet up for lunch or after work one night?"

"Let me check my schedule. Can I call you later?"

"Sure, take your time. I'll be here."

"Okay." Greg paused as he watched a plane fly toward the Philadelphia Airport. "It's good to hear from you, Kate."

"You too. Talk to you soon." Kate hung up and folded her arms across her chest, ready to analyze that conversation, however brief, for all it was worth.

Greg called her back two days later and they agreed to meet for lunch. When that day arrived, Kate took extra time getting ready in the morning, making sure her hair was styled and her makeup was fresh and natural. She chose a skirt and top she felt comfortable wearing that also showed off her figure. She had gnawing in her stomach the entire morning, which became pangs of disappointment when Greg had to cancel at the last minute. They rescheduled, and of course on that day, something came up at Kate's work forcing her to cancel. Kate was beginning to think making plans in advance wasn't going to work, so she called him spur of the moment on an ordinary Wednesday morning in early May and just made it happen.

Greg felt that it was easier not to have lunch with Kate, despite the fact that he truly missed her. He did feel bad when he had to cancel, but a last-minute urgent client meeting came up that he had to attend. He was a little relieved when she had to cancel, and when she didn't try to reschedule, he thought maybe she was just going to let it go.

Over the past few weeks, he didn't sleep well, waking at four in the morning and not being able to go back to sleep. He wasn't eating right, and one night, Heather asked him to please tell her what was so wrong that had him eating ice cream for dinner. He shook it off, telling her work was busy and stressful after a recent layoff left his team short staffed while he was inundated trying to entice new clients to come on board.

Then a couple of weeks later, Greg answered his phone and heard the hope and anticipation in Kate's voice, and he could not say no to her. Right before he left for the restaurant, he felt a twinge of nerves race through his mind. He didn't know how she would be, but her voice led him to believe she was going to be friendly and caring, the same Kate he fell in love with all those summers ago. That meant his will to resist her might never hold strong. It would be easier if she was upset and irritated at him; that way he could hold firm to his decision.

Kate was sitting in the bar area when Greg walked in at one o'clock. She stood up when she saw him, and they walked toward each other, sharing a quick hug.

"It's good to finally see you."

Greg smiled and then frowned. "It's been a while. I'm sorry about that."

"It's okay," Kate said, even though she wasn't okay with not seeing him for three months, not after what happened in Chicago. They walked toward the hostess stand, and Greg led her to the table, placing his hand on the small of her back.

"You look nice." Greg smoothed his tie after settling in the chair.

"Thanks. You too." Kate smiled and placed her hands in front of her on the table.

Their waiter, a guy about their age who easily stood six foot four with short, curly blonde hair and overwhelming bicep muscles came over and told them the specials. Neither Kate nor Greg listened, opting to simply gaze at each other, both of them thinking back to Chicago. *That magical night*, Kate thought, getting lost for a moment in memories. The sexy yet sweet bubble bath, the passionate kisses, the closeness of being wrapped up in each other's arms, skin on skin, all night. The way he picked her up and carried her to the bed was so romantic to her she could only equate it to a bride and groom. Greg held close the softness of Kate's skin, her playfulness, and the incredible way she made him feel. They were so comfortable with each other; she was not self-conscious in any way, and that was so hot to him. He remembered the intense desire of wanting her, of needing her, and knowing the feelings were mutual. Something that surprised him after he came home from Chicago was that he could no longer smell vanilla or lavender without yearning to be with her.

Seemingly at the same time, they looked away from each other and sighed. They started to laugh and then caught up on each other's lives: work, family, their summer plans, and Greg's children. The waiter came back and cleared his throat twice as he stood before them. Kate and Greg absently opened their menus. Kate selected the first salad she saw, and Greg asked for a chicken and pasta dish even though he was not particularly crazy about pasta. Once the waiter walked away, Kate looked up to meet Greg's gaze.

"Kate, listen, about Chicago, I um—"

She cut him off. "It's okay. You don't have to say anything. It was a mistake, wasn't it?" She said it more as a sentence instead of a question.

Greg furrowed his eyebrows. "No. It wasn't a mistake. At least not to me. Was it to you?" His voice was laced with shock and he inhaled sharply.

"No. Of course not. I don't know why I said that."

Greg exhaled. "Good. What I was going to say was, it was an amazing night that I'll never forget. I just hate the circumstances. I wish things could be different, I really do, but they just, they can't. I promised myself I would never walk out on my children." Greg shook his head. "I have to be the adult. The bottom line is my kids come first."

Kate felt tears forming in the back of her eyes, and she bargained with herself with all her might not to cry. "The worst part, the hardest part for me is I know you're doing the right thing. I would be devastated if I were her and you left me. But it's just ..." *You'll never know how sorry I really am.*

Greg cleared his throat. "I hope we can stay friends. I know it isn't the ideal situation but it's the best I can do. It's all I have to offer."

Kate looked down at her hands, gripping the end of the tablecloth, her throat filling with bile. She met Greg's stare but couldn't say a word.

"If I could magically change the situation, I would. In a heartbeat, Kate, I would. You know that, don't you?"

Kate mustered up all the strength in her, determined to at least try. Try hard. "I want more, Greg. I don't think you know how I feel. How I really feel." She swallowed and shook her head gently, a natural smile forming on her lips. "I love you,

Greg Janera. I didn't want to admit it, but I've loved you from the day we met. The moment we met, I knew. Remember at the park with Rocky on that incredibly hot day? I knew I loved you. I have been trying to push my feelings away, bury them for so long now; but I can't anymore. For a while, it was easy to keep pretending I didn't feel that way. But I can't hold it in anymore. I love you, Greg. I just love you." The words tumbled out of Kate's mouth before her brain could process what she was saying, and once they were on the table, it was too late to take any of them back. In truth, she didn't want to take them back. She loved him, and he needed to know.

Greg bit his tongue. He wanted to tell her he felt the same. That he loved her as much if not more than she loved him. But he couldn't. No good would come of it, and it would only cause both of them more heartache. He shook his head softly. "I'm sorry, Kate. I really am so sorry. If I could change things, you know I would. But my boys ..." He trailed off and ran a hand through his hair.

Kate lowered her head, trying to keep the tears from spilling out of her eyes. "I know you would." But even as she said the words, she didn't really know. "I'm sorry, about everything." *More than you'll ever know.*

"You have absolutely nothing to be sorry about. I'm the one who is sorry. I care about you very much. You are so dear to me. I don't want to hurt you in any way. Tell me what I can do. Just tell me, Kate."

Kate gave a small shrug. "There isn't anything you can do."

A few minutes went by with neither one saying anything, both lost in thought about what could have been, the wonderful relationship that never stood a chance. If only things were different. If only circumstances could change with the snap of a finger. It sounded so simple, but in reality it was more complicated than anyone could dream.

"I'd like to stay friends, as long as you're okay with that. I can't imagine not having you in my life." Greg knew this was the only option.

Kate gathered up an inner strength and sat up straighter. "Of course. Of course we can be friends," she said with a fake smile.

Their plates and glasses were still full when the waiter cleared them. Greg walked her out of the restaurant without his hand on the small of her back, and she knew things had changed. It would be different from now on, and that was something she hadn't considered while they were in Chicago. As painful as it was, he was refusing the love that she was more than willing to give him and receive in return. As much as she wanted to be with him, she admired his decision. She understood he had to put his children's needs ahead of his own. Of course he had to put his children first. She loved him even more for that, if that was possible. She was torn over confessing her feelings, but it felt so good to get it off her chest. She felt unburdened and free, yet she felt like she ruined everything. He didn't say it back, and that left a void in her heart. Every time they talked or saw each other, he would wonder if she still felt the same. He might always feel awkward in her presence. She would never truly know.

They hugged briefly before saying good-bye. Greg said he would text her, but she doubted that. The lower her expectations, the less she would be disappointed.

Greg wanted to maintain his friendship with Kate and try to go back to what it once was, if that was possible. He would have to block out Chicago and his feelings, that much was certain. He wanted to be with her as much as she wanted to be with him. He loved her from the depths of his soul. But there was no way he could ever share his true feelings. No way in hell. He would bury them and maintain a friendship. He knew he could do it, as long as Kate was comfortable with it. However, he realized today that maybe she never would be. All he could do now was hope for the best and let some more time and distance pass between them. Wasn't it true that time heals all wounds?

Greg walked back to his office, trying to push away Kate's words. Suddenly, a buried memory came to the forefront of his mind. His dad wouldn't let him ride his bike one Sunday afternoon because he had to write a book report and study for a math test. "It's all about making choices. Sometimes you have to sacrifice certain things, like riding your bike, to be a better person and student in school," his dad had said. Greg whined that he didn't understand what that meant and all he wanted to do was play outside. "You'll understand someday, son," his dad told him while quizzing him on multiplication and division. He never understood. Until now.

Kate stopped at the park before going back to the office. She collapsed on a bench, feeling so hollow she could have been a tin can. He didn't want to be with her. He couldn't be with her. She loved him with all of her heart, but he'd rejected her love. He didn't love her back. If he did, he clearly would have said so. Wouldn't he?

She would have to come up with a way they could stay friends because she needed him in her life. She would never confess she missed him or that she craved his kiss. She would certainly never tell him again that she loved him. She would mentally block out their early dates, all the kisses, and especially Chicago. She would pretend it never happened. Greg obviously was going to do that, so why shouldn't she? If he was okay with being friends, then so should she. How hard could it be? *Impossible.*

It didn't seem difficult for the next couple of months. They started texting on a semi regular basis and talking on the phone once or twice a week. Kate did her best to keep her distance emotionally, and it seemed to be working. They were communicating like comfortable friends; an easygoing, relaxed feeling was always the undertone of their texts or conversations. At one point Greg even brought up the topic of dating to see if Kate had met anyone. She remembered being surprised at his boldness and decided to tell him that she occasionally went on blind dates. She left out that it never went beyond the first date. How could she be romantically interested in anyone else? She couldn't comprehend the thought of kissing or being intimate with another guy. Greg got quiet on the phone when she talked about these blind dates, and Kate wondered if he was jealous or not truly interested in knowing details of her dating life. But then why would he even bring it up in the first place? Jen decided he was probably jealous and just trying to dig for details about anyone she was seeing. Kate didn't think that was it. Her intuition told her Greg was strictly in the friend zone and that he would have no reason to be jealous so it was okay to talk about dating. Kate obviously felt very differently as she certainly didn't want to know any details about Heather or their life together. She didn't want to know how they smiled at each other or how they communicated or how they most likely shared a bed. Then just as abruptly as he brought up the topic, he let it go. But besides those uncomfortable moments, their conversations were pleasant, fun, and happy. Kate felt like their friendship was back on track, destined to go the distance. In her mind, she finally accepted the fact they would simply stay good friends, even though a part of her still wanted more. A part of her would always want more.

CHAPTER 20

Heather had a nagging feeling in her gut that something wasn't quite right. Call it woman's intuition or a sixth sense. She hoped she was wrong, but something had seemed *off* about Greg ever since he came home from Chicago. She wondered if five days away from her and their boys, five days of essentially being a single guy again, had caused him to want his freedom back. No, that couldn't be it, because he did not act any differently around the boys. The boys were asleep when Greg arrived home, and he and Heather had talked briefly about his trip while sitting at the kitchen table. He said the conference went well, that he learned a lot of good information in the seminars and was able to network with other attendees, which would enable him to enhance his work. Greg felt that his career would really take off someday, and he even talked about the possibility of starting his own web design firm. Heather also asked him specifically about Chicago, if he was able to go out and see the city. He had looked away from her for a moment and casually mentioned that he and his colleagues had gone to dinner a few times but that there wasn't time for any sightseeing, and besides, it was too cold to explore the city even if he had had the time. Heather had nodded along, believing she was just being paranoid. But something was not right; she just couldn't pinpoint it. When it was time for bed, Heather put on a pretty pajama set from

Victoria's Secret, lit a scented candle, and had tried to initiate sex. Greg had apologized, saying he was too tired from the week and also the flight home. He gave her a quick kiss, turned on his side, and fell asleep almost immediately. Heather, on the other hand, had lain awake for hours. She thought about what it might mean for Greg to turn down sex, especially since she rarely initiated it. Was he not attracted to her anymore? Was he legitimately too tired? Was he irrationally afraid of her getting pregnant again, despite the fact she was on the Pill? Was he interested in someone else?

Heather did not want to believe any of those scenarios, except for him being too tired. The next morning, the boys had run in and jumped on their bed, and Greg hugged them and smothered them with kisses. He offered to take them out to dinner that night, just the boys, to give Heather a break. Heather didn't want a break. She wanted to spend time with Greg as much as the boys and said she would come along, if that was okay. Greg had said yes, of course, but she sensed a twinge of disappointment in Greg's response.

Heather tried to be extra loving and thoughtful in those couple of months after Chicago. She cooked his favorite dinners and didn't give him a hard time when baseball season started and he was glued to the TV most nights. She took care of the household chores, essentially giving him a break and easing his workload. She knew he was stressed at work after some of his team fell victim to a layoff. After about a month or so, Greg seemed a little better, and Heather was finally breathing a sigh of relief. But then one day out of the blue in May, Greg came home from work and just seemed distraught. Over what, she didn't know. She tried to talk to him, get him to open up, but he wouldn't tell her anything other than there were some issues at work that he couldn't talk about. It was the first time Heather ever thought he was lying to her, and she couldn't shake the feeling that maybe her and Greg were not truly meant to be together. She didn't want to believe that. She loved him and wanted to make their relationship work, not only for the sake of their children but because they had a long history together. Heather wanted to make Greg happy and knew that she could, but she also wanted him to open up and trust her enough to tell her everything that was on his mind. "Communication is key," Clara always used to say. Heather believed it; she just needed to make sure Greg believed it too.

CHAPTER 21

Kate drove home, sobbing nonstop the entire way. She brushed her cheeks, but the tears were coming so fast it would have taken a thick bath towel to make a difference. Her heart was scattered in pieces, her whole body experiencing the effects. She was shivering, even though it was August and her car had been sitting directly in the sun for at least two hours before she got into it. Her windows were rolled down slightly, and a hot breeze flowed in as she drove. She needed the fresh air to keep from passing out. This cut penetrated through her body more so than a knife wound. That could be treated with prompt medical care. But her heart would not be healed by modern medicine. No doctor could fix the stabbing pain she felt in her heart. Doctors would examine her and conclude it was all in her head and send her to a psychiatrist.

She continued driving through the sea of tears in traffic as thick as the haze. An accident by Girard Avenue and construction workers busy in the right lane kept her on the Schuylkill for an extra thirty minutes. She cursed herself under her breath for taking the long way home but she just wanted to get as far away from Fairmont Park as possible. Through her tears, she had zoomed down West River Drive, saw the green arrow to go up Montgomery Drive, and drove up the ramp onto the Schuylkill Expressway. Her mouth was dry, the back of her shirt stuck to the seat, and her stomach felt nauseated. She looked down and saw her mood ring was the color of a raven.

Once she finally got back to Old City and parked her car in a space on the street, she sat numb for at least an hour. People walked by and asked if she was okay, and she absently nodded. She was too spent to speak, and words wouldn't make it past her lips if her life depended on it. Tears and sweat were pouring from her eyes and skin, down her face, her back, chest, and legs. She felt sticky and gross but couldn't fathom taking a step. She was sure her legs would give out and she would fall on the sidewalk, which was probably hot enough to burn her skin.

She eventually pushed herself to gather up as much energy as she could, emerged from the car, and slowly made her way to her apartment. She forced herself to put one foot in front of the other and held onto the railing while climbing the stairs to the second floor. She sat down in the middle of her living room but didn't know what to do. Shower? Sleep? Drink water? She didn't have the strength to do anything except cry. She didn't want to be awake but was too drained to climb into bed and close her eyes. She remained on the floor, softly rocking back and forth, with her arms wrapped around her knees, for the better part of three hours. A few times she laid down in a fetal position with her arms wrapped around her as if trying to keep her heart from breaking into more pieces. She ignored her phone, which rang about five times; two knocks on her door (*I see your car. I know you're home. Are you all right?*); a takeout menu being shoved under her door; and later a flyer advertising something trivial.

Around eight o'clock, Kate gingerly stood, making sure her legs would support her. She headed straight for the shower and stood under the spray of water while soaping away her pain. She ran a huge amount of shampoo through her hair as if trying to wash him away. But how do you wash away a broken heart? She went without conditioner because she simply didn't have the energy to apply it, and she couldn't even think about shaving her legs. The shower refreshed her, and for a fleeting moment she felt like she would be okay. After she patted her skin dry with a towel, she threw on a tank top and boxer shorts and walked to her kitchen with dripping wet hair. Beads of water slid down her back and arms as if they were crying too. She poured herself a glass of water and took a few Saltine crackers from the plastic sleeve but had to force herself to take a few sips and a couple of bites because her insides felt queasy. She reached into the top of her closet and got the polar bear out, if only for a small amount of comfort. She went back to the living room, grabbed the box of tissues, and curled up on the couch under a blanket, still ignoring the phone, which beeped with text messages and rang several times while she was showering. She would call Jen back tomorrow. She just couldn't face talking to anyone right now, not even her best friend. No one would be able to cheer her up, and as much as she loved Jen, she didn't have the energy to go through the story, which unfortunately she couldn't stop replaying in her mind.

She tried not to think about what had happened, what he had said, but something inside her died today. Her heart was being tugged and pulled in a direction she didn't want it to go, but there was no stopping it. He said words she almost couldn't comprehend. She felt he was punishing her for something that was never her choice, never her fault. *"This can't go anywhere. It's too difficult on both of us. I promise you, Kate. You need to move on. This is for the best. For everyone,"* he had said as they walked down West River Drive. As they got close to the Art Museum and the Rocky statue, she thought about Rocky persevering and surviving. She felt a surge of strength to tell him she loved him again, to tell him that she promised to always love him, but the words got caught in her throat. Greg walked, looking straight ahead as if she was invisible. Now, in her apartment, she felt sick. She wanted to die, if only for the pain to stop. She wanted to go to sleep, and sleep, and sleep. Sitting curled up on her couch, her mind flashed back to their conversation.

"Is it really better like this? Ending our friendship? Not even talking anymore?" Kate had said, her voice cracking with shock.

"I'm trying to do the right thing here. You'll be able to move on with your life and meet someone else. Someone who can give you everything you want and need. You deserve someone who will put you first, make you his number one priority. Spend holidays with you. Celebrate birthdays. I just can't be that person. You deserve to be happy, Kate. You can go on and get married and have a family. That is what I wish for you. No one wants that more than me."

"But you're breaking my heart, Greg. I don't see how this could possibly be for the best. You're saying we'll never talk again? What did I do so horrible to make you hate me?"

"I don't hate you. I could never hate you, Kate." Greg looked away for a moment and bit his lip. "We can't go anywhere, and what happened in Chicago … I can't just be your friend; I don't see you like that. It's too difficult. In time you'll understand." Greg paused and stopped walking, and Kate followed his lead. He held her gaze. "I'm so sorry. I never meant for any of this to happen. I wish things were different, but they're not. I don't know what else to say." He wanted to tell her that he loved her and always would, but he didn't. He couldn't. It would have seemed cruel to tell someone you love them and that you want them out of your life in the same breath. "I need to concentrate on my family, my boys. You need to concentrate on your life. It's better for everyone if we just end things now. It might take time, but you'll realize I'm doing the right thing."

I love you, Kate wanted to say. The words slowly slid down her throat, and when she tried to catch her breath, she swallowed, forcing them deep into her gut to a cavernous black hole, where they would stay and never see the light of day. Tears continued sliding down her cheeks. "I don't know what to say. I can't accept this, but you're not giving me a choice. You're making this decision for both of us and ..." She wiped at her eyes. "I'm heartbroken, Greg. You've broken my heart. In a million pieces." She put her hands to her cheeks and then looked Greg in the eyes. "I need to ask you one thing, and I need you to be completely honest."

Greg raked a hand through his hair and nodded.

Kate swallowed and wiped away two more tears falling down her cheek. "I need to know if you ever loved me."

Greg felt his body go numb. He shook his head slightly and faced her. "Kate, please don't do this. Don't ask me that. You know how I feel."

Kate crossed her arms and a fierce energy came up from inside her. "No, Greg, I really don't. Go ahead. Tell me the truth."

Greg turned to look down the parkway toward City Hall. He cracked his knuckles and wiped sweat from his forehead. "I can't, Kate."

Kate unfolded her arms and put her hands on her hips. "I need to hear you say it, Greg. Did you ever love me? I won't leave until you tell me."

Greg swallowed and bit his lip. He then looked Kate square in the eyes and lied, one of the biggest lies he ever told in his life. And he felt as horrible as he imagined, telling the woman he loved, the woman he was in love with, that he never loved her at all. That the years of knowing her and the time they spent together had all meant nothing.

Kate opened her mouth and closed it. She wanted to yell at him or slap him in the face. Her eyes remained fixed on his; she didn't even blink. Her insides felt hollow, as if she had been detonated. She felt like the trash floating in the river. Her mouth was dry, but tears started streaming down her face. She swallowed and found a drop of moisture on her tongue. "You really said it." She trembled, and her lips quivered. "I have to go." Kate turned to leave and started running down the path, not even knowing if she was heading in the right direction to her car. She didn't remember parking let alone driving there.

Greg ran after her to catch up and screamed for her to wait, but Kate was too fast. The adrenaline coursing through her body to get away from him and the situation was overpowering her pain. She didn't hear him yelling her name over and over through the hazy air. She didn't hear anything but the sound of her own feet hitting the pavement. She reached her car and didn't look back.

***

She grabbed another tissue and wiped new tears from her eyes. She was curled up on the couch in a fetal position, the polar bear on the table. Her mood ring would probably remain black permanently. How could he, after four years, cut her out of his life? She thought about what he had said and now understood. He never loved her. Of course he could cut her out of his life if that is the way he felt. He didn't care that her heart was in more pieces than a jigsaw puzzle. Bottom line, he didn't want her in his life anymore. She couldn't say good-bye forever. But she had to respect his decision. This was his choice—a choice she did not agree with. Ironically, she understood why and knew how important his boys were to him. But couldn't she and Greg stay friends? If he didn't love her, why was he so adamant about cutting all contact? She had no choice but to somehow learn to accept it. Brokenhearted. Alone. Without even his friendship. The person she felt was her soul mate, the one person she felt closest to, kicking her out of his life.

When Jen got her on the phone, she tried to console her as best she could. "In time you will be okay. Time heals all wounds.

And really, it is his loss. You have to remember that most of all. I hate him for doing this to you, and he clearly isn't worth your time," Jen had said. This is actually what her mom told her ever since she was a teenager when her first boyfriend broke up with her after two months. Pat was a decent enough guy, but a teenage guy is a teenage guy. Greg was different. Greg was a man, someone who was mature. She loved him, and she wanted him to be happy, more than anything. That is what love is: considering the needs and wants of the other person before your own. And if this was what Greg wanted, what he really wanted, she would have to accept it.

Greg was shaken up the most by his outright lie. He slowly walked around the park after watching her drive away. He stood across from Boat House Row, watching the water rush over the edge, feeling like he was going with it, down, down, down. As much as he racked his brain for an alternative solution, there was none. If he told Kate the truth, she would never accept his decision. She would never even accept a platonic relationship. She would want what they couldn't have, and how would that make anyone happy? It would destroy them both; it would cause them more pain than they ever knew possible. Even though it was ultimately his decision, it was never the choice he wanted to make. Not by a long shot. His feelings for Kate were so strong, it scared the hell out of him, and he didn't want to lead a double life or hurt her any more than he already had. He also didn't want to hurt Heather; she didn't deserve that. It wasn't fair to anyone. Heather had been hinting since before the twins were born that she wanted to get married. She wanted Greg to make the full commitment to her and the boys. She loved him, they had children together, and she wanted nothing more than for them to make their relationship official. He would have to decide, and he couldn't do it if his mind was still fixated on

Kate. His Kate. He would have to stop saying that. He would try; that was the best he could do. Eventually, he reasoned, Kate would be okay. She would realize he was right, move on, meet someone else, fall in love, get married, and have children. He knew she would be a wonderful wife and mother, and he wanted this for her. She deserved someone who would love her and be able to give her one hundred percent.

If he stayed in the picture, even as a friend, he knew Kate would never move on. She would always hope things would work out between them. And he couldn't live with himself if she wasted her most precious years waiting for something that would never come. He just couldn't leave his boys, ever. He couldn't go from living with them, seeing and playing with them every day, experiencing all of their firsts, to seeing them every other weekend and one night a week. It would break his heart if they grew up thinking even for one second that he didn't love them, that he didn't care enough about them. That he cared more for a woman who wasn't their mother than he did for his own flesh and blood. He would never know the emotional damage this would cause them throughout their life. And Heather was a good mother; she would be a good wife too. She deserved his commitment. She deserved his honesty. He realized he was trying to justify his decision about Kate, make himself feel better. Of course he loved Kate. He loved her with all of his heart, and it tore him up to see Kate cry when he spoke those awful words. He felt like residue from the bottom of the Schuylkill River as she ran away from him. But he knew Kate was strong and resilient. It was for the best. For everyone. If he said it enough, maybe someday he would believe it.

CHAPTER 22

August was winding down, but Kate's pain was still evident on her face. She rarely smiled anymore; it was as though the joys of life had been sucked out of her with a vacuum. She had a difficult time sleeping and would lay awake for hours at night, listening to sad love songs, wishing her heart and her head would come together and heal. *Maybe tomorrow things will be better* became her new mantra. She went from someone who was healthy and fit to having to force herself to eat. She dropped ten pounds without blinking. After work, she would try to zone out with a book or movie or by listening to music, but her mind would always come back to one thing: Greg. Was it all her fault? Chicago? Did that ultimately destroy any hope of a normal friendship? The only thing she knew with certainty was that she could not accept this, even though she understood it. Deep down, she understood it. Coming to terms with it would be a different story.

One particular night, she lay awake in bed, staring at the ceiling. Streetlights left little circles of white light on her walls, and when the trees swayed, the shadows bounced around like ping pong balls. Kate had so much inside her, so many feelings to get off her chest that she was overcome with emotion. She climbed out of bed and sat at her little kitchen table, pen and paper in hand. She wrote for the next several hours, crumpling papers in a ball, throwing them in the recycling bin and reaching for a clean sheet. She kept writing and crumpling until her bin overflowed with scrunched up papers that looked like snowballs. Exhaustion overcame her around four in the morning, and after the last sheet was balled up, she climbed back into bed and clutched the polar bear that Greg had won for her on a day so long ago it felt like another lifetime. She couldn't keep the bear hidden away. Holding the stuffed animal to her chest somehow comforted her for the few moments before she fell back asleep, making her feel less hollow inside, like her heart was going to mend after all. But once she woke up, the pain revealed its ugly self and her heart was once again scattered throughout her chest, like confetti on New Year's Eve.

By mid-September, she was determined to try to put the past behind her. A couple of times she went out with coworkers after work, had a drink, and even flirted with a guy who lived just a couple of blocks from her. She started taking walks again after stopping for most of August. In the back of her mind, she was afraid she would run into him, or worse, he and Heather would be there with their kids. She didn't want to take that chance while she was still wallowing in self-pity. But enough was enough; she couldn't live the rest of her life pining over someone who didn't even want to be her friend despite the plain and simple fact that she loved him. She knew a small part of her would always love him, no matter what.

Jen told her from their first conversation that she needed to put the past behind her and get on with her life. She needed to meet someone new and start a real relationship with a guy who was physically, mentally, and emotionally available. Jen would text her randomly, reminding her it was his loss, that he didn't deserve her even if he came back begging for forgiveness. She did stop setting her up with guys from the hospital after not one first date turned into a second. Instead, Jen tried to get her to double date with her and her new boyfriend, Todd, but that was even worse as far as Kate was concerned. Some of Todd's friends were very nice and had serious dating potential, but Jen and Todd were in the beginning honeymoon stage, and although Kate was happy for her friend, she couldn't sit and watch the PDA while her mind was still fixated on Greg.

Kate's heart would always hold a very small hope that her friendship with Greg could be salvaged, even if they were the type of friends who only talked once in a while. Why did Greg not want this at all? More important, if he was so repulsed by her friendship, why didn't he unfriend her on Facebook? She refused to unfriend him, but she was not the one to make that harsh decision in August. She used to check her account daily, figuring that day would come sooner or later when he would see her post on his News Feed and fully erase her from his life. But so far, as crazy as it sounded, they were still Facebook friends.

One day in late September, as the air gained that familiar fall crispness and the leaves started to change from deep green to red, gold, and orange, she sat again with pen and paper in hand, this time at Rittenhouse Square. Over time she slowly came out of her depressed funk, but she couldn't understand why her mood ring refused to change from the deep onyx color it had turned on that last day with Greg. Right there in Fairmont Park, her life had changed, and her ring was somehow fixated on that day. She wondered if it would ever change colors, even if she won the lottery or opened her own PR firm. But she knew her ring was somehow attached to her heart, and as sad as it was to admit, it was a possibility her ring would stay black forever.

CHAPTER 23

"Daddy!" Hunter screamed in his most ear-piercing "outside" voice.

Greg walked into the kids' room and picked him up, planting a kiss on his cheek. "Hi there, buddy. Remember to use your *inside* voice, okay?"

"Okay, Daddy," Hunter said quietly.

"What are you doing?" He put Hunter back down on the floor.

"We're playing police. See? Cole is the bad guy, and I'm going to get him." He turned to his brother. "Busted!" He rammed the police car right next to the race car, picked it up, and let it fall to the floor.

"Yes, I see that." He looked down to see little police cars, an ambulance with blinking red lights, fire trucks, a bunch of race cars, and a sheriff's van littering their bedroom floor.

"I'm hungry! Mommy said you would make us breakfast." Cole picked up his stuffed green turtle and threw it in the air.

"She did, did she?" Greg winked at Heather and gave her a peck on the cheek as she put the boy's clean laundry away in their drawers.

"Can you watch the boys today?"

"Daddy, I wanna go to the playground!" Hunter was clutching his stuffed grey dog named Sam.

"We'll see, Hunter."

"But I wanna go now!"

"Greg?"

"I can't promise the playground today." He looked at Heather. "Right, watch the boys. What's up?"

"Why, Daddy?"

Heather turned toward her son. "It's going to rain, sweetie." She then faced Greg. "I need to help Aunt Clara this morning with some Christmas shopping, and remember Kelly's baby shower is this afternoon." She dusted the tops of the dressers and then started cleaning up some toys and puzzles that were on the floor.

"I wanna go with Aunt Clara! She always brings us toys," Hunter screamed. Greg and Heather gazed at him but chose to ignore his request.

Greg ran his hand through his hair and wiped the sleep from his eyes. "Kelly?"

"My friend from work. I told you her shower is today. I have to run out and get her gift. I have been so bad keeping up with stuff like that."

"Rain, rain, go away. Come again another day. Little Hunter wants to play. Rain, rain, go to Spain; never show your face again!" Hunter and Cole sang at the top of their lungs. They giggled profusely over putting Hunter's name in the song as they did each time they sang it. Greg and Heather smiled at their budding vocalists, appreciative they were learning songs in day care. They turned to each other, unable to hide how proud they were of their sons.

"Wait, did you say Christmas shopping? Today?"

"I know. But Clara's busy for the next two weekends, and she wants to get a jump start before Thanksgiving. You know how she hates crowds. You shouldn't complain. At least she moved here so I don't have to go to Scranton anymore. Plus"—Heather walked over to whisper in his ear—"she needs me to pick out stuff for the boys."

"Yeah, okay. I would love to spend the day with my two favorite little men." Greg picked them up together, and the boys hugged him with all their might. After putting them down, the boys climbed on their beds, giggled, and jumped up and down.

"Good." Heather yawned. "You know I love Clara and I'm happy to go with her, but I wish I could take the rest of the day off and just sleep. No work. No laundry. No cleaning." She laughed.

Greg smiled. "Mother's Day is coming."

Heather put the kids' books back on their bookshelf. "And, Greg, don't let them eat too much of their Halloween candy."

"Mommy!" Hunter and Cole cried. "No fair!"

Heather sighed and brushed hair out of her face. "Okay, boys, Daddy will give you each one piece later."

"One piece? But, Mommy!" the boys moaned in chorus.

Heather leaned over to Greg. "They'll turn into a sugary, hyper mess. Don't give in."

Greg winked at the boys, and they squealed.

Heather whipped around and put her hand on her hip. "Greg, I saw that. I mean it, one piece. You'll be sorry—I'm telling you. Remember Easter when they ate that chocolate bunny and then talked you into giving them jelly beans? We couldn't calm them down for a week."

"Right, right. I got it. One piece each."

"Thank you." Heather sighed. "I'll pick up something for dinner on my way home."

"Okay. Enjoy shopping, and don't worry about us. I'll take care of everything. We'll be fine. Right, guys?"

"Daddy! We wanna go to the zoo!"

"I'm hungry!"

"Okay, Daddy's going to make a special breakfast. How about blueberry pancakes?"

"Yay!"

Heather was just finishing cleaning up the boy's books. "No syrup, Greg. The dentist said it's bad for their teeth."

"Mommy won't let us do anything fun, will she?" Greg joked.

"Greg!" Heather crossed her arms.

"Sorry, sorry. No syrup. Got it." Greg rolled his eyes, his back to Heather.

Heather went back to their bedroom, took a shower, and got dressed. When she came out, she was wearing black pants, a cherry-red blouse, and a silver-and-black scarf. Her naturally straight blonde hair came past her shoulders. Her makeup was natural with a hint of eyeliner and lipstick.

The boys and Greg headed to the kitchen where Greg made Bisquick pancakes with bananas and blueberries. The boys started picking at their pancakes *sans* syrup and drinking their milk.

Heather came in the kitchen, adjusted her purse on her shoulder, and jingled the keys in her hand. "You sure you'll be okay?

"Of course. You know I love spending the day with the boys."

"Okay. I'm going to leave now, so I'll see you later." She bent down and gave each of her sons a big hug and kiss. She leaned over and gave Greg a peck on the lips and then she was gone.

"Daddy, I don't want pancakes!"

Greg let out a sigh. "Well, that's what we're having."

"No!" Cole took his pancake and threw it on the floor right by Rocky, who picked it up and hightailed it out of the kitchen.

"Oh Jesus ... Rocky!" Greg ran after Rocky, but it was too late. The dog stuffed it in his mouth and inhaled it in less than ten seconds.

Greg patted Rocky on his rear end and returned to the kitchen. He didn't want to be double-teamed by his two three-year-olds, so he decided to bite his tongue and do whatever he needed to do to get through the day in one piece. "Pick your battles," he heard his mom say when she had given him advice after the twins turned two.

"I want cereal with milk, Daddy!"

"I need milk in a cup!"

"I want cereal too!"

"I need my milk!"

"Okay, okay." Greg took Cole's empty plate and Hunter's plate with the pancake leftovers and walked to the sink. He put both plates down and stretched his neck from side to side. He poured two bowls of Cheerios and set one in front of each child. He then poured milk into two plastic cups, red for Hunter and blue for Cole because they wouldn't drink it in any other color cup. "Here, but remember this is the last—" He looked to the ceiling for strength. "Boys, just eat your cereal."

Greg sat back down at the kitchen table and opened the sports section while the boys sloshed milk and cereal with their spoons. He glanced over at them and didn't say anything when he saw more cereal on the table than was going in their mouths. He made a mental note to get a plastic tablecloth and thought about calling Heather to pick one up but decided he'd do it later. He ignored the boy's giggling when they started having a war with their spoons. Greg just sat back, drank his coffee, and decided to clean up the mess later.

"Daddy, can we play at the park today?"

"Not today, Cole. It's going to rain." Greg looked over toward the kitchen window to see if the rain had started.

Hunter and Cole moaned. "Why?" they said in unison.

"It's going to rain," Greg repeated. "And it's cold."

"But why?" Cole griped.

"Because, if we play outside, you'll get sick," Greg said as he turned the pages of the newspaper.

The boys looked at each other. "Let's go to Chuck E. Cheese!"

Greg flipped another page. "Not today, but how about we build stuff with your Legos or play with your cars and trucks. How does that sound?"

The boys glanced at each other and then each got up and ran to collect their toys. Greg was still drinking coffee as his two boys sat on the floor playing with their trains, cars, and trucks. They also had a few toy musical instruments, blocks, and games. They were still in their pajamas even though Heather had asked Greg to get them dressed by ten o'clock. It was close to eleven, but it was a dreary Sunday and the cold rain was now coming down in sheets. Greg looked out the window, thinking it was the perfect day to sit next to a roaring fire and snuggle with the one you love. *With Kate. His Kate.* He wondered if she was doing okay and thought maybe he should call her and try to mend their friendship. There wasn't a day that went by since August that he hadn't thought of her and wished things could be different. Sometimes he woke up in the middle of the night thinking he heard her voice. He would quietly go into the closet, pull out the photo box, and find her picture tucked away in a little envelope. His fingers would softly trace the curve of her face and her smile. He couldn't fathom how he never once told her he loved her. Of course he loved her, but not everyone can have what they want; not everyone gets the happy ending. He shook his head, folded up the newspaper, and joined his kids on the floor.

"Here, Daddy." Cole stood up, grinning from ear to ear as he handed his father his favorite little blue truck.

"Thanks, buddy." He scooped up Cole and hugged him tight. Hunter walked over and put his little arm around his dad, and Greg wrapped his arms around both boys and held them for as long as they allowed it. When they suddenly squirmed away, Greg readjusted himself to be more comfortable.

"I don't wanna play cars anymore!" Cole shouted.

"Me neither!"

"Okay, how about Legos?" Greg suggested.

The two little boys looked at each other with wrinkled noses.

"Okay, how about you guys watch Sprout for a little while?"

The boys raced to the TV with Greg trailing close behind. Once the familiar Caillou theme song began, Greg quickly cleaned up the spilled milk, put the dishes in the sink, and sat back down with another cup of coffee, hoping for at least fifteen minutes of peace and quiet. That is exactly what he got, and when the fifteen minutes were up, the boys started chasing each other around the house.

"Sit down and I'll read you a story. I have your favorite here, *Harry the Dirty Dog*."

The boys looked at each other and kept running. "Mommy read it yesterday."

"How about *Curious George*?"

"No!"

"You love *Memoirs of a Goldfish*. Let's read that."

The boys stopped in their tracks and looked at their dad. "No!" they screamed and started chasing each other again through the living room and kitchen, under chairs and over the coffee table.

"Okay, how about painting or playing with Play-Doh?"

Suddenly the boys stopped and smiled. "Yay! Painting," they yelled in unison.

Cole and Hunter loved to paint, and Greg reasoned it was because they liked to make a mess. But they were three-year-olds, and that is what three-year-olds were supposed to do. They were supposed to get into everything. It was a phase, and Greg knew it would eventually pass. Soon they would grow up and learn to clean up after themselves. He smiled, shaking his head at the thought.

"Okay. But first, let's go put on your play clothes so Mommy doesn't get upset when you get paint all over."

The two boys took off for their room with Greg right on their tail. Greg pulled out each of the boy's paint-stained play clothes while the boys started ripping off their pajamas. Greg handed each one their sweatpants and sweatshirts. Greg smiled at them in their rainbow-colored clothes with so much paint on them that you could no longer tell the original fabric color. They looked cute: messy little boys, but irresistibly adorable. He picked up their pajamas from the floor and folded them, placing them back on their beds. They liked to finger paint, much more than Heather or Greg or even Rocky liked it. Greg then changed quickly into his own paint-stained sweatshirt and an old pair of jeans.

The boys stampeded to the kitchen where Greg grabbed the stack of old newspapers and laid them out to cover the kitchen table. He pulled the construction paper from the drawer and set it on the newspaper. "Okay, what are you going to paint today?"

"An airplane!" Hunter screamed.

"No! I want to make an airplane!" Cole shouted.

"You can both make airplanes if you want. Remember to use your *inside* voice." Greg turned around to grab a roll of paper towels and heard an ear-piercing scream.

"Ow! Daddy! Hunter hit me!" Cole started to cry, and Greg had to bite his lip not to laugh. The boys reminded him of him and his brothers when they were kids.

"Hunter Damon Janera, stop hitting your brother. You know there is no hitting in this house."

"But he's taking the airplane."

"I told you, you can both paint an airplane."

"No! I want to paint a dog," Cole screamed.

"Okay, a dog like Rocky? That's a good idea."

"Now I want to paint a train," Hunter yelled.

"Okay, okay. Please use your *inside* voice. You can both paint whatever you want. Sit here and be good while I get the paints. No hitting or you're both going to get a time-out."

Greg found the paints in the arts-and-crafts container. He glanced at the clock and figured he had a good five hours to go before Heather got home. No problem.

Once he came back, he placed the paints in front of each child and let the boys go to town. In a matter of minutes, they had paint on their clothes, their hands, their faces. Even their short brown hair now looked like a clown's wig, and Rocky was polka-dotted and striped in red, green, and blue. At least it was washable paint, and why not let them have fun? They were two rambunctious boys after all, stuck inside on a rainy Sunday. He would have to come up with a physical activity after lunch because they needed to be let loose and use up all their energy before Heather got home. He just hoped this would distract them from their Halloween candy. Greg helped each child paint an airplane, dog and train, and once they were finished, he set them aside to dry. Afterwards he would hang them on the refrigerator with alphabet magnets. Greg then got the boys in the tub and gave them a bath, washing away all traces of paint. The water turned a rainbow of colors, and when he drained it, it left pale colored rings around the tub. For a second it reminded him of the different colors in Kate's mood ring. With that thought, he left the tub, deciding he would clean it up later. Once he got the boys in clean clothes and combed their hair, he gave Rocky a quick bath as the boys looked on, giggling at their multicolored dog. Greg fed the boys chicken nuggets and leftover macaroni and cheese for lunch, and set them down to watch *Roary the Racing Car* on Sprout.

Greg cracked his neck from side to side before he began cleaning up the paint-covered newspapers. He folded them up and threw them back in a cardboard box for recycling. He had one more layer of newspapers to throw in the box, and since this was the bottom layer, there wasn't too much paint on it. He slowly scooped up the papers, folding them as he went, and without warning, Kate's photo was staring back at him. Surprisingly, there was no paint on the article. When he saw it, he dropped the papers, his mouth went dry, and the blood drained from his face. His eyes couldn't comprehend what he was seeing, and he could only make out certain words which would go on to haunt him for the rest of his life. He stared at her photo and then the headline. He felt his blood pressure drop, his head went light, and he saw spots when he blinked. His hands trembled and then turned clammy as he held the paper while tears started to form and then slowly roll down his cheeks.

Philadelphia ... Fatal
Katherine Shuster ... blinding rain ... Schuylkill ... overturned ... deer ... police ... totaled ... paramedics ... scene ... dead ...

His eyes were transfixed to the date of the accident: October twenty-fifth. Greg immediately thought back to last Sunday when he and Heather took the kids to the pumpkin patch. He felt a knot of shame and regret in his stomach because he was having fun on the day she died. He looked at the end of the article and saw Kate's funeral was scheduled for Monday, November second. Tomorrow.

Greg used to think that the worst thing he could see in the paper regarding Kate was her listing in the engagement section. Her photo, taken with a doting fiancé with his arm around her, both of them smiling, blissfully happy, optimistically looking forward to their new life together. Or Kate, featured in the wedding section in a beautiful white gown next to her equally handsome groom, their arms around each other proclaiming their love. He would have to read every detail of how the happy couple met, how her mom cried during their vows, the romantic luxurious honeymoon on an exotic island and the song that they first danced to as husband and wife. Despite the fact that he wanted this for her, he knew it would break his heart to see Kate with another man. But he also knew the mature side of him would have to be happy for her, even though he was the one who should have been her husband. He would later call her with his congratulations, as painful as that would be. He would do it because it was the right thing to do. But never in all his life did he think he would open the newspaper to find her photo in an article about her tragic death.

Greg wiped at his face, shaking, clutching the article in his hands when Cole and Hunter came running back into the kitchen. "Daddy, Daddy!" they yelled. "The rain stopped. Take us to the playground!"

Greg sat on the floor, tears rolling down his cheeks while Cole and Hunter hung on him like he was a jungle gym. "Daddy's sick." Greg swallowed and hugged his boys tighter than he ever did before. "If you promise to play quietly until Mommy comes home, you can each have three pieces of candy. Just don't tell your mother."

CHAPTER 24

A few weeks after Kate's funeral, Ellen Shuster and Jennifer went to retrieve Kate's belongings from her apartment. Her landlord told them to take their time; he too was upset about the loss of Kate and he wasn't going to try to rent the apartment until after the holidays. *Difficult* didn't begin to describe what it was like to have to clean out your only daughter's apartment because she was never coming home. *Heart-wrenching* was more like it—absolutely the worst nightmare of a mother's life. But Ellen decided to take care of the apartment now because the longer she waited, the more painful it would be. She found Halloween decorations and unopened bags of candy set neatly by a giant plastic pumpkin, novels on her coffee table with bookmarks sticking out, clean laundry in a basket waiting to be put away, piles of mail shoved under her door, overturned coffee mugs in her dish drainer, holiday catalogs with tiny post in notes peeking out on some of the pages, a Redbox movie that was more than a month overdue. Everything in its proper place, simply waiting for Kate to come home and pick up where she'd left off.

Why couldn't she have made it home that night, safe and sound? Why did that deer have to run out on the highway right in front of her car? Why did there have to be monsoon rain? Why couldn't she have just stayed at her mom's until Monday morning? She could have called in to work, letting them know she'd be late if the morning traffic was bad. Ellen winced, thinking of the phrase, "Better late than never." She would carry these questions to her grave. She would never know why this had to happen to her daughter, her baby, the person she loved more than anyone else in the entire world. Everyone told her it was a terrible, tragic accident and not anyone's fault. Ellen shook her head at those people and told them she simply could not accept this. There's always a reason. There has to be a reason, if only for her daughter not to have died in vain.

"I can't imagine how difficult this is for you," Jennifer said. "If you want me to handle this, I can bring her things to your house and ..."

"Thank you, Jennifer, but I need to do this. For Kate. I love my daughter so much ... I just don't know ..." Ellen choked back tears.

Jen was quiet for a moment and handed Ellen a tissue. "Okay, but if you change your mind, you know I would do this for you. In a heartbeat."

Ellen sniffled and wiped her eyes and nose. She brushed her auburn curls away from her face. "I will, Jennifer. Thank you for being such a good friend. Kate loved you, and I know you loved her ... still love her."

"I'll always love Kate, and I'll always miss her. I don't know what I'm going to do without her." A few tears trickled down her face. "There will always be a huge hole in my heart, in my life, without Kate."

Ellen embraced her. They hugged while tears ran down both of their cheeks. "We need to be strong, Jennifer. For Kate. It's what she would have wanted. We need to still make her proud of us, okay?"

"Okay." Jennifer took a deep breath. "I can do that for her." She grabbed a couple of tissues, handed one to Ellen, and then wiped her own eyes.

Ellen crumpled the tissue in her hand and shook her head. "Okay. This isn't going to be any easier in an hour or tomorrow or next week, so let's start now, and whenever you need a break, you just let me know."

Ellen went to the kitchen, taking two empty boxes and a few old newspapers with her. She opened the cabinets and began wrapping dishes and mugs in newspaper and putting them in the boxes one by one. In one drawer she found the floral pink insulated oven mitts and apron that she gave Kate over five years ago when she first moved in. Ellen picked up the mitts and held them tight. Her hands shook as she held them and she had to sit down at the table. Her daughter died, and with that a part of her died as well. She would never be the same; there would be sadness in her heart for the rest of her life. Her daughter was too young. No one should ever have to bury their child. How could God let this happen to her baby, her pride and joy? How do people go on after losing a child? She realized there was probably no answer to that question. A few friends had suggested counseling or joining a grief support group. It was too raw to think about that. She knew she would grieve her daughter for the rest of her life, support group or not.

She put the oven mitts in the box and then slowly wrapped glasses and silverware, trying to keep her mind focused on the task at hand. After she emptied a couple of cabinets and drawers, she went into the living room and sat on the couch. On the coffee table, she found a small photo album and held it tight in her hands.

Opening it with caution, she found the first photo to be of Kate in her cap and gown on the grounds of West Chester University. She smiled, remembering how proud her daughter was to earn her college diploma. Ellen closed her eyes and heard Kate say, "Now I'm going to conquer the world, Mom." Ellen turned the page and saw a picture of Kate and Jen as teenagers acting goofy for the camera. She was glad her daughter had had Jennifer as a best friend. The next photo showed Kate at one of her ballet recitals when she was about six. Ellen cherished those memories of Kate as a little ballerina, dancing and twirling on the stage. She looked away and noticed it was windy outside, bare tree branches being pulled by the wind under an overcast sky. She pulled a blanket from the top of the couch and wrapped it around her, breathing in the scent of her daughter. She flipped another page in the album to find a photo of herself holding Kate when she was just a baby. She stopped, overcome with emotion. Her daughter would never know this kind of joy. She would never fall in love with a man who loved her for being the wonderful woman she was. She would never be a bride, walking down the aisle amid family and friends. She would never experience the bliss of being on a honeymoon. Kate would never know the pure joy of holding her child in her arms for the very first time. She would never experience all that life has to offer and as her mother; this was the hardest part for Ellen to accept. She wiped new tears from her cheeks. She shook her head, not wanting to believe she was really gone. Her heart was broken beyond repair. She would never see her daughter again.

Jen was busy packing up Kate's bathroom and linen closet. The tears came and went as she packed up the towels and sheets, shampoos and soaps. Her hair dryer had still been plugged in and her makeup sat on the counter as if she had just used it. Jen glanced out the window, remembering how she and Kate would paint each other's nails, apply mud masks, and soak their elbows in lemons when they were teenagers. She recalled the day when they were eight and agreed to be each other's maid of honor. She remembered endless shopping trips to the mall and marathon phone conversations. Unlimited friendship

206 Sue Krawitz

and love. She missed her best friend more than words could describe. How would she go on without Kate by her side?

After Ellen finished looking at the photos, she walked into Kate's bedroom not knowing how she should begin. There were three empty boxes on the floor and a suitcase from Kate's closet. She scanned the room. Clothes. Shoes. Jewelry. Knickknacks. Bedding. Stuffed animals. Pictures. She knew this had to be done, so she opened the suitcase and started folding clothes from Kate's dresser, putting them in one by one. Kate's favorite jeans, her beloved West Chester University sweatshirt, random shorts and shirts. She opened the closet and found suits, skirts, and dresses, all freshly dry cleaned and ready for her to wear to work. There were fun tops and sweaters ready for Kate to wear on a date. On the floor were dress shoes and heels, chunky boots and sneakers. She remembered how much Kate loved her new job and was looking forward to going on the upcoming business trip to Orlando—a trip that now would never happen. Ellen gently closed the closet door and sat on her daughter's bed. She picked up a bottle of perfume on Kate's night table and held it tightly in her hands. She breathed in the fragrance and then set it back down. She turned and picked up a soft white polar bear with little black eyes. Was it her imagination or was the bear smiling at her? She held the bear for a minute, set it back down, and then absently opened the night table drawer and pulled out a necklace she remembered Kate loved to wear. She held it in her hands: a thin silver chain with heart design pendant that emanated the word love. There was also a small bottle of hand lotion, lip balm, some old birthday cards, and stationery. She remembered buying the stationary for Kate when she moved to Philadelphia so she would write letters to her. Ellen was old fashioned, and while she knew they would visit, e-mail, text, and talk on the phone, she looked forward to getting a letter in the mail every so often. And Kate did not disappoint her. Ellen received a letter every few months and she smiled thinking of all the letters stored in a keepsake box at home. She was thankful even more now for those letters that she could read anytime she wanted. She picked up the box of stationery and a white envelope slipped out, falling to the floor. Ellen bent down to pick it up and almost threw it away, but then realized it was sealed and felt like it had a couple of pages inside. She turned it over in her hands and looked at the name on the front. It was one she didn't recognize and tried to remember if Kate ever mentioned that name. She hadn't, Ellen Shuster was sure of that. She looked at her daughter's dresser and scanned the framed pictures that sat on top. There was no one she didn't recognize in those treasured pictures of family and friends. *But who was Greg?*

"Jennifer, dear, could you come here for a minute?"

Jen appeared in the doorway of Kate's bedroom holding one of Kate's teddy bear's that she'd had since she was a little girl.

Ellen stared at the envelope, her hands with a firm grip, and then looked up at Jen. "Who's Greg?"

Jen stood without reaction as she watched Mrs. Shuster turn the envelope over and over in her hands. She traced Greg's name with her finger, awaiting a response from Jen. Jen slowly stepped in the room and sat beside Ellen on the bed. She put her hand on Ellen's shoulder. "Let's go into the living room. I'll make you tea and tell you the whole story."

CHAPTER 25

Greg walked into the little coffee shop near Jen's apartment in Manayunk. He arrived first, and when he didn't see her, he took a seat at the last empty table near the front window. The café was crowded with people, most with shopping bags beside them on the floor. There was also a group of people toward the back who seemed to be in a heated yet friendly discussion for a book group. A solo guitarist playing light rock music sat in the front, his wavy brown hair down to his shoulders. Greg wasn't sure why Jennifer had called him and racked his brain all day thinking of different scenarios. Maybe Kate had told her something personal that she felt Greg deserved to know. Or maybe she wanted to yell at him for hurting her best friend the way he did, and that Kate said she would never forgive him. And now that Kate was gone, he would have to live with the remorse for the rest of his life. He hoped this wasn't the reason, and pushed the thoughts out of his head. As he sat in the coffee shop, he couldn't concentrate between the music and his thoughts about Kate, so he ordered a coffee and stared out the large window as crowds of shoppers walked by. Main Street was in full swing for the holidays. Even though it was pitch dark outside, lights lit up the shops and restaurants while white twinkling Christmas lights outlined the row of trees, making their branches glow in the night. He cringed looking at the cheerful people; they were not grieving over the death of someone they loved.

Greg's pain from the loss of Kate was apparent in every aspect of his life. Coworkers had been asking him what was wrong for weeks, but all he could manage to say was that there was a death in his family. His colleagues had patted him on the back and offered to do anything they could to help, but he didn't want to get too personal, especially about Kate. Heather noticed a sadness and lethargic tone in his behavior, but after a week of trying to convince him to talk and getting nowhere, she decided to give it a rest and figured he would eventually tell her what was wrong. Greg wasn't ready to talk to anyone, not even Tom, who offered to listen day or night whenever he was ready. Even though he knew it wasn't healthy, he kept his feelings and pain bottled up. What he and Kate shared had been between them, and not too many people knew about it, except for Tom and Jennifer. However, in order to get everyone off his back, he started putting up a good front, for himself and his family. His boys needed him, and so did Heather. He couldn't simply vanish from the realities of life until his heart healed, if it ever healed.

But more than anything, he couldn't bear the pain he caused Kate in August. He would never forget how she cried and told him he was making a mistake. He would remember her words until he died. *"What we have is rare and beautiful. Some people search their entire life for this kind of passion, this love. Someday you're going to realize it, and I hope it won't be too late."* Greg realized it now; he knew he would never find this kind of love with anyone else. But at the time, he couldn't say the words. He had stood there while she poured her heart out and didn't even give a response. He had lied to her face that he never loved her, that what they shared had meant nothing. He would regret that for the rest of his life.

"Hi, Greg." Jennifer had walked in without him noticing and startled him to life. She took off her jacket and rubbed her arms. "It's getting cold, isn't it?"

He looked up at her and stood. "Hi, Jen. It's really feeling like winter now. I guess we're in for a long one."

"I hope not." She peeked at Greg's coffee. "Are you okay or can I get you another one?"

"No, I'm fine. But please, let me get one for you. What would you like?"

"Thanks, just a regular coffee is fine."

"Okay, I'll be right back."

Jennifer sat down while Greg went to the counter. She pulled the letter out of her bag and placed it on her lap, hoping whatever it said wouldn't be too hard on him. She knew how much Kate loved him and how devastated she was at the end.

Greg placed a steaming mug in front of Jen along with a tiny pitcher of milk.

"Thank you." Jen added some sugar and milk and gave it a quick stir. She wrapped her hands around the cup and let the warmth seep into her skin.

"That's Kate's." Greg gazed to Jen's right ring finger as he stared at the oval stone set on the thin silver band. Unmistakably, it was Kate's mood ring.

"She was wearing it, you know, when ..." She struggled to say the words. "She had it on the day of the accident." Jen paused. "But somehow it came through without a scratch, and her mom wanted me to have it. I can't believe it didn't get crushed, but Kate always told me it had magical powers."

The stone was midnight black. He looked closer, as if he was looking for a sign of life.

"I don't remember it ever being pure black before August. It hasn't changed color since ..." Jennifer trailed off. Greg suddenly realized it turned black on the day he broke her heart. She shook her head. "I would give anything for this ring to have saved her."

Greg didn't say anything right away, apparently lost in thought. "Me too." He'd give anything for Kate to come back, alive and well. He wouldn't make the same mistake twice; he would immediately tell her how much he loved her, that he couldn't live without her, and beg her forgiveness. He thought about what could have saved her. Maybe if the deer did not jet out on the highway? Or if the roads were dry instead of being flooded? She should not have been out on the roads; she should have been home or should have stayed the extra night at her mom's instead of trying to drive back to the city in the middle of a storm.

"I'm so sorry you had to find out the way you did. It must have been awful," Jennifer said.

"It was. I just, I couldn't believe it." Greg shook his head slightly.

"Her Facebook page was filled with messages; I'm surprised you didn't see that before the paper."

"After August, after I last saw her, I stopped going on Facebook. I just couldn't look at it anymore. I figured she unfriended me anyway and assumed she would have blocked me."

Jen nodded. "I would have called sooner, but I didn't get your number until her mom gave me Kate's cell, and that wasn't until the night before her funeral. I can't believe a few months ago, Kate and I were talking about taking a vacation this winter; actually it was more me trying to convince her to come with me. And now here I am, talking about her funeral. I wish I could go to sleep and wake up and Kate would be here, happy and healthy."

"It must have been horrible for Kate. I hope she wasn't in pain when ..." Greg looked away, the words painful in his own ears.

"I don't think she was from what the reports said. I know it would have meant a lot to her that you came to her funeral. She really loved you, you know?"

Greg put his hand on the back of his neck and met Jen's eyes. "I cared about her more than she'll ever know." He picked up his coffee and put it back down without drinking.

They were both quiet for a moment. Jen tucked her hair behind her ear. "So, I bet you're wondering why I asked you to meet me."

"I wasn't sure if you just wanted to talk or if there was something Kate said that you wanted to tell me."

"Kate's mom and I were cleaning out her apartment and we found something. Actually her mom found something that you should have."

Greg sat up in his chair a little straighter and raised his eyebrows.

Jen placed the letter on the table in front of him. "She must have written this to you. It was in her night table and ..."

Greg looked at the envelope and saw his name written in script. It was Kate's handwriting, and for a moment, he felt as though she were still here. He got a slight chill in his spine. "Oh. Do you know when she wrote it?"

"I have no idea. We didn't open it, and she never mentioned it to me."

"What did her mom say? What did she ask?"

Jen took a sip of coffee. "Well, you know Kate never mentioned you, right?"

Greg nodded.

"She asked me who you were and when I saw the look on her face while she was holding the envelope, I knew I had to tell her the whole story. Well, almost everything. Kate was my best friend, and we talked about everything. I'm sorry I made her break her pact to you, but when she came back from Chicago, she was like a different person, and I just had to know what happened. But I didn't tell her mom about Chicago. I think some things are better left unsaid."

Greg felt himself blush. "You two were lucky to have each other. I'm glad she had you as her best friend."

"I was lucky to have her. I don't know what I'm going to do without her."

Greg reached across the table and put his hand on Jen's arm. "I'll never forgive myself for what happened, Jen. I hurt her so much; I'll regret it for the rest of my life." He shook his head. "I never told her how I felt, how I really felt, and worse than that, I lied to her when she needed me the most. I just lied, straight to her face ..." Greg trailed off and looked out the window. He turned back and looked directly into Jen's eyes. "I loved her, Jen. I fell in love with her, from the beginning." He shook his head. "If I could change what happened in August, I would. I should have told her. I was such a coward for feeling I would hurt her more if I said the words, but I know she just wanted to hear them come out of my mouth. I let her down for no reason, and I will always carry that regret. It will always be inside me. No matter how much time passes, the love I feel for her will never die."

"Greg, it's okay. Deep down in her heart, I think she knew how you felt. Despite what happened in August, I think she knew you loved her. I really believe that." Jen pushed her coffee mug to the side, and Kate's mood ring caught her eye. "Oh my God! Look." She held out her hand, and the two of them watched the black immediately turn to pink and then to teal before settling on bright indigo blue with specks of violet. "Kate's favorite color," they said simultaneously.

They sat lost in thought for a minute. "It's like she's here, watching us, knowing I love her ... that I would do anything to change what happened. I would do anything to make things right." Greg couldn't take his eyes off the ring, but when he looked up at Jen, she was smiling.

"I think she is. She's giving us a sign that it's okay, that she forgives you. She wants you to be happy," Jen said. They sat for a few minutes, realizing that Kate would always be with them and they with her. They relaxed a bit, comforted by this revelation.

Greg broke the silence when he picked up the envelope and held it in his hands. "Thank you for bringing this. It means more than I can tell you."

"You're welcome. She would have wanted you to have it."

"Will you be okay? If you ever need to talk, you can call or text me. Day or night," Greg offered.

"Thank you. I will. You do the same, okay?"

"Yes, I will. Thank you."

Greg gave Jennifer a hug good-bye and held the envelope tightly in his hand as he walked back to his car. As he drove back downtown, he thought of all the different things she could have written. She hated him for hurting her and would never forgive him. She wanted to salvage their friendship. She hoped that someday things would work out and they would be together. Greg flipped through the radio stations as he made his way down West River Drive and remembered that last day they were together in August. He would regret that day for the rest of his life.

He got into the city and decided to read Kate's letter at Rittenhouse Square where they'd met. Even though it was dark and cold, there was no other place where he could consciously read a letter that she had written him. He parked, zippered up his jacket, and threw on a hat. He walked over to the park and smiled when he saw the exact spot where he and Kate sat together over four years earlier. He kept walking until he found a bench near a lamppost. He slowly opened the envelope to find two pages tucked inside.

September 19, 2015

Dear Greg,

It is the most beautiful day, and I am sitting at the exact location where we met. I remember that day as if it were yesterday: the easy conversation, the innocent flirting. I felt an instant, undeniable connection with you and knew you would have a profound effect on my life. I was so full of hope of the man who stood before me with his adorable dog by his side. My heart beat faster as the day went on and we began to learn about each other. As I look at the bright sky and see the tree branches and leaves dancing in the breeze, I see so many different people: walking, talking, and holding hands. I see children with wonder in their eyes as they play with siblings and their parents. I'm still amazed that I've never run into you here with your own boys.

When you ended our friendship last month, I realized something. The person who did that was clearly not you. He was not the Greg I came to know and love. He was not the Greg who was always so sweet and kind, sexy and funny. It was most definitely not the Greg who shared the most romantic night of my life. This person was someone else. He was mean and hurtful. He made tears slide down my cheeks for weeks. I don't know where he came from, but he was not you. At least I realize that now. It would destroy me if that person who stood in front me with those harsh words was really you.

I know your boys are most important. Of course they are. They are your children and they deserve to come first. I would honestly be worried if they weren't at the top of your list. I would never try to take a father away from his children. I know they need a father who is there for them, one hundred percent. Nothing less is acceptable. You are their hero. They depend on you, not only for basic needs but to be there for them in all aspects of their lives. You are teaching them every day so they grow up to be responsible, productive, caring members of society. I admire you and love you even more for that.

However, speaking as the woman who loves you, who is in love with you unconditionally with my whole heart, I will always wish we had a real chance. I imagine what our life could have been like, and it brings tears to my eyes, yet a smile to my face. I know how amazing we could have been together, and this breaks my heart. I love you with every ounce of my being and know without any doubt that you are the one for me. Even though you assured me we will never be together, I take comfort in knowing I found you. Some people search their entire life for a love this powerful. My body aches to be with you, my lips crave yours, and my mind hungers for the connection we share. Even if we never speak again, I will die knowing that I found my soul mate here on earth. I found you and I loved you, but tragically, it could never be.

My soul will always hold the very special memories of our beautiful night together in Chicago. It was so comforting to fall asleep in your arms, my head resting on your chest while I listened to the rhythm of your heartbeat. I treasure every second of that night. Your soft yet passionate kisses, the way your eyes looked deep into my soul, the incredible feeling when our bodies became one. Your actions that night, the way we made love and the way you held me in your arms, told me you love me. At least that is what I choose to believe. It is less painful to believe you want to be with me as much as I want to be with you. My mind cannot bear to believe anything less.

You have always done the right thing, made the right choice, came to the right decision, except for this decision to end our friendship. But even now that we are no longer talking, I can never be angry with you. I love you unconditionally. You are the man I was supposed to share my life with, have children with, and grow old with. You are the man who was supposed to be my best friend, confidante, and lover. When I go to sleep at night, these are my dreams, coming to life while I'm in a different realm. I wake up smiling, wondering if you have ever had this dream of our secret life together. I like to believe that everyone comes back after they die, so maybe we will be together in our next life. I hope you will wait for me, because I will without a doubt be waiting for you.

In our next life, I dream that we wake up in each other's arms on Christmas morning as our children come running in, jump on our bed, and plead to open their presents. We take vacations to the exotic places we talked about—Italy, the African Safari, and Hawaii—exploring all of the magnificent attractions. On winter nights, we curl up on the couch next to a roaring fire and watch a movie together, playfully kissing and sharing popcorn. In the summers, we dance under the stars at Rittenhouse Square, as if no one exists but the two of us. Our hearts are united, our fingers are intertwined, our ears delight in the sound of each other's voices. We kiss first thing in the morning and the very last thing at night. In my dreams, we stand up in front of our family and friends, declaring our love, reading our vows, and kissing for the first time as husband and wife. For now, I can only hold onto these dreams, but rest assured, I will be waiting for you to make them come true in our next lifetime.

You made the right choice to stay with Heather and your boys. You are a good guy, Greg Janera, one of the few left. Don't let anyone tell you any different. Never think anything less.

Please know that while I respect your decision, it is near impossible to truly believe we will never talk again. I treasure the bond we share, and I sincerely hope that someday you will have a change of heart. If that day comes, I will be here for you. I love you from the bottom of my heart and always will.

Love,
Kate

Greg sat hypnotized on the bench, tears flowing down his cheeks, the pages firmly in his hand. He stared out at the empty park and wished she was here so he could hold her in his arms and tell her the truth. He would say all the things he should have told her in life. He would confess his true feelings: that he loved her, that he has been in love with her since the day they met. He would tell her she was right; it had been a horrible mistake to end their friendship. Greg would plead how sorry he was for hurting her, for lying to her. He'd beg for a second chance. He would try to make their relationship work. Somehow. Someway. If only she was still alive, maybe everything she wrote could have come true. Couldn't love conquer all?

He sat for several minutes, wiping away the tears and staring at the park. He then folded her letter, placed it back in the envelope, and put it in his pocket. Greg stood up and aimlessly started walking back toward the spot where they'd met.

He wiped away more tears that had seeped down his face. When he reached the spot, his mind flashed back to their first hellos, Rocky licking her toes, the two of them sharing their first iced teas. This is where it began, as innocent as it was in the beginning, to become something so profound and so strong that Greg couldn't put it into words. He kneeled on the ground, his eyes transfixed on the sky. *Toward heaven. Toward His Kate.* He whispered a prayer and a promise to her. He would never forget her. He would always love her. Someday he would see her again.

EPILOGUE

Greg sat eerily immobile. However, his mind whirred with thoughts of what to say. They were zooming through his head like heat lightning illuminating a dark summer sky. He put his hands on the ground to steady himself. Greg rose slowly, wiping away fresh snow from his jeans, brushing his hands together to free them of snow and dirt. Ellen Shuster held her gaze on him for a few seconds, dabbing at her eyes with bunched up tissues before glancing toward Kate's headstone.

She had the same eyes that he knew so well, the same eyes he had looked into hundreds of times: chocolate brown with flecks of amber that glittered in the sunlight and shimmered in the moonlight. Eyes with the uncanny ability to reveal thoughts and emotions. Eyes that at one time had looked deep into his soul to uncover thoughts that were never spoken aloud. Sadly, Greg would only see these eyes in photographs now.

He cleared his throat and took a step toward Kate's mother. "Hi, Mrs. Shuster."

Ellen put the tissues in her pocket. She moved the bouquet of flowers to her other hand. "It's nice to meet you, Greg, although not under these circumstances. Jennifer told me a lot about you. And please, it's Ellen."

"I wish we were meeting under different circumstances too." He looked toward Kate's headstone. "Jennifer told me about your conversation. I can't express how sorry I am about Kate. About everything. I just—"

"It's okay. I know." She took one step closer to Greg.

They were both quiet for a moment as the snow suddenly tapered off. The winter chill lingered in the air, and Greg nervously rubbed his hands together and then cupped them over his mouth and blew gently into his palms.

He shook his head. "I'm so sorry that she died in such a horrible way. I should have been there for her, to protect her. I love her so much. I am so sorry she'll never know; she'll never know how I really feel."

Ellen looked at Greg and saw what her daughter had seen in him: a tender, loving young man who would never intentionally hurt anyone. The type of man who always did the right thing. A man who loved her daughter and who her daughter had loved in return. "Greg, there are some things I need to tell you." Greg looked at her as if wanting to ask a question, but said nothing.

"I want to thank you for being the man my daughter fell in love with. I can see what she saw in you." Ellen glanced toward the sky. "When she died, a piece of me died with her. My heart broke, and ever since, I've been in utterly unbearable pain. She was taken away from me without warning for absolutely no reason. But I also had unbearable grief because I thought she'd never experienced the wonderful feeling of falling in love. Ironically, she never told me about you even though we were very close." Ellen hesitated for a moment.

"When Jennifer told me about when you two met, I thought back to that time and remember noticing a difference in her. She seemed so happy, like everything in her world was perfect. Then there were dark days that followed, and even though I asked her what was wrong, she never said anything more than things were not going the way she wanted. I wish she had confided in me because I could have helped her deal with the pain. But finding love without getting hurt in some way is extremely rare, and most people risk something when they love another person, as she did, with her whole heart. Jennifer told me what happened, and at first I was angry at you for breaking her heart. But then she told me about Heather and your boys, and I need to tell you that you did the right thing by staying with them. I don't know if Kate ever told you, but her father left us when Kate was a little girl. He just decided one day he didn't want to be a dad or husband anymore and that was it. Every birthday and every Christmas until she was sixteen, all she wanted was for her dad to come back. He used to send me sporadic checks—maybe two a year. But never so much as a birthday card or Christmas present to his only daughter." Ellen shook her head. "He just never came back, at least not until it was too late. I tracked him down from an old address, and he came to her funeral. He said he'll always carry a lifetime of regrets, and I can never forgive him for not being the father that Kate deserved. I always suspected she felt it was her fault that he left, that he didn't love her enough. Just knowing she felt that way breaks my heart."

"It's terrible to break someone's heart, but it is worse to walk out on your family, your spouse, your children. You are a respectable young man, and I see why she chose you. And I feel more at peace knowing about you. As difficult as this is, to lose my only child, something I'll never fully heal from, I take comfort in knowing that she fell in love with a good and decent young man. You."

Greg's eyes filled with tears as he listened to Kate's mother. He wiped his face with the back of his hand and then looked directly at Ellen Shuster. "I loved her so much. I fell in love with her from the first day we met and wanted to be with her more than I've ever wanted anything. But my twins, I couldn't leave them. I know Kate and I were meant to be together, but we just met at the wrong time." Greg paused. "Maybe in our next lifetime, Kate and I will find each other." He gave a half smile. "I'll know it's her because it'll feel like coming home."

"Greg, please know that you did the right thing. It wasn't your time with Kate, but you're right … maybe in your next lifetime. I believe that we're all given another chance at life, especially now. I believe that I will see my daughter again. I have to. For now, you have to be strong for your family. They need you, and you have to concentrate your energy on them. Of course you are going to mourn Kate, but you need to look ahead to your future too."

"Thank you, Ellen. I know why Kate was so wonderful. She had you."

"Thank you." Ellen bowed her head and then looked back at Greg. "Can you give me a minute with her?"

"Of course." Greg stepped away as Ellen walked toward her daughter's grave. He turned his back to give her privacy and looked out into the deepening night air. There were no stars in the sky, but he could feel Kate's presence shining down on him from heaven. He turned slightly and saw Ellen crouched down, her coat lying like a blanket over the snow-covered grass. He could make out only a faint whisper. She had placed the bouquet of flowers down, and he noticed her hand on Kate's headstone. He turned away again to give Ellen the time she needed with her daughter.

Several minutes later, she stood up and turned to Greg. "I'm going to let you be with her now, to tell her what you need to."

"Thank you. I want you to know that I'm going to miss her for the rest of my life, that I will always love her."

"I'll always love and miss her too. Take care of yourself, Greg. I'll never forget you."

Greg leaned over and gave Ellen a hug. They embraced with tears falling onto each other's coats. Then she walked away without another word.

Greg was transfixed for several seconds as he watched her walk away. The vision of what Kate might have looked like in twenty-five years was fading farther and farther away from him until he could no longer see her. But he knew Kate's presence and memory would always be in his heart. Greg slowly walked back over to Kate's grave and he kneeled down. He took the letter from his jacket pocket and opened it. He smiled at her photo and looked to the sky. Toward heaven. Toward His Kate.

My dearest Kate,

As I sit down to write you this letter, I am at a loss. I know what I want to tell you, what I need to tell you. For the past two hours, I have reflected on all of our memories, sifting through the moments as if they were grains of sand falling through an hourglass. Treasured memories. Unique unspoiled seashells. Rare hidden gems. Moments that stand still in time. I know that you can hear my words in heaven as you watch over your family and friends, all the people you love.

I fell for you right from the start, from the moment we met at Rittenhouse Square. I was taken away by your beauty, your sense of humor, your kindness, your loving nature. As I got to know you through conversations and dating and simply spending time with you, I fell deeper than I ever thought possible. I grew to love you, a love that came from deep within my heart. I'll always regret that I didn't come out and say the words "I love you." Three little words that mean more than any other three words strung together in the English language. I can't apologize enough for that. The words always seemed to be on the tip of my tongue, but for one reason or another, never made it out. I would have given anything to have seen the glowing smile that would have appeared on your face if I had said, "I love you." Or the big hug and kiss you would have given me. Deep down you knew I loved you, but the experience of seeing your face light up as you heard the words will escape me forever now. I take comfort in knowing you were, and always will be, my one true love, and that I was yours.

I never doubted my feelings for you despite the curve balls life threw at me. I'm sorry that we never had a real chance for a future, a future that would have turned out as happy and bright as you dreamed. Even more so, I apologize from the bottom of my heart for what happened in August: the outright lie I told when you asked if I ever loved you. I can never get that moment back, to make it right. But let me tell you now: I love you. I did from that first day at the park and I never stopped. I take full responsibility for the unspeakable decision on my part to end our friendship and for not having the guts to call you and make things right. I should have shown up at your apartment and begged you to forgive me. I had no right to do such a thing to the woman I loved with my heart and soul. But at the time it seemed like the right decision for both of us. I wanted you to be happy and be able to move on, and I needed to concentrate on my boys. It was never my intention to hurt you in any way, and I hope that you know that. I hope you can find a way to forgive me.

I picture what our life could have been like, which brings me both joy and despair. We could have had a wonderful marriage and shared all of the moments you wrote about. But I'm holding you to your promise that we will be together in our next lifetime. I will be waiting for you, you can count on that. So until we meet again, and we will, Kate, for this I am certain without a shadow of a doubt.

My love always,
Greg

Greg sat motionless. He wiped his eyes with his fingertips and sighed heavily. After a moment, he placed his hand to the right of her photo, the cold of the stone seeping into his skin. Greg gave a half smile as he looked at her picture and then closed his eyes in an attempt to shut out the pain and heartache.

When he opened his eyes, he saw the sky was now shimmering with tiny snowflakes. He gazed back at Kate's photo and let his tears flow freely. "I'll always love you, Kate." He trembled with emotion. "And I'll be there someday, waiting for you. I promise."

Appendix

Mood Ring Color Chart

Black: Fear, Nothing, Angst, Serious, Overworked, Stormy, Depressed, Intense

Yellow: Anxious, Cool, Cautious, Distracted, Mellow, So-So

Orange: Stressed, Nervous, Mixed, Confused, Upset, Challenged, Indignant

Green-Peridot: Mixed Emotions, Restless, Irritated, Distressed, Worried, Hopeful

Green-Light Green: Normal, Alert, No Great Stress, Sensitive, Jealous, Envious, Guarded

Blue-Green: Upbeat, Pleased, Somewhat Relaxed, Motivated, Flirtatious

Blue: Normal, Optimistic, Accepting, Calm, Peaceful, Pleasant

Indigo-Darker Blue: Deeply Relaxed, Happy, Love-struck, Bliss, Giving

Violet-Burgundy: Love, Romance, Amorous, Heat, Mischievous, Moody, Dreamer, Sensual

Pink: Very Happy, Warm, Affectionate, Loving, Infatuated, Curious

Reader's Guide

It is clear that the two people in the prologue both loved the woman who died. Who did you think the woman was at the cemetery? Why do you think she and Greg never met? What are Greg's regrets?

In the beginning of the story, Greg and Heather are on a break in their relationship. What do you think Greg would have done if he never met Kate? Would he have gone back to Heather or ended the relationship? What are the reasons for your answer?

Heather and Greg have been together for three years and she wants their relationship to move forward. Greg has doubts about their relationship. What are your thoughts on Greg and Heather as a couple?

Greg and Kate meet at Rittenhouse Square and seem to hit it off. What qualities does each have that make them a good fit to be a couple?

Greg decides he wants to be with Kate and end his relationship with Heather. What do you think would have happened if Heather was never pregnant? What would Greg and Kate have been like as a couple if they had the opportunity to pursue a relationship?

Greg is nervous about being a father at the young age of twenty-five. He chooses to stay with Heather after learning she is carrying twins. Would he have made the same choice if there was only one baby? Why, or why not?

How do you imagine Greg's life to be as a single dad if he chose to be with Kate? How would Kate have been as a stepmom?

If Greg and Heather did not stay together, how do you imagine Heather's life would be as a single mom? How would her rough early childhood affect her as a single mom?

How do you feel Heather and Kate would have gotten along if Greg and Kate developed a relationship?

Jennifer and Kate have been best friends since early childhood. How do you feel Jen's friendship influenced Kate's life?

Aunt Clara rescued Heather as a young girl and gave her a good life. How do you feel Aunt Clara has influenced Heather's life?

Greg and Tom met in college and became good friends. How do you feel Tom's friendship influenced Greg's life?

Heather never knew her father, and Kate's father left her when she was a young girl. How do you feel Heather's and Kate's lives would have been different if they'd grown up with loving fathers? Do you think Greg was somehow unknowingly drawn to both of them in an attempt to heal them?

Greg was torn over his decision about what to do after finding out Heather was pregnant. Do you think Greg made the right choice in staying with Heather and the twins? Why, or why not?

In the book, Greg and Kate are deeply in love. How did you feel when Greg was intimate with Kate in Chicago? Did you feel he cheated on Heather, and if so, were you able to still like his character? Was it right or wrong that Greg and Kate were able to share that experience together?

How do you feel about the fact Heather never knew about Kate? Do you feel Greg was being deceitful, just a typical guy, or that his love for Kate overtook him? How would Heather have reacted if she found out about Kate? Would she have ended her relationship with Greg? Would she have forgiven him? Why, or why not?

Why do you think Kate never told her mom about Greg? Do you think she had internal conflicts about telling her? Why, or why not?

Kate's mood ring changes throughout the story based on what is happening in her life. How does Kate's mood ring play a part in the story?

Greg's dog Rocky has been with him since he graduated high school. How does Rocky play a part in the story?

What do you think Kate's life would have been like if she hadn't died? Would she have moved on from Greg? Would she have gotten married and eventually had children? Would she be working in the same field? Do you think it's possible she and Greg could have been together someday?

What do you think Kate's mind-set was like when she died? Was she sad? Lonely? Heartbroken? At peace? Something else?

Ellen Shuster is devastated over the loss of her daughter. How will she mourn? How will she eventually be able to go on with her life?

How will Jennifer heal from the loss of her best friend? How will she go on with her life?

How do you feel Greg's life will go on after the death of Kate? Will he and Heather get married? Will they have more children? How will Greg get over the loss of her? How will he forgive himself for all of his regrets?

CPSIA information can be obtained at www.ICGtesting.com
Printed in the USA
BVOW05s2057250416

445579BV00001B/1/P